WYONATION

ISBN: 978-0-9990017-3-8

Library of Congress Control Number: 2023913984

Printed in the United States of America

First Printing, 2023

This book is a fictional work written without assistance from artificial intelligence. The names, characters, places, and incidents are products of the author's imagination, or the author has used them fictitiously.

Published by Guy Talk Press

Highlands Ranch, Colorado

www.guytalkpress.com

WYONATION

Dallas Jones

CHAPTER 1
TARGET CONFIRMED

(Many Years from Now)

WITH HIS EYE pressed to the rifle's scope, the man in a long-sleeved, drab-olive shirt and worn jeans scanned the dense landscape for his target. He detected movement in the willows and focused. Simultaneously, an elk raised its trophy head as if it, too, sensed something about to happen. The magnificent bull turned slightly, showcasing a six-point set of antlers. Moments later, a gun barrel appeared through green foliage.

"See it?" Yurdy asked. "Eleven o'clock, just beyond the huge boulder."

Johnny, looking through a government-supplied range finder, responded, "Got it. Ooh, long shot."

Estimating a five miles-per-hour wind speed, Yurdy combined the distance and wind data with his memorization of ballistics tables to quickly calculate his shot. Accordingly, he adjusted his scope to mitigate the bullet's anticipated drop.

"Confirming the target," Yurdy whispered.

"Confirmed," Johnny said.

The gun barrel inched forward, and a hunter's face appeared in a small patch of sunlight. Still peering through the scope, Yurdy clicked off the safety. He inhaled and then slowly squeezed the trigger. A thunderous boom roared, and the frightened elk dashed into the pine forest and disappeared.

The target lurched backward before dropping to the ground with a gaping chest wound. His gun lay next to him.

Fifteen minutes later, the two Wyonation Protectors stood over the dead man. Blood not only drenched his plaid shirt at the sternum but also trickled down the left side of his face, presumably a scratch from a branch as he had fallen.

"Ready to call this in?" Johnny asked.

After a long, sobering gaze at his regrettable handiwork, Yurdy answered, "Yeah."

"Okay, start documenting the immediate scene. And check for some identification. I'll report in." Johnny then pulled a cell phone from his pocket and called the district office.

⋲

In a one-story government building on the outskirts of Spearfish, Grayson Woodley waited for a call. When the phone rang, he answered.

"Wyonation Treasures. Woodley speaking."

"Grayson? Wasn't expecting you," Johnny's voice said on the other end.

"Got a heads-up after the alert was issued. Is it serious?"

"Yeah. We have one suspected poacher, now deceased."

Grayson bit his lip. *Damn*, he mouthed.

"Yurdy's documenting the scene now."

"Have you confirmed the deceased belongs with the vehicle?"

"Not yet. Haven't been to his truck. Not exactly sure where he's parked. We'll search for keys on his body and take a look."

"Okay." Grayson tapped his finger on the desk. "Johnny, minimal disturbance, you understand? Get the keys and ID him if you can. That's all. I'll call Criminal Investigations and get them out there as soon as possible."

"Right."

After a pause, Grayson asked, "Who fired?"

"Yurdy."

"Is he doing all right?"

"I think so. Hey, Grayson, we didn't intercept the vehicle. By the time we got the alert, we figured we had about three minutes before we'd run into it. We were close, you know, but… Anyway, we never saw a truck. We were on this ridge and pulled over to see if we could spot anything. Well, you know Yurdy, him and his sixth sense. Damned if he didn't see the elk immediately. Spotted the poacher with his rifle maybe eight hundred yards from us a few seconds later. After I saw him, we confirmed, and Yurdy fired."

"Impressive shot."

"It was a helluva shot!" A dull groan from Johnny's end passed through the phone. "Just a minute," Johnny said. "Yurdy's found something."

Grayson mindlessly doodled on a notepad while waiting.

"Uh, Grayson, we may have a complication. Yurdy found some identification on the poacher. It's an ID card from the Chinese consulate."

Grayson's aching hip barked as he limped across the office for some coffee. He continued digesting Johnny's unsettling news as he poured cream into his morning salvation. When he considered the situation's gravity, Grayson frowned and tried to remember the last occurrence of a poaching fatality. *I thought we were past all this nonsense.*

He strained to remember the last incident. Three years ago? Maybe. At least three years. Was it the Utah guy who'd taken down a grizzly east of Baggs? Possibly, but Baggs wasn't in his district, so Grayson was fuzzy on the details. He shook his head slightly when he thought about Baggs and grizzly bears mentioned in the same sentence. The notion of grizzlies even residing that far south had been laughable not so long ago, but then, a lot had changed since The Birth.

Grayson knew he'd have to contact Doolin back in DC, but did the complication of Chinese involvement require notification of others? Maybe, but that was Doolin's problem. As US secretary of the interior, Doolin would determine whom to contact.

Grayson loathed making a phone call to Doolin. He hated the son of a bitch. Yet, an audio-only interaction would eliminate subjection to that little weasel's condescending gestures. Still, a video conference would surely follow, probably many of them.

Yep, the government boys and girls on the East Coast were going to pitch a fit when they heard the news about the no-poaching enforcement. The Washington, DC, pooh-bahs considered the practice barbaric. Then again, they were far removed from the consequences suffered from unauthorized animal killings. The simple fact was they could bitch all they wanted, but in the end, it wouldn't matter. It wouldn't matter because this wasn't their country—not anymore.

Thanks be to Stella.

THE CASE OF LIN LOK

"YOU NEED TO apologize publicly to the Chinese," Barry Doolin demanded. "That and a quick synopsis of events is all I want from you."

"Not gonna happen," Grayson replied from the desk chair in his Washington, DC, hotel room.

"What do you mean it's not gonna happen? This fiasco is your shit show. I'm telling you exactly what you're going to do."

Grayson's agitation doubled. First, a thunderstorm delayed his flight for three hours in Chicago, and now he was engaged in a midnight telephone argument with an overbearing administrator who had forgotten he wasn't Grayson's boss. "My guys did their job. They enforced the law. It doesn't matter whether the perpetrator was from California, China, or Mars. They enforced the law as is our right. That's what I'll communicate at tomorrow's hearing."

"Damn it, Grayson! We have a potential foreign-relations crisis on our hands!" Doolin screamed.

"That's the State Department's problem. As you know better

than anyone, Wyonation isn't permitted to have a relationship with foreign nations. You'll need to coordinate whatever political spin you're planning with O'Leary and her people."

Through the phone, Grayson listened to Doolin's loud, rapid exhalations and pictured his long-time adversary seething on the other end. Then, in a measured tone, he said, "Look, Barry, the facts are on our side. Sovereign nations are allowed to determine and enforce their own laws. The Chinese certainly do. I'll present the case details, and then you and O'Leary can remind our Asian friends about sovereign rights. Let's stick together on this, and we'll be fine."

"I won't be in attendance," Doolin announced. "Lionel Brown and Theresa Cicci will represent Interior."

You little worm. Given Doolin's plan to be a no-show, Grayson understood Brown's meeting assignment. He was Doolin's deputy. However, Grayson was puzzled by the second name mentioned.

"Why Cicci?" he asked.

"If you recall," Doolin teased, "she has an extensive history with Wyonation."

That she does.

⋙

The next afternoon, Grayson sat patiently in an elegantly adorned State Department conference room. While waiting to narrate the event sequence from the ill-fated poaching attempt, he stroked the executive-style chair's fine leather arms with his palm.

The primary door to the conference room swung open. Three gentlemen entered and proceeded to the side of the table opposite Grayson. All wore dark suits. All were Chinese.

Besides the Chinese representatives, roughly ten others sat at the table. As Doolin had promised, Lionel Brown and Theresa Cicci represented the Interior Department. Grayson doubted

Cicci would add anything to the briefing. Still, it was nice to see a familiar if not always congenial face.

Being the session host, State Department officials occupied the other seats. Under Secretary of State Norma O'Leary led the contingent—a necessary assignment, given the Chinese involvement. Her chair, positioned at the far end of the large cherrywood, conference table, telegraphed a silent yet emphatic message. Today, she was in charge.

The other State Department civilians filled the perimeter. These individuals each possessed an impressive master's degree in government or foreign-policy studies. Yet today, none would rise above the rank of flunky.

O'Leary began the meeting. "Good afternoon. I want to thank everyone for making hurried arrangements to be here today. I sincerely appreciate your efforts and your willingness to come together to discuss this serious matter."

While she introduced this afternoon's participants, Grayson studied the woman. Had he passed her anywhere outside this building, he doubted he would have taken notice. Her pencil-thin frame was physically unremarkable. Yet in this domain, the American foreign-relations official stood out. With her cropped gray hair, she carried her authority as easily as she wore her tailored navy jacket and skirt.

O'Leary began reading from a prepared summary. "On Monday, June 11, Mr. Lin Lok, a citizen of the People's Republic of China and employee at the Chinese consulate in Chicago, died tragically while traveling on a personal excursion."

Mr. Wu, as identified by his name placard, wasted no time intervening. "Mr. Lin, a member in good standing within China's diplomatic core, was savagely murdered while innocently vacationing within the jurisdictional boundaries of the United States. We demand the murderer be prosecuted and punished for this heinous crime. Further, we demand the United States apologize and pay full restitution to his family for their loss."

Grayson noted the position immediately taken by the Chinese team. The first part was obvious: our boy, Lin Lok, did nothing wrong; he was innocently sightseeing and was murdered. The second part was more subtle: he did nothing wrong, but even if he had, he couldn't be prosecuted due to diplomatic immunity.

Grayson also observed some personal dynamics in the Asian contingent. Mr. Wu was their mouthpiece, but he wasn't the senior official. Body language suggested the stoic man on Mr. Wu's left, a Mr. Tang, held supreme authority.

"We share your concerns and sympathize with your loss," O'Leary responded. "We are conducting a full investigation. However, as I'm sure you're aware, the shooting occurred in Wyonation, a unique entity within the United States. Though Wyonation shares the legal principles founded by the US, it has established and enforces some laws particular to its circumstances for existence."

"China does not maintain a relationship with Wyonation nor do we recognize its sovereignty," Mr. Wu replied. "Our relationship is with the United States, and it is you we hold accountable. Still, we would like to hear from the representative of the rogue region where the crime was committed."

"Of course," O'Leary answered. "Mr. Woodley, please brief us on the shooting details."

Upon hearing the "rogue region" barb, Grayson restrained himself from marching over to Mr. Wu and kicking him squarely in the balls. Instead, he drew in a breath and summoned his vast experience as a communicator.

"Thank you, Madam Under Secretary. Before I get into Mr. Lin's case details, I'd like to refresh everyone's understanding of Wyonation and the vital role wildlife plays in its culture.

"Wyonation is classified as a natural range region, or NRR.

It consists of Wyoming, one of the fifty states prior to Puerto Rico's admission to the Union, and a large section of the Black Hills. During its formation, the United States Government and Wyoming citizens agreed the newly created NRR would function as an autonomous US enclave, with some exceptions—"

Mr. Wu interrupted, "What do you mean by exceptions?"

"For example, Wyonation does not maintain relations with any foreign country. It interacts only with the United States."

"Are you regarded the same as an Indian reservation?" This question came from a new voice, Mr. Chen, the third person representing China.

"No, but there are some similarities," Grayson answered. "Wyonation is unique in its existence. I guess you could say it's part US territory, part national park, and part aspects that are all its own."

"And do you have a season for shooting human beings?" Mr. Wu added.

That warrants two kicks to the nut sack. However, Grayson quickly realized he wouldn't have to act. Mr. Tang's embarrassed facial expression torpedoed Mr. Wu with a hard stare.

"Forgive my colleague's rudeness," the senior member said in flawless English. "Please continue."

With a slight head nod, Grayson acknowledged his statement. "In a nutshell, Wyonation is a vast land area returned to its natural state. It is intended to be a place where humans have minimal impact on the native animals, plants, and topography. We refer to all these amazing natural resources as Wyonation Treasures and are committed to their full protection. Sustaining these magnificent wonders represents the NRR's core vision. Additionally, this practice is vital to the people who reside in Wyonation."

"How so?" Mr. Chen asked.

"Per our agreement with the US, commercial agriculture and large-scale mining and drilling ceased when Wyonation came into existence. That left us with tourism as our primary revenue generator. Our unique natural sites and wildlife draw millions of visitors annually from around the world."

Grayson sipped some water and then continued.

"Charging fees to observe our animals in their natural setting is one way we generate revenue. Another is from our managed hunting program. We harvest our wildlife in a responsible manner. Our citizens receive first priority to meet basic needs; wild game is a significant portion of most families' diet. Next, we allow licensed operators within Wyonation to sell wild game products—meat, hides, artistic works made from bone, that sort of thing—to customers outside our borders in limited quantities. In a given year, and if there are still excess animal populations identified for culling, particularly big game—bison, deer, pronghorn, elk, moose, and sometimes bears and wolves—they are made available for nonresident hunting through a fee-based lottery system. Though not as much as our tourism program, hunting fees bring in substantial revenue for the NRR."

"That is all fine, but I fail to see the need for lethal enforcement," Mr. Wu argued.

Grayson's jaw clenched as his patience waned. "During Wyonation's brief existence, we've suffered great economic hardship from illegal hunting. At one point, the situation became so dire we had no choice but to take drastic action." He turned away from the Chinese delegation and directed his next comment toward Theresa Cicci. "Some described our preventive and punitive measures as draconian; we believed then and still do they are justified means of self-preservation. As a last resort, those measures include lethal force to prevent an illegal killing." Grayson paused to let the last point sink in, and Cicci's scorching stare verified the message had been received. "Now, I would like to address the details pertaining to Mr. Lin—"

"Before continuing," Mr. Wu interrupted, "Madam Under

Secretary, we would like to state for the record China believes taking human life for such an arbitrary reason is unjustifiable. No other country practices such inhumane activity."

Grayson jerked backward in his chair. He scanned the faces of the State Department officials for any hint of incredulity regarding the brazen accusation but found none. Mr. Tang remained silent as well. The emotional void catapulted Grayson into a retaliatory frenzy.

"Sir!" Grayson boomed. "China has no standing to dictate morality. Your founder wiped out forty million people, his own people. And where was the regard for the lives of students at Tiananmen Square or the Uyghurs in Xinjiang?"

Now O'Leary, Brown, and the rest of the American contingent reacted—with mouths wide open.

"Also, for the record," Grayson added, "preemptive lethal force *is* practiced in other places. Specifically, India permits it at its tiger preserves, and countries in Africa have intermittingly used it to reduce elephant poaching."

In continued bold defiance, Grayson absorbed the hate-filled lasers emitting from Mr. Wu's eyes. He expected similar contempt from the other Chinese officials but was surprised by Mr. Tang's odd expression. *What was that? Admiration?*

Mr. Wu protested, "Madam Under Secretary, we are deeply offended by this outlandish behavior! Please remove Mr. Woodley from the room."

"I've been insulted, too," Grayson answered. "Mr. Wu has been picking a fight since this hearing began. I'm happy to oblige."

"Enough!" O'Leary interjected while slapping the papers stacked to her right. "Mr. Woodley, you will refrain from any more outbursts. Do you understand?"

"I came here to relay the case facts," Grayson said. "May I do that, please?"

O'Leary paused, then said, "Gentlemen, I understand tensions are running high. I'm asking you to exercise professional courtesy for the remainder of the afternoon. Agreed?" She glanced at the Chinese diplomats, and Mr. Tang nodded. Then Grayson met her gaze as she turned toward him. He nodded, too.

"The practice in Africa is meant purely for self-defense," Mr. Wu said. "Well-armed poachers are killing game wardens at an alarming rate."

Grayson grimaced at Mr. Wu's renewed needling and turned to O'Leary for support. All he received was a don't-you-dare warning from her raised hand. He swallowed hard. "I'm sure that's true."

O'Leary redirected the conversation. "Mr. Woodley, you were going to present the facts in Mr. Lin's case."

"Yes, Madam Under Secretary. Thank you."

Grayson's finger swiped the monitor assigned to his seat and brought up Lin's file. "I'll present the case in two parts; the first part covers the events starting when the Treasures Department received a trespassing alert and runs through the post-shooting documentation at the scene. Part two pertains to the department's follow-up and background investigation."

He surveyed the room and received a nod from O'Leary to continue.

"On Monday, June 11, at 6:27 a.m., the Spearfish office of the Treasures Department received a trigger alert from Tracking Station 36 within Sector 14, about eighteen miles west of Hot Springs. A trigger alert indicates an unauthorized vehicle has entered into a controlled area. The accompanying image was a blue General Motors EV333 pickup with Illinois license plate identification V456XG22."

"How did you determine the vehicle was unauthorized?" Brown asked.

Grayson explained, "In Wyonation, every vehicle residing in or entering our jurisdiction must be registered. At registration, the vehicle is issued a transponder allowing us to monitor its movement. At that time, travel-area permissions are granted. For example, a long-haul interstate truck might only be granted permission to move along the I-80 and I-25 corridors, while a non-resident, personal vehicle may access all primary but no secondary roads. As the vehicle moves, tracking stations throughout Wyonation communicate with the transponder to track its location and ensure the vehicle has authorization to be there."

"So this pickup didn't have authorization to be where it was?" Brown asked.

"Correct. But not only that, the alert message indicated no transponder connection happened."

"Meaning?"

"Meaning either the transponder wasn't working—a very low probability—or the vehicle had no transponder because it hadn't been registered."

"Thank you. Please continue."

"At 7:03 a.m., a second trigger alert was received from Tracking Station 31, same sector, about six miles from the first station. At 7:05 a.m., a Spearfish office dispatcher directed a protector unit in the vicinity to intercept the vehicle and investigate the trespass. The protectors were unsuccessful, so they stopped at a high vantage point to survey the landscape for any sign of the vehicle. During this scan, they spotted a person with a rifle pointed at an elk. One protector fired his weapon, killing the suspect."

With the last statement, a few people shifted uneasily in their seats.

"The protectors then proceeded to the suspect's location. He was confirmed to be dead from a gunshot wound to the chest. Lying near the deceased was a Weatherby Mark V Deluxe rifle with a bullet in the chamber. The deceased also carried a Buck hunting knife. The protectors reported the incident to the Spearfish office at 7:42 a.m."

Mr. Wu spoke. "That is a fantastic tale, Mr. Woodley. You would have us believe that, in the span of a few seconds, your officers were able to exit their vehicle, miraculously spot a person in the forest, and determine his guilt for a crime that had yet to be committed."

"The protectors are trained to identify active threats and, if necessary, take preemptive action to protect our wildlife. They were on alert for illicit activity. The fact the suspect was spotted so quickly was unusual; it rarely happens that a poacher is caught in the act. Honestly, I'd call this particular incident a fluke."

"What would have happened if Mr. Lin had not been shot?" O'Leary asked.

"Well, assuming Mr. Lin had reasonable hunting skills, the animal would have been killed and Mr. Lin arrested after the fact."

"But not shot?"

"No, assuming he didn't resist arrest."

"You're assuming Mr. Lin was more than just a sightseer!" Mr. Wu cried. "There are many other plausible explanations. Maybe he carried the gun for protection. Maybe it wasn't his gun but that of another person who intended to shoot. You've conveniently failed to mention the truck identified by your tracking system did not belong to Mr. Lin. Another person was involved."

"Both protectors stated the man shot was holding a rifle and in a position to fire at the animal. On-site examination by our Criminal Investigations Unit corroborates their claim," Grayson answered. "I'll address vehicle ownership and an additional suspect next."

"Let's hold off on any other questions until we've heard the whole report," O'Leary advised.

Grayson scrolled through the text on his monitor.

"After notifying the Spearfish office, the protectors searched the surrounding area for the vehicle in question but found nothing. However, at 8:48 a.m., Wyonation Highway Patrol pulled over a truck bearing a similar description and headed south on Highway 71. Only one person, the driver, was in the vehicle. Pierre Robidoux, a Caucasian male, age forty-three. Mr. Robidoux resides in Naperville, Illinois, and is the vehicle's registered owner. Items found either inside the cab or in the pickup bed included a box of ammunition compatible with the Weatherby rifle, rope, tarps, a field dressing kit, and topographical maps of the Black Hills area. Also, a suitcase full of personal items belonging to Mr. Lin was discovered."

"Has a relationship been established between Mr. Robidoux and Mr. Lin?" O'Leary asked.

"As I understand, Mr. Robidoux hasn't been cooperative," Grayson answered. "However, we've ascertained that Mr. Robidoux and Mr. Lin traveled together to Wyonation from Chicago. They initially met a few years ago at a shooting range. Mr. Robidoux has not revealed how he entered Wyonation without registering, but we have confirmed he stopped at a battery recharging station in North Platte, Nebraska, prior to crossing our border. Our best guess is the vehicle entered Wyonation on some unmaintained road running through open-range land somewhere north of Crawford."

Mr. Wu challenged him. "Your poor border security is yet another unreliable law-enforcement example. How can we have any confidence in the merit of your officers' work?"

"We have an enormous border to watch over, and sometimes a determined party can breach it. Yet on balance, we are effective in controlling our borders due in large part to our strong working relationship with the United States," Grayson said while gesturing toward the Interior Department representatives. "Also, we maintain concentrated security in critically valuable areas such as the Black Hills. Our enforcement record in these sensitive areas is outstanding."

"Could you please describe the technology used in your

tracking system?" Mr. Chen asked. "Is it entirely land-based, or does it incorporate satellites?"

Wow! These pricks never stop probing for intel. "The actual technology employed is classified and, frankly, not germane to this investigation," Grayson answered.

After a brief pause, O'Leary asked, "Do you have anything else to add, Mr. Woodley?"

"No, that covers the report."

Mr. Wu spoke. "Madam Under Secretary, Mr. Woodley's report fails to exonerate the officers involved in the crime. The fact is his men acted recklessly, and now an innocent man is dead. They must be held accountable. Our demands made at this session's onset have not changed."

In a steady but forceful voice, O'Leary answered, "To the contrary, Mr. Wu, I believe an impartial judge would find the information presented by Mr. Woodley to be quite compelling. Still, the investigation is ongoing, so I'll refrain from making any final conclusions." She paused, glanced at Grayson, and then returned her gaze to the Chinese. "Though sometimes unorthodox in its tactics, the US recognizes Wyonation's autonomy concerning natural resource management and its right to enforce its laws. Today, I believe Mr. Woodley adequately conveyed Wyonation's involvement. This matter is now for China and the United States to resolve. I want to thank Mr. Woodley and the Interior Department representatives for their participation. You are excused. The rest of us will remain for a few minutes to schedule next steps."

CHAPTER 3

REFLECTIONS

GRAYSON CLEARED THE State Department building's front doors. His eyes adjusted to the bright sunlight as he surveyed the street. Cars played a stop-and-go game while pedestrians hurried along the semi-shaded sidewalks. To a visitor from the High Plains, the afternoon felt noticeably humid, but native Washingtonians didn't seem to mind. Today's moisture in the air was nothing compared with what the city would soon endure in July and August. Grayson was always surprised how quickly he forgot about the muggy discomfort when he wasn't in the region. Like they said, out of sight, out of mind.

Grayson loosened his blue-and-silver-striped tie as he continued to ride a game-on, emotional high from the meeting. He suspected when it wore off, he would crash pretty hard. Since taking Monday's poaching-incident call, the man whose career was on the downhill side had been hustling nonstop. Between coordinating the investigation and communicating with all the affected parties, he had fed off adrenaline. Fatigue would soon show its face.

During his contentious back-and-forth with the Chinese representatives, Grayson had faithfully communicated the Wyonation Treasures report's details, but he hadn't revealed all he knew. Case information trickled in daily. In fact, he had received additional tidbits about Mr. Lin this morning.

Lin had been on a four-year assignment at the Consulate General of the People's Republic in China in Chicago. During his time in America, he had developed a great fondness for outdoor recreation, particularly hunting. He had met several acquaintances, including Pierre Robidoux, at a local shooting range and had participated in a few hunting excursions to the upper Great Lakes region of Michigan and Wisconsin. At some point, he had taken a vacation to Wyonation and become infatuated with the abundance of wildlife. He had planned to enter the hunting lottery this coming autumn.

Unfortunately for Mr. Lin, his assignment in Chicago had been unexpectedly shortened. Now scheduled to finish on July 1, he had apparently panicked about missing out on a big-game-hunting opportunity and solicited Robidoux's help. Though evidence of a monetary exchange between the two men had yet to be established, investigators still believed Lin had paid, or had promised to pay, Robidoux for help in bagging an animal.

Because the data hadn't been fully vetted, Grayson had held off from sharing it. When it came to making statements, the public-relations veteran practiced caution and refrained from saying anything he couldn't back up. Still, it didn't really matter that this latest information wasn't released. The Chinese already knew. Grayson was sure of it. They knew all about their employees' habits and happenings—and they didn't say a damn thing.

He doubted O'Leary or anyone in her community knew, but they would in time. He considered the under secretary of state's carefully measured behavior during the meeting. She had failed to deliver on her reputation as a diplomatic tigress. Was she scared? Maybe. Hell, rumor had it the entire State Department operated on pins and needles concerning any matter related to China. The Taiwan affair had changed the world order—and not in America's favor.

Grayson questioned his characterization of the twenty-first century's most significant event to date. It had been far from an affair, and it hadn't been a standoff, though the Western world had painted it that way. Had it been a surrender or a capitulation? Mmm, not that drastic. Then, it dawned on him. It had been a consumption. China had simply consumed Taiwan.

China's action had been completely predictable to anyone who'd been watching the signs. They had swallowed Hong Kong whole and aggressively reinforced their military positions in the East and South China Seas. Assimilating Taiwan into communist control had been a long-stated goal. After the Chinese had attacked the island nation and a confrontation with the Western powers seemed inevitable, the US blinked faster than anyone imagined. They had to. They were outmatched and overextended. A nuclear strike was the only possible military counter to the aggression, but America balked on taking the fight to that level.

Essentially, the US relinquished their long reign as enforcer in East Asia. In return, China agreed not to endanger Japan, Australia, and South Korea. However, Singapore, the Philippines, and the remainder of Southeast Asia remained up for grabs. China exclusively managed its own backyard. The pressing question was exactly how large that backyard would be.

Given the seismic political shift, the American diplomatic core was now engaged in a tentative dance to reestablish some normal semblance in this new equilibrium. Enough time had passed since the Taiwan consumption to soften heightened sensitivity between the parties, but the US remained hesitant to overtly challenge its Asian rival. O'Leary's restraint proved as much.

Well, to hell with that. Grayson replayed his tirade against

Wu's ridiculous assertions and tingled with self-satisfaction. He refused to let China manipulate him like a puppet.

Grayson glanced at his watch. The time read 3:50 p.m., a no-man's period in the office workday, as it was too late to meaningfully start something new yet too early to call it a day. Because Wyonation had no formal presence in Washington, DC, he had nowhere to go. The NRR's lone office outside of Wyonation resided in Denver. Still, Grayson had outlined some other matters requiring attention.

Screw it. I'll deal with those issues tomorrow. I'm tired, and it's too nice an afternoon to waste haggling with those jokers.

Grayson began walking and immediately became reacquainted with the pain in his hip. Last night's cramped flight had done him no favors. He crossed Constitution Avenue and entered the National Mall. As he strolled by the Vietnam Veterans Memorial and headed toward the Lincoln Memorial Reflecting Pool, the unmistakable cry from *The Good, the Bad, and the Ugly* sang from his jacket pocket. He reached in and retrieved his phone.

"Hello."

"Hey, loser. Where'd you go?"

Grayson recognized the voice in an instant. "Why, hello, darlin'. I didn't get the chance to rave about your beauty. It looks like you've been eating well."

"Stuff it, Cowboy!"

"No, really. You have that just-finished dinner—and dessert—satisfied glow going for ya."

"Now you're really pissing me off. Like you're one to talk. Did you bring a dolly to carry that belly around?"

"Hey, now, Ms. 'Chi-Chi.' Let's be civil."

"What the hell was that little self-righteous spiel about in there?" Cicci then quoted Grayson verbatim: "Some described our preventative and punitive measures as draconian; we believed then and still do they are justified means of self-preservation."

"Wow! I said that? I'm impressed."

"Shut up. Since when have you ever used the word *draconian?*"

"I'll use it right now," Grayson said. "Dumping your pasta into my lap was a draconian response to my reminder about our infamous little wager."

"You are one sorry son of a bitch. Now answer my question: where are you?"

"I'm down on the Mall, soaking in the national heritage of the country that abandoned me. But now I'm feeling a little bit thirsty."

"Thirsty, huh? Are you gonna do something about it?"

"Thought I might head to the old watering hole. Is it still there?"

"It is. Hey, stick around until I get there. I have to make a few calls, but then I'll be over."

"I'll count the seconds."

"You suck. Bye."

The old watering hole was a little bar called Gerry Manders. It had weathered the test of time, meaning it had an established customer base. While newcomers were always welcome, the venue wasn't compelled to employ trendy marketing gimmicks to attract business. Located a few blocks north of the Capitol, it stood just beyond the tourist region. The establishment was frequented mostly by people involved in government work—contractors, lobbyists, federal employees. Patrons could count on potent libations and above-average grub including some regional Chesapeake Bay specialties.

Grayson meandered along the National Mall and toward the Capitol. As he passed the National Museum of American History, he noticed prominent banners displayed on the building's façade. They advertised the museum's newest exhibit in bold letters on a vertically-divided background of blue and red. From top to bottom, they read: *Puerto Rico, America's Newest State, America's*

Latest Star. Unlike the visiting thousands who passed by daily, Grayson considered what the banner didn't say. The American flag hadn't changed a bit; there were still fifty stars. It was just that the star representing Puerto Rico used to belong to Wyoming.

Adding a new state to the Union was a happy affair; removing one, not so much. He wondered how the exhibit explained Wyoming's expulsion from the United States or if it even bothered to mention it at all. The Equality State had been the first one to get booted. That distinction in itself deserved some acknowledgement.

Further, he pondered whether Wyonation received any recognition—probably not. Though never confessed publicly, many bureaucrats who had dismantled Wyoming carried a sense of guilt. However, those same politicians treated The Birth of Wyonation like a bastard child's arrival. To the best of Grayson's memory, the most public acknowledgement of Wyonation was on a tourism website. The region's boundaries were marked, and a simple inscription was printed within those boundaries: *Wyonation: A Natural Range Region.*

⁊

As Grayson entered Gerry Manders, he savored the air-conditioned chill seeping into his garments, a temperature ten degrees cooler than outdoors. Like old friends, the smells of draft beer and aged wood welcomed him back.

The hostess greeted him with a warm smile and offered a menu. "Will you be dining with us?"

"A cocktail to start," he answered.

"Perfect. Seating's open."

"Thank you."

Grayson scanned the room and considered his options. He had beat the happy hour crowd's arrival by twenty minutes, so open spots were plentiful. He passed on a stool at the U-shaped bar and the high-top tables running along the establishment's front window. Instead, he decided on a quieter table in the back of the room. He had endured center stage enough for one day.

Momentarily, a man with close-cropped hair and wearing black slacks and a black button-down shirt walked over to the table. "Hey, man, how's it going? My name's Billy. Can I get you something from the bar?"

"Hi, Billy. How about a Tanqueray and tonic?"

"It's two for one on well brands."

"I'm going for the good stuff."

"Right on." Billy grinned. "You want some water, too?"

Grayson thought for a moment. "Yeah, why not. That'd be nice."

Billy cast his eyes toward the empty chairs. "Is anyone joining you?"

"Maybe later. Just me for now."

"Cool. I'll keep an eye out." Billy smiled and left.

As Billy headed toward the bar to place the order, Grayson watched and envied the younger man.

Handsome guy in his twenties. Smooth and friendly. He won't be lonely tonight.

Grayson checked the time on his watch and examined the back of his own worn, rugged hand. He blew out a heavy breath and interlocked his fingers behind his head. The emotional high from this afternoon's hearing was quickly dissipating. He deliberated closing his eyes for a few minutes but feared he would fall asleep.

Billy soon returned with his cocktail, served in a balloon gin glass. As he anticipated tart satisfaction trickling down his throat, Grayson carefully grasped the stem and raised the drink to his lips. For him, tonic water and gin weren't simply flavors; they were memories of past days, crazy days in Washington, DC.

For the next fifteen minutes, Grayson imbibed until ice cubes were the only thing left in his drink. He tipped the glass and allowed a couple of cubes to slide into his mouth. Suddenly remembering his dentist's warning about chewing ice, he stopped himself in mid-crunch. *Yet another surrender to the aging process.*

He pulled his cell phone from his jacket pocket and began skimming through assorted news stories. A crisis here, a storm there, but nothing suggesting the world would end today. The stock market was up slightly, and, oh yes, on their West Coast, road trip, the Colorado Rockies blew a four-run lead in the eighth inning to extend their losing streak to five games.

Consumed by the streaming information on his phone, Grayson didn't notice the tall figure standing over him and was startled when a voice asked, "May I join you?"

Grayson paused and focused on the newcomer. It was Mr. Tang.

CHAPTER 4

LEROY LIKES HIS BEER

"BE MY GUEST," Grayson said and gestured to the empty seat across from him.

"Thank you."

Before sitting, Mr. Tang placed his hors d'oeuvres plate on the table. His selections included carrot and celery sticks with a dollop of blue cheese dressing, some pita bread triangles with hummus, and mixed nuts. He finished by setting down a tall, sweating mug of amber-colored beer.

Grayson studied Mr. Tang as he became situated. The man was thin but not frail and dressed conservatively in a dark suit and tie. He kept his short, black hair neat and combed it back revealing a broad forehead. He wore wire-rimmed glasses. Grayson had not spent much time around people of Asian descent but admired how flawlessly they tended to age. He guessed Mr. Tang to be five years his senior but then added another five years for good measure.

"Warm, isn't it?" Mr. Tang said.

"It is. Happy to be inside." Whatever relaxation Grayson had felt minutes ago flitted away.

Mr. Tang motioned to his snacks. "Please, help yourself. I can't possibly eat all this food."

Grayson politely declined and then contradicted himself a moment later when he grabbed a carrot stick. "On second thought," he said.

Mr. Tang seemed pleased by his decision. His thin lips parted in a smile revealing front teeth in need of orthodontia.

Grayson considered how to interact with his adversary from just a short time ago. Should he dance around a subtle edge, or should he approach with blunt force? When he bit into the carrot stick, it snapped between his teeth. The sound reminded him of a starting gun at a one-hundred-meter dash, and he made his decision. *Off to the races.*

"Excuse my frankness," Grayson began, "but our meeting can't possibly be a coincidence."

Mr. Tang's eyes revealed nothing as he swallowed his last pita bite. Then the corners of his mouth turned upward ever so slightly.

"I fully understand your suspicion, and the answer to your question is yes and no." He paused and then modified his response. "Technically, it is more accurate to say no and yes. I was taking care of some other matters after our meeting when I saw you walking one street over. That's North Capitol, yes? I wondered where you were going, so I followed. When you entered this bar, it struck me that I was thirsty, too. A beer sounded appealing."

Grayson listened intently to his explanation and tried to pick up subtle clues about the man. He spoke in a casual manner, and his English was remarkably good, devoid of the stereotypical Chinese miscues spoken in classic TV shows. If anything, Grayson thought he detected a hint of southern drawl but decided that was crazy.

"And your beer is good?"

Mr. Tang's face brightened. "It's the best! So satisfying."

The earnest, emotional spill caught Grayson off guard. "What makes it so special?"

"It is Yuengling, the beer of my happy youth."

Grayson recalled what he knew about Yuengling. It was one of America's oldest beers, perhaps *the* oldest, with its brewery located in Eastern Pennsylvania. Though it had existed as long as the big boys, Budweiser and Coors, it had remained a regional beer for a long time. In fact, he vaguely remembered Yuengling hadn't expanded its distribution to west of the Mississippi River until well after the craft-beer revolution. Given Mr. Tang's estimated age, Grayson was surprised to learn Yuengling had been available in China so long ago.

"I didn't realize Yuengling was exported to Asia," Grayson confessed.

"Oh, it isn't. Nowhere that I am familiar with, anyway."

Now Grayson was really confused. "I'm sorry. I thought you just said you drank it when you were young."

"Yes," Mr. Tang said, and his face illuminated even more after comprehending Grayson's misunderstanding. "I've only had Yuengling in the US, but I've been here for a long time."

"Ah," was Grayson's one-word response, enough verbiage to both acknowledge Mr. Tang's statement and indicate the floor was now his to continue the story.

Recognizing his cue, Mr. Tang sat up straight and placed his hands in his lap. "I was raised in Suzhou, a city near Shanghai. You have probably never heard of it, but it is almost the size of New York City. My father was a professor and encouraged me to do two things: pursue a technical career and think globally. Like many of my countrymen, I was mesmerized by the United States and wanted badly to study here. I applied to several schools, but the competition was intense, and I was not accepted to the most prestigious universities. Still, I had a choice of four schools, one of them being the University of Alabama. Even in China, we had heard of the Crimson Tide, and being part of that experience excited me." He paused and then added with a defensive note in his voice, "Despite what the elite class in Washington and New York think, Alabama is a fine university."

Grayson smiled upon hearing the last sentence. "I'm quite familiar with regional bias."

Mr. Tang nodded. "Yes, well, when I came to Alabama, I was very well prepared academically. My parents insisted I speak excellent English, so I had a big advantage over other international students. But I had no idea about the university culture and how it was tied so much into football. I immediately caught the fever, as they call it, and fell in love with the whole Saturday experience. Roll Tide!"

"You went to the right place for football."

Mr. Tang babbled away. "Yes, and did you know, they put hand and shoe imprints of their football heroes into concrete at Denny Chimes?"

"Denny who?"

"It's the giant bell tower near the stadium." Mr. Tang now rocked in his seat with pure enthusiasm. "And after a win, we would go out to celebrate. My favorite place, The Stockade, sold Yuengling on tap, thirty-two ounces for three dollars. Can you believe it?"

Grayson whistled. "You can't beat that. I'm surprised. Did most international students embrace the football craziness?"

Mr. Tang took a swig from his mug. "Some did. Not so many Chinese. Most stayed in their own small groups. Their English was not good, and they felt intimidated."

"But not you?"

"Oh, no." Mr. Tang grinned. Like I told you, my parents insisted I learn perfect English. Not only that, I had an American roommate my freshman year. His name was Billy Ray Penders.

He was a tall, friendly guy from Mobile. Loud. I moved into our dorm room the Friday before classes started, and he was already there. He was sitting on his bed, drinking a beer. I don't remember what kind, but it wasn't Yuengling. He opens a small refrigerator and gives one to me. Then he asks me my name."

Mr. Tang took another swallow.

"I tell him my name is Tang Dingbang, and he says that name is no good. Billy Ray says I will get beaten up if I use that name. Then he says I need a proud Southern name instead, and he sits on his bed thinking. Suddenly, he jumps up and grabs me by the shoulders. 'Your new name is LeRoy,' he says. 'LeRoy T. if someone asks you for your full name.' Then he makes me laugh. Billy Ray says, 'Hot damn, I like it.'"

For a few moments, Mr. Tang gazed at nothing. When he turned his attention back to Grayson, he smiled. "And now you and I are friends. Please call me, LeRoy." He raised his mug. "Cheers."

Grayson responded in kind. "Call me, Grayson." He caught Mr. Tang looking at his almost empty gin glass.

"May I buy you another?" Mr. Tang asked.

"I'll wait until you're ready for one, but I will snag a few of these nuts."

Grayson reached over and grabbed a handful. As he popped the nuts into his mouth, he considered Mr. Tang's—er, LeRoy's—tale. It was a good story. He would grant him that, but it still didn't explain why he was here.

"So you drank your first Yuengling in Alabama?"

"Yes, yes. Those are happy memories. They were better days. Our countries got along well then." Mr. Tang's face expressed a bittersweet sentiment. "Now I'm delighted whenever I find Yuengling available." Slowly, his melancholy smile faded, and his face grew serious. "Grayson, when I saw you outside, I felt as if I'd been given a chance to clear the air about this afternoon's meeting."

Grayson placed his elbow on the table, allowing his chin to rest between his thumb and index finger, but he stayed silent.

"I wanted to apologize for my colleague's rudeness in his questioning. He was out of line."

"I've dealt with worse."

"Not that it's an excuse for his behavior, but I thought you should know that Mr. Lin was Mr. Wu's close friend. I made an error in judgment by allowing Mr. Wu to be part of the panel. He was too excitable, and I am truly sorry."

"Mmm," Grayson acknowledged.

"I thought your account of the incident was straightforward."

But are you going to admit your guy was in the wrong?

"Under Secretary O'Leary is a reasonable person. I am encouraged we will reach a mutually acceptable solution."

Guess not.

Billy stopped at the table. "How are you gentlemen faring? Need a refresher?"

Grayson responded, "LeRoy, you told me about your friend, Billy."

"Yes, yes. Billy Ray."

"Well, this is my friend Billy. He's a magician. He can make more alcohol appear in our glasses."

"Abracadabra, baby." Billy wiggled his fingers and laughed. "So, two more?"

Affirmative nods on both sides of the table.

"Tanqueray and tonic, and what kind of beer?"

"Yuengling," Mr. Tang gushed, now back in LeRoy mode.

Billy's appearance relaxed the atmosphere. Mr. Tang sat back in contented silence, and Grayson followed suit, permitting the alcoholic spirits to warmly blanket him. Just as a doze hinted as a possibility, Mr. Tang's voice startled him.

"I've been to Kaziranga."

"Huh?"

"Kaziranga National Park. In India. You mentioned the tiger preserves in your briefing. Kaziranga is one of the biggest reserves and an absolutely fascinating place. Lots of rhinos, too"

"Oh." The revelation piqued Grayson's interest. "Why were you there?"

"I was on a diplomatic team. We had a few extra days, so we visited the states of Northeast India."

Grayson couldn't claim geographic literacy with regard to India, but when the northeast area was mentioned, he remembered it and other parts of the Himalayan region had been another successful expansionary quest for China. *I bet that was a most interesting diplomatic trip.* "You are clearly a man of the world."

"I have been to a few places. Yes, yes."

"Do you have a favorite?"

Mr. Tang paused to formulate a reply. "I appreciate different places for different reasons. Of course, my home carries a special place in my heart. And Alabama, as I've told you. The Caribbean is beautiful, too." Grayson watched him mentally cataloging his prior destinations. "I've never been to the American West. Perhaps it is the most beautiful of all?"

"Well, I'm not the international traveler you are, but I like it."

"I saw a Western movie once. It starred Clint Eastwood."

Grayson's attention perked. "Which one?"

Mr. Tang grinned. "Oh, I don't remember the name. He was a preacher, and he saved some gold miners."

"*Pale Rider,*" Grayson said while leaning in and applying a three-quarter fist-pound on the table. He loved many types of movies, but his favorite genre was Westerns, particularly Clint Eastwood Westerns.

"Yes, yes. That sounds right."

"I know it's right." Grayson beamed. With an impatient prod, he queried his new friend, LeRoy. "Is that the only Clint Eastwood film you've seen?"

"Let me think. It has been many years." Mr. Tang paused. "I watched *Gran Torino*."

"No, I mean Westerns. His Spaghetti Westerns. You didn't see any of those? When I was little, I spent entire weekends watching them with my grandpa. He told me he'd watched them in the theater when he was a boy."

"I do not believe I've seen them, Grayson."

"Man, they're fantastic! I've seen each one so many times I can recite the dialogue." He looked at LeRoy with disappointment. "I'm sorry you haven't seen them. We could have so much fun playing trivia."

"I would not provide good competition for you. You are clearly an expert."

"It's not about winning. It's about sharing. Here, let me show you. I'll say a famous line and then tell you which movie it's from." Grayson began reciting lines from *High Plains Drifter* and *A Fistful of Dollars*. Then he pulled out his cell phone and played *The Good, the Bad, and the Ugly* ringtone. Grayson reveled in delight as he pontificated about one of his favorite pastimes.

Silently, Mr. Tang reveled in delight as he uncovered a key to opening the Westerner's chamber of trust. Now that Grayson was in a sharing mood, it was time to probe his drinking companion for more relevant information. "You have incredible recall, Grayson. I have no talent to match yours."

Grayson eagerly accepted the compliment.

Mr. Tang kept quiet, allowing Grayson to extend his period of self-admiration. Finally, he spoke. "Do you think one day they will make movies of Wyonation?"

Grayson paused to consider this novel question.

Mr. Tang pressed on. "I mean, to be nullified by your own country. That is an amazing story and one few people outside the US understand. Just how did the break up begin?"

CHAPTER 5

CHANGES IN THE WIND

(Eighteen Years Earlier)

"WE ARE BEGINNING to make our descent into Washington, so I've turned on the fasten-seat-belt sign," the captain said from the cockpit.

"Drink up, Grayson," Smitty ordered his youthful counterpart.

Grayson rattled the ice cubes, then tipped his clear, plastic cup. The last ounce of his Seven and Seven flowed down his throat. After the satisfying swallow, the twenty-eight-year-old man tipped the cup again and slid an ice cube into his mouth. Immediately, he began crunching on the frozen cube, a lifelong habit.

"I wonder what Claude has in mind for dinner," Smitty said as he polished off his second Dewar's during the flight. "I'm hungry."

The flight had originated in Denver around noon and was scheduled to land at Reagan National Airport at 5:50 p.m. Eastern Time. Grayson occupied the middle seat while George Smith, aka Smitty, sat along the aisle. Chronologically, Smitty was Grayson's senior by twenty years.

Smitty continued. "I hope it's a seafood joint. Some spiced shrimp would do me just fine. You ever had spiced shrimp?"

"No. I don't think so."

"Good stuff," Smitty assured him. "And then maybe we can head out to a gentlemen's club. DC has some great ones. Watch those fine ladies dance around the pole. You can show off that new fuzz around your mouth." Smitty nudged Grayson with his elbow, then he belched.

"Geezer, you would go into cardiac arrest at the first sign of skin. Then Mary would blame me for your heart attack," Grayson responded while stroking his dark goatee. "You know she slipped me fifty bucks to babysit you?"

"Bite me. We might as well have some fun on this trip. The governor has sent us off on a wild goose chase. It's a big waste of time if you ask me."

"Well, he's the boss."

"Congress is gonna do what they're gonna do with oil and gas. We can't stop that. I say let them freeze their asses for a while, and then we'll see how loud they huff and puff."

"No argument from me, there," Grayson replied. "But if we lose energy jobs, we've got to replace them with something. I think exploring the environmental tourism idea is worthwhile."

Smitty folded his arms and heaved a sigh. "It's a bunch of horseshit." Then his face contorted into a "Eureka!" expression. "Tell you what: Let's convert that fifty Mary gave you into a bunch of five-dollar bills. We'll use 'em to decorate those sexy garters. At least that would be productive use of our time."

"You're hopeless," Grayson muttered.

⌘

At 7:05 the next morning, Grayson sat at a table in the hotel café and watched Claude Mullin steep his tea. The chief of staff for Wyoming's US Senator, Emma Shelton, attended to his hot beverage with the same diligence he devoted to his personal grooming. The gray-eyed man kept his wiry, brown hair short and neatly trimmed. In his carefully pressed, yellow dress shirt with a coordinating herringbone tie, Claude personified poised confidence. Even the faint hint of pleasing aftershave suggested this man was a class act.

"Did you ever drink coffee?" Grayson asked, feeling somewhat out of place in his simple outfit—a tan suit, plain white shirt, and embroidered Justin cowboy boots.

"I used to, but I had a bout of acid reflux, so I switched to tea. I think it's helped." Claude poured a splash of cream into his cup. "Did George and you go out after I dropped you off?"

"For a little while. I talked him out of the strip club. We hit a bar a few blocks down instead. Man, there are some pretty ladies in this town."

"And they outnumber men by a sizable margin."

"Nice," Grayson said while scanning the room. "Do you think Smitty got the message about breakfast being moved up to seven? I'm happy to go get him."

Claude waved him off. "George will be joining us at seven thirty. I wanted to speak to you alone."

"Oh. Okay."

Claude drew in a deep breath and began. "So, yesterday, I had a long conversation with Hogan." He stopped abruptly as if he'd been buzzed for giving an incorrect answer. "Grayson, do you mind if I call your boss Hogan? It's tough for me to refer to my old college roommate as Governor Linsey."

"You were roommates?"

"Yeah, we had some wild times. Stories that will have to wait until he's out of office. Anyway, the governor and I chatted about your visit here. I take it you're up on your current events?"

"I think so."

"Good. Then you're aware Cran Fran's scandal not only led to his own political death, it also decimated the entire Republican Party in this past election."

Grayson knew former Congressman Cranmer Francis' saga well. The lone House representative for Wyoming, not so affectionately known as Cran Fran, carried tremendous sway in the nation's capital. He referred to himself as the Capitol Watchmaker; he made Washington, DC, tick. During his forty-plus years of House service, he'd perfected techniques for getting what he wanted and scuttling opponents who dared to challenge him. Politicians from both sides of the aisle agreed they needed Cran Fran's blessing to advance any meaningful legislation. So, when a reporter from a national tabloid caught Cran Fran leaving a Thermopolis motel room with a fourteen-year-old Shoshone girl, decades of pent-up resentment seeped out of the Capitol woodwork. Enemies buried him in a public-shaming landslide. Paybacks are hell.

Initially, fellow Republicans circled the wagons around their most senior member. That decision proved disastrous. Americans were infuriated by the old man's lechery and the party's willingness to excuse his behavior. During last autumn's election, they spoke with clarity. In all but the reddest states, voters swept Republicans out of office and cast them into a political purgatory. The action resulted in a Democratic super majority of both congressional branches not seen in modern times.

"Representative Francis' troubles and their impact are well known," Grayson answered.

"I don't feel a bit sorry for him," Claude said, "but the rest of the country is associating all of Wyoming with that asshole. There are folks on Capitol Hill who'd like to stick it to our state."

"Well, everyone I know working in oil and gas is really worried. They're sure the Dems are going to stop all the drilling. Our energy folks think the state will continue losing jobs, thousands more than we've already lost."

Claude nodded. "Hogan sent you here because he's worried about Wyoming's energy infrastructure."

"Right. He wants us to do some lobbying—and get a feel for people's reaction to our environmental tourism idea. What do you think?"

"I told him the stakes are far greater than just energy jobs. Dems want to take the state."

Grayson's face went blank. Finally, he said, "I'm not sure I follow. As mad as people are at Cran Fran, it's still a Republican state. I don't see that changing."

Claude shook his head and said, "No, I mean they want to take the state away from us. Though no one will publicly admit it—yet—there are backroom discussions to remove Wyoming as one of the fifty states. And there's a related movement to replace us with Puerto Rico."

"W-w-what? I m-m-mean, how? Why would they do that?" Grayson stuttered. Irrational but dizzying images of the state capitol imploding shuffled through his mind.

"It's a political play, a power play. Like you said, Grayson: Wyoming's a Republican state. It always has been. Dropping Wyoming and replacing it with a place like Puerto Rico gives the Dems two more reliable seats in the Senate. It's something they've had their eye on for a while, and right now, they have overwhelming numbers in Congress to give it a go."

"But how does something like that happen? I mean, the libs have been crying about California and Wyoming having the same number of senators for years. So what? Maybe they should read the Constitution—two legislative houses, one based on population and the other with equal representation."

"Currently, the Constitution contains no specific language about removing a state from the Union, but that's not to say something couldn't be added to address that topic," Claude answered. "Again, the numbers throughout the country right now are skewed so far to the Democrats' advantage, a new amendment proposal is a real possibility."

As Grayson grasped a greater realization of the potential situation, he grew more flustered. "What happens to the people? I mean, we're American citizens just like anyone else. Are they gonna kick us out of the country?" He winced at this uncertain possibility.

"Fair questions," Claude conceded. "I don't how it would play out. I don't know if it will play out. At this point, I think that's what they're trying to figure out. If they try, we'll do our damnedest to stop it in its tracks." He looked hard at Grayson and then turned his head toward the outside window before returning his attention to his table partner. "I know George and you were told this was going to be a public relations task on the state's behalf, and it is. But it's more than that. If the Dems decide to make a move, we'll be campaigning for our survival. To succeed, we need to gather some intelligence." He sipped his breakfast tea. "Grayson, you'll be taking the lead in this effort. Not right away. I'll groom you into the position. Introduce you to the right people. But you'll be the point person sooner than you think."

At first, Grayson was surprised by the new assignment but soon realized he was a suitable fit. After all, he was currently the public relations lead for Wyoming's Office of Environment and Natural Resources. His combined degree in agriculture and applied economics had not gone to waste. "Uh, yeah," he thought aloud. "Between Smitty and me, we'll get things going."

"About that," Claude began. "George is a fine person, and he knows regulations inside and out. He also knows lots of people in government and industry, and that will be useful, but he's not the kind of person I need in this task. Frankly, he's crass and lacks the necessary tact. You're my guy."

Grayson's eyes widened. Claude's assessment wasn't wrong, but Smitty was a good friend, not just a coworker.

"I'll speak to George and explain the situation," Claude assured him. "Meanwhile, after breakfast, I want you to see Leslie at the senator's office. You've met her, right? She will show you around the Capitol. You'll need to understand how the legislative docket works. Start there, and we'll touch base this evening for next steps. This week, meet as many folks as you can as quickly as you can. Gain an understanding of what they do on the Hill and how they relate. It's a little overwhelming at first, but you'll catch on."

A waiter appeared. "Do you gentlemen know what you'd like?"

Grayson knew he would like to be back in Wyoming. Claude's political bombshell stunned him. He struggled to comprehend the possibility and ramifications of such a brazen ploy. *What effect would it have on me? My family?*

Further, Claude's intention to separate Smitty and him caused added angst. His buddy hadn't been keen on this trip's purpose, but getting officially demoted would sting. This was going to be uncomfortable. Grayson ordered a Denver omelet with sourdough toast. His meal arrived just as Smitty joined them at the table.

"Did I misunderstand our meeting time?" Smitty asked with a gaping-mouthed yawn.

"No," Claude answered. "I needed Grayson to run an errand, so I woke him up a little early."

Grayson said nothing and quickly downed his food.

Grayson met up with Leslie Moore, Senator Shelton's administrative aide, at the Russell Senate Office Building across the street from the Capitol. Per Claude's instructions, Leslie led Grayson to preselected senators' offices within the building.

With one exception, Grayson's initial contact with the respective offices was limited to staff members. He was introduced as Governor Linsey's special envoy for Wyoming's exploratory program in environmental tourism. He shook hands with folks from Nebraska, Arkansas, Alabama, Montana, and Iowa. The exception was South Dakota, and there he met Senator Swede Mendenhall, a grizzled political veteran who carried excessive girth around his middle. He was serving his third term as senator after spending six years as South Dakota's lone congressman.

"How is that old son-of-a-buck boss of yours?" Mendenhall asked. "Last time I saw him was at the one-shot antelope hunt a few years back. Did you know he sneezed just as I was starting to fire? Messed up my shot and cost me the trophy."

"The way he tells it is a little bit different," Grayson said with a sly expression. "He says he saved you the embarrassment of shooting a heifer."

"A man with moxie," Mendenhall said while complimenting the comeback. "I seldom see that around here. All I usually get from junior staff is this maddening servile mousiness. Drives me nuts."

Grayson was pleased his retort had drawn the senator's surprise and amusement. He credited his father for the positive encounter. Daryl Woodley had stressed the importance of first impressions to his children. "A friendly wave and a smile are your best allies in dealing with strangers," he would say. "When you're talking to someone for the first time, try to put them at ease. Humor comes in handy; people like to laugh. Just make sure it's friendly. Don't be mean about it."

The senator continued. "So besides spreading vicious lies about my hunting skills, why did Hogan send you here?"

"We're looking into starting an environmental tourism program. The governor thought it would helpful if I came here and picked some people's brains, other folks who've tried this sort of thing."

"And to see if there might be some seed money lying around?"

Grayson watched Mendenhall closely. His words fit the

conversation, but his crooked half smile betrayed his immediate understanding. *He sees right through this flimsy cover story.* "I'm sure the governor would be open to funding contributions," Grayson answered. "Mostly, he wants me to meet influential people who might have an environmental interest in Wyoming."

"I'm sure." Mendenhall laughed in one snort. "I'm surprised you're working this matter on the Senate side. Normally, the House is a better place to start."

"Senator Shelton offered to give us a hand."

"Emma's a good person to have on your side," Mendenhall agreed. "She's your best option. Hell, your only option really, given Cran Fran's disaster."

Grayson nodded but remained silent.

The senator went on. "Still, my advice is to meet up with members of the House Committee on Natural Resources. Congressman Williams from Maryland heads that up. Leslie can introduce you." Mendenhall then turned to Leslie. "You know who he is, right?"

"Yes," she answered. "I've met him."

"By the way, Leslie, you look especially spectacular today. Grayson, did you know you have the prettiest redhead on the Hill escorting you?"

Leslie blushed at the unsolicited compliment. "Thanks for your time, Senator."

With quick steps, she exited. Grayson also thanked him and followed Leslie but stopped when Mendenhall called after him.

"And Grayson, keep your eyes open when you're meeting the natural resources folks. You'll find they're a lot more interested in Wyoming than you think—and not just its environmental tour-ism program."

More than his words, the grave expression on the senator's face put a knot in Grayson's stomach.

That afternoon Leslie and Grayson walked to the Cannon House Office Building located south of the Capitol. They met with House members residing on the Natural Resources Committee, and the receptions ranged from standoffish to borderline hostile. At Wyoming's mention, Democratic committee members clammed up. Grayson wasn't an expert in legislative procedure, but he could certainly read body language. *Why that reaction?* Was it people's disgust with Cran Fran's ordeal and his association with Wyoming? Possibly, but Grayson doubted it. No, their congressional hosts behaved as if they'd been caught in the act of doing something. *Doing what?*

At four thirty, Grayson parted ways with Leslie and walked back to the hotel. He'd received a text from Claude saying they would meet for dinner at six o'clock across the street. Grayson worked through his other messages—office matters back in Cheyenne and a reminder from Mom that Friday was his younger sister Cindy's birthday—like he'd forget. When he finished, it was 6:02 p.m. He hustled down the stairs, out the door, and across the street to The Gavel. Claude and Smitty were already seated. Claude waved him over while Smitty stared down at his napkin like a scolded puppy. *Eeesh! Guess gentlemen's clubs aren't in tonight's plans.*

During his two-course meal—tossed salad and then a seared tuna steak with a wild rice pilaf—Grayson briefed Claude on his day. He conveyed Mendenhall's cryptic heads-up and the ensuing awkwardness over in the Cannon House Office Building.

"Well, Grayson," Claude said, "tomorrow, I think the best course for you is to continue your meet and greet. I'm hearing more rumors about a challenge to Wyoming, but until we know what rationale they're going to apply, we can't really establish our defense."

Grayson nodded. "Got it."

Turning toward Smitty, Claude continued. "Meanwhile, George the Wise will become our resident expert on any regulations concerning statehood. Why you haven't been on *Jeopardy!* is beyond me. I can't believe your memory for details."

Grayson watched Claude's attempt to mend the hurt, but Smitty was having none of it. When the meal was finished, Claude paid the waiter and excused himself to work on some other matters for Senator Shelton. Grayson glanced at Smitty and attempted to break the awkward silence. "Buy you a whiskey, sailor?"

Smitty declined with an old man's pout. "I'm only allowed to put water in my sippy cup while I'm stuck in time-out."

Grayson's shoulders shook with laughter.

"I mean, damn, am I that much of an oaf? How humiliating."

"Yours is a special kind of charm. It just takes some getting used to."

"To hell with that! I can do all of Claude's research back in Cheyenne. I'm flying home tomorrow."

Grayson's eyes widened in surprise. "So how about that whiskey?"

"Not tonight," Smitty answered. "I'm beat. I think I'll watch a little TV and call it good. I'd forgotten morning happens two hours earlier here than at home. It kinda kicked my ass today."

"Me, too." Grayson's mood darkened. "Hey, Smitty, something big is going down around here, and I'm worried. These people are serious, and they're dangerous."

"What can I do about it? I've been cast into the netherworld," Smitty replied with his arms in a tight fold.

"Keep your head up, buddy. The guv selected you for a reason. I'm sure you'll have a role to play somewhere along the line." Grayson noticed Smitty didn't agree, but he didn't disagree, either.

As Smitty stood to leave, he said, "Do me a favor. If you see any hot legs over there at the Capitol tomorrow, don't tell me."

Grayson laughed.

"No, I changed my mind. Do tell me. Tell me every gorgeous detail."

"You're incorrigible, Smitty. That's what I love about you."

❧

The next morning, Grayson and Leslie resumed their congressional tour with mixed results. Grayson mingled smashingly with Moses Brown, Southern Illinois' representative and agricultural committee chair. Conversely, Berkeley representative Blossom McKenzie verbally accosted him. McKenzie, an influential member of the Select Committee on the Climate Crisis, drubbed the Wyoming novice mercilessly for suggesting mineral exploration and environmental management could happily coexist. By day's end, Grayson was exhausted and a bit demoralized. Some kind words from Leslie revived his spirits.

"I'm meeting a friend for happy hour," she said. "Why don't you come along? I think you could use a little fun."

I could indeed. Grayson watched Leslie tidy her desk and place some papers into her briefcase. He appreciated her assistance during the past two days. She understood the nuances of working in federal government's top tier.

A few minutes later, the pair reached their drinking destination, a hopping little spot called Gerry Manders. Grayson smiled at the name play as he watched Leslie embrace a male friend with an enthusiastic kiss. After a moment, she separated from him but still held his hand.

She turned toward Grayson and said, "Thomas, I'd like you to meet Grayson Woodley. He's visiting from Cheyenne and doing some fact-finding for the governor of Wyoming."

Thomas, perhaps six foot two with medium-length blond hair having just the right amount of tousle, cast a classic New England prep image and eagerly extended his hand.

"Hi, Grayson. What do you think of Washington?"

"It's busy. Energetic. I'm just hoping I don't get run over."

"By a vehicle or a politician?" Thomas teased.

Grayson laughed. "Too late for the latter. I probably got flattened at least six times today." He looked at Leslie for confirmation.

"At least six," she agreed.

Thomas grinned. "I know the feeling."

"I'm sorry," Grayson apologized. "I didn't catch your last name."

"Darling. Thomas Darling. I work public relations for Senator Anderson."

"Massachusetts Anderson?"

"No, Connecticut. The male senator, Reggie Anderson. Trudy Anderson is Massachusetts. Can I get you something to drink? I already know Leslie's poison."

"I'll take a beer."

"That narrows it to fifty possibilities."

"Um, you have a local lager?"

"I'll take care of you."

Grayson watched Thomas squeeze between huddled groups to reach the bar. Beyond Thomas, the room bustled with numerous conversations from crowds varying in age. The barely legals opted to stand while a handful of silver hairs seemed more content sitting at tables.

Grayson checked the time on his watch. When he raised his head, he thought he caught a woman's glance toward him. She wore her dark-brown, curly hair in a sassy, short cut. The contrast between her dark hair and cream-colored skin reminded him of Snow White. She turned slightly, affording Grayson a side profile. She was definitely attractive. No, more than attractive. She was hot, sultry in a white-collar, Washington, DC, sort of way. Her navy skirt and jacket paired nicely with the multicolor scarf atop her white blouse. Yet something about her was odd. She seemed uptight, like she was trying too hard to belong to the power crowd.

During his extended stare, he had yet to see her smile. Grayson felt as if he'd seen her before but couldn't place when or where. Though his gaze lingered beyond the bounds of polite etiquette, she never looked at him a second time. Maybe he had imagined the first.

Grayson turned his attention back to Leslie, who had begun chatting with another acquaintance. After a minute, the woman excused herself by patting Leslie's hand and shuffled away to greet another friend. Leslie looked at Grayson and smiled.

"So, how long have Thomas and you been an item?" Grayson asked.

"Well, let's see. I've known him about a year and a half. We went out for the first time just before Christmas and had our first wild sex on New Year's Eve, so I guess we've been an item since then." Leslie smirked.

"Man, I'm just trying to have a conversation. Is everyone here such a smartass?"

"Ask a personal question…"

Thomas returned with the drinks, and Leslie sipped from her wine spritzer. Grayson thanked Thomas for the beer and took a swallow from the frosty glass.

"It's called Potomac Autumn, a popular local beer around here," Thomas explained.

"Tasty," Grayson agreed.

After quickly downing his glass, Grayson offered to buy the next round, but his companions ignored him, preoccupied in their own courting ritual. He walked alone to the bar and ordered a second beer. The tightly bunched crowd along the railing left no space for Grayson, so he grabbed his foamy-topped glass of Potomac Autumn and searched for an open area. Partway across the room, he spotted a clearing, and on its edge stood the mystery girl. This time, eye contact was a certainty. He smiled at her, and she nodded—barely—then turned away.

Looks like an invitation to me. The stirring in his stomach prompted Grayson's recollection of his college bar-hopping days. Back then, the prospect of a coed encounter had revved his imagination. Here at Gerry Manders, he enjoyed a similar vibe. He eased in her direction, and the woman turned toward him. Grayson stopped two steps from her, admiring her button nose and soft, brown eyes. Then he noticed an etched name pin on her jacket lapel: *Theresa Cicci*. Despite unfamiliarity with the last-name pronunciation, Grayson attempted an introduction.

"Hello, Theresa Something? I'm sorry, but no one told me I needed a nametag."

Frowning, she responded, "It's pronounced 'chi-chi.' Theresa Cicci, and as for your nametag, let me help you." She pulled a pen from her purse, grabbed a cocktail napkin from the nearest table, scribbled something, and passed it to him.

Grayson chuckled as he read the inscription aloud. "Yura Dumazz. Aw, shucks, I thought only my dad called me that. People I've just met usually call me Grayson. Grayson Woodley."

"And judging from those shiny cowboy boots on your feet, you must be from Hawaii."

"Right again, and you know what? The surfing here is lousy."

Almost smiling, Cicci paused to sip her clear cocktail which had a lime wedge resting on an ice cube.

"What are you drinking?"

"Gin and tonic."

"Good?"

"Oh yeah, if you like something tart, that is. A couple of these bad boys erase all my troubles." Her tone suggested she had already imbibed some of those bad boys. "Do you like them?"

Grayson shook his head. "Never tried one."

In a snap, Cicci flagged down a waitress. Pointing at her glass, she signaled for two more G&Ts. When the drinks arrived, she offered a toast. "Time to graduate from groundling swill and onto the nectar of sophisticates."

Grayson placed his beer on a nearby table and accepted the gin glass. He took an exploratory swig and instantly approved. "Thank you for the education, Miss Chi-Chi. I owe you one."

"Oh no. You're buying, buster." Now she really did smile. Cicci coddled her glass, rocked slightly in a semi-bliss stupor, and then resumed the conversation. "You're a total bullshitter, but I'll give you this much: you are resilient. When I saw Congresswoman McKenzie beating you like a drum a few hours ago, I thought the janitor would have to wipe you off the floor. Yet here you are. Pumped up and cocky as hell."

Grayson's eyes narrowed. "You were there? I thought you looked familiar. Do you work in her office?"

"No. You passed me in the corridor. If you remember, the congresswoman carried her tirade into the hall for public display."

"I remember." It was now Grayson's turn to toss out a zinger, but he held off. Noise from the bar surrounded the two. Cicci downed another swallow. Then, without prompting, she said, "I work for Congresswoman Edelman, Minnesota Fourth District."

"I haven't met her. Doing what?"

"Legislative assistant."

"Mmm. So, you're from Minnesota?"

"Yeah, but not the Fourth District. That's Saint Paul. I grew up in Eden Prairie, west of Minneapolis. When I first came here, I worked for the rep in the Third District, my home, but then my boss lost the next election, and Nancy—that's Congresswoman Edelman—had an opening in her staff."

"I see." Grayson said. "I have a confession to make. Despite my stunning suntan, I'm not really from Hawaii. I'm here from Wyoming."

"I know where you're from, Cowboy. And we know why you're here. You're an advanced scout."

The statement puzzled Grayson. He guzzled some gin and regrouped. "Who is 'we,' and what is it I'm scouting for?"

Cicci harrumphed.

"What is that supposed to mean?" he asked.

"Don't play stupid. You know what's going on. You're here to save your state." With the gin now assuming the lead, she bent forward and whispered in his ear, "But it's not happening. The winds of change are upon us, and not you, not Senator Shelton, not even that goddamn Cran Fran can do a thing about it. Sooner than you know, my friend, Wyoming is just going to be a memory."

Now incredulous, Grayson fired back, "You can't just wipe out a state. You need some rational reason. And you forget, lady, states are protected by the Constitution."

"Ah, but not for long, and we have a very good reason to act. In the land where the deer and the antelope play, you've got a big problem. You have too many cows and not enough cowboys."

"What are you talking about?"

"People, Cowboy. I'm talking about people, and you don't have enough of them."

CHAPTER 6

THE 1/700TH RULE

"YOU'RE SURE THAT'S how they're going to play it?" Governor Linsey asked on a breezy Cheyenne morning.

"Yes," Claude answered. "We anticipate draft language of the proposed amendment to be finished by the end of the month. They're already beginning to organize ratification groups in the states they are counting on."

Grayson watched as Wyoming's power players absorbed Claude's shocking revelation. They were seated at an oval conference table in the governor's office. Joining Linsey in this session were Wyoming Senate President Carl Biddle, Wyoming Speaker of the House Winnie Lopez, and the ad hoc committee comprising Claude, Smitty, and Grayson.

Since Grayson had returned from Washington, Theresa Cicci's ominous warning a few weeks earlier had fully sprouted into DC's juiciest rumor. Yesterday, the rumor had become official. The Dems were launching an effort to strip Wyoming's statehood. The campaign phrasing adopted a more benign tone. The purpose wasn't to screw Wyoming; it was to ensure equitable representation across the land.

Specifically, a new constitutional amendment, the Twenty-eighth Amendment if passed, would establish a minimum population necessary to gain admittance or continue as a state. This amendment would be known as the 1/700th Rule and would require each state to maintain a population greater than or equal to one-seven hundredth of the total US population.

Two primary arguments drove the amendment's push. First, if states were to be regarded equally, they should be reasonably similar in key characteristics, with population being one of those characteristics. If the US population was evenly spread among the fifty states, each state would contain one-fiftieth, or two percent, of the population.

Of course, state populations aren't perfectly equal. From the country's origin, the founding fathers recognized there were states with large populations and states with small ones. Each group advocated a style of representation favoring the member states in its group. Large states wanted representation based on population, while small states pushed for an equal allocation among the states. The solution to this political quandary was a compromise—one of the greatest success stories in American civics. Two sets of lawmakers were created. The US Senate would allocate two senators to each state—equal representation. Meanwhile, the US House of Representatives would divvy up seats based on a state's percentage of the country's total population.

The compromise worked well for more than two hundred years. However, no one had anticipated state populations varying to such an extreme. Proponents for the 1/700th Rule now argued it was unreasonable and unfair to grant an inordinate amount of sway to such a tiny fraction of the country's people.

The second argument revolved around the actual one-seven hundredth number. With the US population having just exceeded three hundred fifty million, supporters pointed out that a minimum requirement of one-seven hundredth was equal to one-half million people. This figure represented a nice round number everyone could understand, and it was a generous minimum standard for maintaining statehood. A state only needed five hundred thousand citizens to maintain its status. If it couldn't achieve that level, amendment proponents argued the state was really little more than a sparsely populated territory.

The second argument's more important implication to its advocates, but never actively mentioned by them, was the number of states who currently failed to reach the one-seven hundredth standard. That number equaled one. That state was Wyoming.

To Wyoming's detriment, the numbers didn't lie. While the nation as a whole grew rapidly, the state's population was headed in the opposite direction and falling hard. Throughout its existence, Wyoming had ridden the energy industry's wild boom-and-bust economic cycles. However, the current multiyear political push to squash fossil fuels exacerbated any previously known business decline. First, coal was effectively purged from the domestic list of energy options. More recently, federal regulations severely restricted oil and gas exploration. When technological green-energy innovations had broken into the mainstream, the livelihood so many had known for so long quickly dissipated, much like the sudden disappearance of the prehistoric plants and animals the fossil-fuel industry was based on.

All these shutdowns cratered jobs in the energy industry, but the impact didn't stop there. The state's infrastructure, particularly its school systems, suffered devastating cuts to its budget—forty percent in some cases. With few options for work and little money available for schools and other basic services, families began moving away in droves. In less than a decade, Wyoming's population dropped from a peak of five hundred eighty thousand to a current reading of four hundred seventy-five thousand, a whopping eighteen percent decline.

Biddle spoke. "Claude, refresh my memory. What are the major steps involved in passing an amendment?"

"First, the amendment is introduced in Congress, where it has to pass both houses. A two-thirds majority is required in each. If that happens, then the proposed amendment is presented to the states for ratification. To be ratified, three-quarters of the states—thirty-eight states, as it currently stands—must vote for it."

"And what is the president's role in this effort?"

"He plays no part, not that Garcia would ever be on our side."

"Numbers-wise, how does it look in Congress?" Linsey asked.

Claude answered, "The Democrats hold 312 seats in the House, and they have sixty-nine senators. That's sixty-nine percent of the Senate, and let's see. He paused a moment to calculate and resumed. "Almost seventy-two percent of the House."

"More than two-third majorities in both branches," Lopez observed.

"Yeah. Hmm," Governor Linsey mused as he chewed on a fingernail. "The Senate's numbers aren't completely overwhelming. Any chance of defections on this issue?"

"Maybe Senator Terry in Arkansas, Garrett in New Mexico," Claude said.

"What about Ralston, our northern neighbor?"

"Don't think so. Cran Fran ripped him on a bipartisan agriculture bill a few years back. He hasn't forgotten."

"Cran Fran—he's killing us."

Grayson chimed in. "The scuttlebutt I'm hearing is all the Dems are going to tow the party line. People who might be on the fence like Garrett are okay with passing the amendment in Congress and then letting their home state make the final call."

"So assuming it gets to the states," Lopez said, "who's the next-smallest? Who else is vulnerable?"

"Vermont," Smitty answered. "They're at roughly six hundred thirty thousand in population."

"Rumor has it they're in line to get a massive government contract for a new data warehousing center. Could be as many as five thousand new jobs," Claude said.

"We answered that request for proposal," the governor complained. "We even argued hardship status because of the drilling cuts. Never made it to the second round of bids."

"After Vermont, Alaska and the Dakotas are next. Alaska and North Dakota are in the same boat as us with energy cuts," Smitty continued.

"Yeah, but Anchorage is a big place and has become fairly diverse industry-wise," Biddle said. "North Dakota could be nervous, but their eastern half is stable enough. I don't see them falling under five hundred thousand."

"True," Claude answered, "but as the total US population increases, they could drop below the one-seven hundredth requirement over time."

"So they should at least be sympathetic to our plight," Linsey said. "Who else is on our side? Claude, how many friends do we need?"

"We need at least thirteen 'no' votes from states."

"Mmm. Okay. Grayson, man the white board!" the governor barked. "All right. Let's list our possible allies. If we go straight Republican, who do we have?"

The group took turns identifying conservative states, and Grayson placed them in one of two columns: solid allies and possible allies. When he had finished, seven states, including Wyoming, had been placed in the first column, and a dozen more had been written in the second.

Grayson noted the group's disappointment about other small-population states absent from either column. The Northeastern states of Vermont, New Hampshire, Delaware, Rhode Island,

and Maine were all deep blue in their allegiance, and Hawaii was basically a socialist paradise. Of Wyoming's bordering states, only Colorado hadn't been listed. Grayson was hopeful it had been overlooked, but Biddle and Smitty effectively dashed his hopes.

"The northern counties and western slope would support us, but the Denver/Boulder metropolis has the population and political muscle," Smitty explained. "It's the same problem in the Plains states. Rural populations sympathize, but the eastern border cities—Kansas City, Omaha, and Sioux Falls—dominate with sheer numbers."

Governor Linsey summarized the situation. "So it looks like a forgone conclusion the amendment will pass Congress and move on to the states for ratification. At that point, we have a fighting chance to stop it." He scanned the room for agreement and received it in the form of nodding heads. He asked, "Do we even make a stand in Washington?"

"Of course, we do," Claude answered. "We battle this campaign every damn step of the way."

The governor pressed his tongue into his cheek. "Okay, but I'll leave that to Senator Shelton and you. I'm going to concentrate my energy and Wyoming's resources on convincing enough states this is a bad idea."

"Except for Grayson," Claude said.

"Huh?" Linsey asked.

"All your resources except for Grayson," Claude clarified. "I need him with me in Washington."

"Oh, right," Linsey agreed. "Grayson, you are on loan indefinitely."

"Okay," Grayson said. *Indefinitely?* His stomach hollowed with uncertainty. He glanced at Smitty, who offered an infantile buh-bye wave.

Claude and Linsey stared hard at each other. Had Grayson

converted the men's eye contact into language, it would have said, "Man, this sucks!"

Lopez broke the silence. "We've also been hearing about a Puerto Rican push for statehood. Will that be part of this effort?"

"It won't be part of this amendment or any constitutional amendment," Claude informed her. "The Puerto Ricans simply need to formally decide they want to become a state and then petition Congress. Congress can accept the request with a majority vote. No amendment required."

"How long does the amendment process take?" Grayson asked.

"It varies," Claude said. "The Twenty-sixth Amendment, the one that set the voting age at eighteen, was passed in just over two months. At the other extreme, the Twenty-seventh Amendment took more than two hundred years to pass."

"That's the one dealing with congressional salaries," Biddle said. "Any raise in salary doesn't take effect until the next congressional session."

"Don't want the politicians padding their own bank accounts," Smitty blurted out. His face reddened when he realized who surrounded him in the room. "Present company excluded, of course."

"Like that amendment shut off the money spigots in DC," the governor remarked.

"In fairness, I can understand other states being concerned about our drop in population," Lopez said. "Do we know if another state has ever been this skewed to the low side?"

Smitty replied, "Nevada had barely any people the entire first half of the twentieth century. It was well below the one-seven hundredth minimum for over fifty years. Also, Alaska, when it was first admitted as a state. It wouldn't have met this new criterion."

"So this is an arbitrary level," Lopez concluded.

"Yes, but so what?" Linsey answered. "A political play is being made here. They're just making up a rule to support their desired outcome."

"I wonder," Lopez pondered, "what if we lobbied for a minimum number that's absolute rather than relative?"

"What are you thinking?" Governor Linsey asked.

"Well, we could offer a number—say three hundred fifty thousand—as a floor. That way we're acknowledging a minimum population should be set, but we remain a state because we're still above that number."

"Why does population have to be included as a requirement at all?" Claude argued. "It's never been a criterion before."

"Because at some point, population matters," the governor answered. "You can't justify a state with only a thousand people, or ten thousand, or even fifty thousand."

As Linsey made his point, Grayson saw Claude messing with his cell phone.

"Here's some information from Washington," he announced to the room. "It couldn't be timelier. Leslie has obtained proposed language for the amendment." He shared the proposal.

Amendment XXVIII

SECTION 1. Any proposed state petitioning for admittance to the Union must have a citizen population greater than or equal to one-seven hundredth of the total United States population.

SECTION 2. Every existing state in the Union must maintain a population of at least one-seven hundredth of the total current population of the United States.

SECTION 3. Failure of an existing state to meet the population requirement in Section 2 will result in its loss of statehood, and the geographic area of that state will be declared a __________.

SECTION 4. Congress will be empowered with discretion in managing the newly dissolved state.

Everyone in the room paused in quiet reflection. Smitty was the first to break the silence.

"Why did they leave a big blank in Section 3?" he asked.

"Good question," Claude mused.

"It's because they don't have an answer," Grayson offered.

"They don't," the governor agreed. "There's general agreement about getting rid of us as a state, but they don't know what to do with us in the aftermath."

"Oh, you can bet some folks back there have ideas," Claude said. "It's just that nobody has the same idea. That's a big holdup for them and might buy us some time."

The governor agreed.

Grayson considered the proposed amendment. That blank line put a lump in his throat. *What will Wyoming be years from now? Who will I be? An American citizen with voting rights? Maybe. Maybe not.*

CHAPTER 7

FILLING IN THE BLANK

AS A DREARY November afternoon waned, Grayson stormed through the front door of Senator Shelton's office and flung himself into a waiting room chair.

"Whoa! Easy there, Mr. Woodley," Leslie said, waiting for a document to print.

Grayson glanced Leslie's way and then audibly exhaled. "Man, what a bunch of bastards!" he shouted.

The noise drew the senator and Claude from the adjoining room. "You're looking a bit unsettled, partner. What's up?" Claude asked.

Slowly, Grayson recognized the other's concern over his fuss. He closed his eyes and attempted to regain his composure. Yet when images of the just-completed committee session reappeared and dangled in his head, he erupted once more. "Those guys are impossible! They won't even try to reason."

By "those guys," Grayson meant a handful of congressional assistants serving on the House Committee on Natural Resources.

This committee was taking the lead in writing and advancing the amendment proposal. Grayson lacked any designated political clout, so getting actual face time in the same room with house members—or senators, for that matter—was a pipe dream. Still, Grayson had persisted in his quest to pitch Wyoming's case. He coaxed and pestered the lead committee designees until they relented and permitted him to sit in on the proposed amendment meetings. At these sessions, the legislative underlings hashed out details, crossed t's, and dotted i's.

"Would you like some water? Or tea?" Shelton asked. At six feet in height, the farmer's daughter of Dutch descent stood tall when Grayson was upright. Now looking up at her from his chair, she assumed a redwood's status.

"Or cyanide?" Claude joked. His remark drew a snicker from Leslie.

Grayson declined the senator's offer and rejected Claude's with a smirk, but the gestures from his superiors grounded him.

"Give us a rundown of the meeting," Shelton said, a golden-aged lady with wise, blue eyes and a dozen-plus years of Washington under her belt.

Grayson considered how to best summarize the afternoon's session. "Basically, they're assuming Wyoming loses this battle in Congress. That enables them to focus on the fill-in-the-blank part of the amendment—you know, what happens after we're booted. They started tossing out some pretty radical crap, so I spoke up and tried to rein them in with some common sense—at least I thought so."

"What did you suggest?" the senator asked.

"I said the simplest solution would be to relegate us to a territorial status, just like we were before Wyoming became a state and just like Puerto Rico and Guam are now. That way we no longer have direct representation in Congress, but we are still under the domain of the US. Going forward, we use the Wyoming

Constitution to self-govern. I also pointed out that making us a territory enables us to regain statehood if our population rebounds and meets the one-seven hundredth threshold."

"And how did that go over?" Claude asked as he poured a cup of tea for himself.

"Like a lead balloon. They said this situation is a once-in-a-generation opportunity to… Now get this. These are their exact words: 'to right some historical wrongs.' I asked them what the hell that even means, but they just smugly blew me off and went back to Operation Crazy."

Now seated with her hands in her lap, Shelton asked, "What specifically are they considering?"

"Well, the group consensus was to give Wyoming back to nature. They vary in opinion as to exactly how that might be done and to what extent. They definitely don't want any more coal or oil or gas production, which we already knew and is pretty much already a done deal."

Claude pressed, "What about renewable energy? Are they planning to keep the wind farms? What about any solar projects?"

"Didn't say specifically," Grayson replied. "Also, some people don't want to allow ranching or farming."

"You're kidding?" Leslie said.

"No. I'm not."

"What about tourism?" the senator asked. "Are they thinking of making the entire state a wilderness area?"

"No one actually said, 'Wilderness area,' but I think many of them envision large portions of the state going untouched. Also, I got the impression they planned on leaving Yellowstone and the Tetons alone. The public would flip out if they couldn't visit Old Faithful."

"Surely they're not planning to close I-80," Claude said. "It's a major trucking route."

Grayson just shrugged.

After a pensive, silent moment, Claude said, "Okay, so how exactly are they proposing to govern this novel, back-to-nature region?"

Claude's question jogged Grayson's memory. "Oh yeah. Interesting story. One lady recommended keeping the amendment simple by saying Congress will have the authority and responsibility for deciding how the area will be designated and governed. I thought that sounded reasonable, but a couple of others jumped all over it. They were adamant the designation and governance piece be fully described in the amendment. I didn't get it."

The senator half-smiled and half-grimaced. "They want to ensure the new Wyoming, whatever it is they decide upon, will be a permanent fixture. If they specify precisely what Wyoming is to be in the amendment, then that's what it'll be forever unless the amendment is changed or repealed. We all know how hard that is. But if they simply gave that power to Congress and the makeup of Congress were to change, say from a Democratic-dominated one to one that is Republican, then the new Congress could change Wyoming's status as they see fit."

"Ah," Grayson said in comprehension. "That's smart on their part."

"Yes, it is," Shelton agreed.

"And a designation to some other kind of entity closes the door on Wyoming ever returning to state status," Grayson concluded.

"Bingo," Claude said.

Shelton steepled her fingers. "Did they say how they're planning to handle the displacement of people? If they get their way, almost one-half million bodies will have to go somewhere."

Grayson considered her question for a second. "Not really. They briefly talked about the need to allocate some government monies for the transition, but that would be a budget discussion after the amendment passes."

"To hell with the affected population as long as you eliminate two Republican senators!" Claude groused.

The remark rekindled Grayson's ire. "The thing that really upsets me is no one in that room seemed to care about the plight of the average Westerner. It's like they don't see individuals getting hurt. Instead, they throw up some faceless image of a greedy driller, Mr. Polluter, or a redneck hunter, Mr. Murderer." He stood and began pacing as Leslie, Claude, and Shelton listened attentively to his outburst. "They don't understand our livelihood. They've never seen a roughneck freezing in the January darkness while he's pulling up a thousand feet of pipe from a drilling hole just so they can turn their thermostat to seventy-five degrees. They don't feel the pain in their wallet when a pack of wolves devours a couple of your steers."

"Welcome to our world," Shelton said.

From his seat, Grayson evaluated the senator's plight and began to appreciate the challenges a person in her position faced.

"So, how do we change our image?" Claude asked.

Leslie spoke. "Well, maybe we should make our legislative friends see us for who we are. We could focus on individuals, profile their stories, maybe call the campaign 'Everyday Wyoming' or something like that."

The senator's eyebrows raised. "Leslie, I can't possibly be paying you enough."

"No, ma'am, you're not," Leslie replied with a smile.

Grayson waited patiently while Leslie completed her pitch. When she finished, he tossed a new complication into the mix. "Not to burst your bubble, Leslie, 'cause I think you've got us moving in the right direction, but I just remembered something else that drives me crazy."

"What's that?" Claude asked.

"Many of them have adopted animal rights as their new religion." Grayson's remark was answered with anticipating faces.

"They believe it's their moral duty to expand animal ecosystems at whatever the cost."

"How does that relate to Leslie's idea?" Claude asked.

"I'm just saying when we profile Joe the sugar-beet farmer outside of Worland, we need to understand that serene shots of Max the Moose chomping on moss at the base of the Tetons will be playing on five different social media channels."

"But you do agree that telling our human story is important?" the senator asked.

"For sure," Grayson agreed.

Shelton continued. "Speaking of the 'go natural' offensive, yesterday, I learned Senator Doolin has invited the CEO from Great Outdoors America to speak with the Senate Natural Resources Subcommittee next week. And, get this: he's bringing Extravaganza along for the show."

"Extravaganza the singer?" Claude asked.

"The one and only."

"Since when did she become an expert in land-use policy?" Claude protested.

Shelton gestured toward Grayson. "Like our man in the war room said, you just need a smartphone and a devotion to furry critters."

"Oh, great."

⟡

In a packed senate conference room one week later, the Senate Subcommittee for Conservation, Forestry, and Natural Resources convened. Unlike the somber, all-business tone usually permeating the conference room during a typical testimonial session, today's affair carried a festive mood. And why not? This gathering had little to do with fact-finding. Instead, it was a pep rally disguised as information collection.

Two environmental "experts" sat at the guest-speakers' table.

Hector Devine served as CEO for Great Outdoors America. The head honcho—a lean, fit man who was pushing fifty but could easily pass for thirty-five—wore an open-neck, button-down shirt of forest green with khaki trousers. His arguably too-casual attire raised the eyebrows of some in the room; however, more attendees were struck by his hairstyle: a ponytail stub riding in back of an otherwise shiny, bald head. He was accompanied by Extravaganza, one of pop music's most iconic artists and an honorary organization member.

In accordance with senate custom, Democratic and Republican subcommittee members alternated turns in speaking with their invited guests. Using this format, a guest speaker could typically expect badgering from one senator and tender loving care by the next or vice versa.

Yet today's proceedings went differently. The Democrats, true to form, tossed out softball questions and gratuitous raves. The Republicans, however, limited their interaction to requests for clarification or expansion on the finer points of the environmental organization's presentation. No one was willing to contest an issue already decided. No hawks in the room today—well, except for one. Senator Shelton's turn to query came last.

"Good afternoon, Ms. Extravaganza. Thank you for taking the time to share your input."

"Thank you, Senator." The singing diva radiated an entirely different clothing vibe. She was decked out in a tight, gold pantsuit ornamented with scattered ruby- and pearl-colored sequins. She had unzipped the top of her garment low enough to share a generous view of her voluptuous breasts cradled in a black lace plunge bra.

The senator continued. "I'd like to better understand your involvement with Great Outdoors America. How did you get started with the organization?"

"Hmm. Well, I guess the first time I heard of Great Outdoors America was at a rally down in La Jolla to protect the sea lions."

"Could you expand on that, please?"

"Sure. You see, someone in the city wanted to take the sea lions off the endangered list, and my friends and I knew how beautiful these creatures are and felt that was wrong. We learned Great Outdoors America was staging a protest, so we joined in."

"Do you have a background, say any education or training, in marine biology or any type of natural science? How did you think you might help?"

"Well, I've watched a lot of documentaries about climate change and animal extinction. Watching all these animals getting killed off upset me. I decided getting involved and trying to help was the right thing to do. I met Hector in La Jolla, and he said I could be very useful to the effort 'cause people recognized me and all."

"Because you're famous?"

"Yeah. At first, I was thinking about maybe writing a song about animals on the endangered list, but Hector said we should concentrate on ways for people to associate my name and face with Great Outdoors America."

"I see. So have you attended rallies in other places?"

"Sometimes."

"In Wyoming?"

"No."

"Have you ever been to Wyoming?"

"Yes, a couple of times. We did a concert at a university once. I don't remember what city it was in, but it was awfully cold, and the wind blew like crazy."

"Laramie can be very cold in the winter."

"Laramie. Yeah, that's right. I remember now. I've been so many places on tour, it's hard to keep 'em straight. Oh, I've also been to Jackson Hole. Now, that place is beautiful, sitting in that valley with the mountains shooting straight up. And the little town is so cute. It's got that park in the middle with all the antlers piled up in an arch."

"Did you do any camping while you were there? Pitch a tent? Sleep in a sleeping bag?"

"Me? Oh, goodness no, Senator. I stayed with my friend, Millie Skidoo, the actress."

"Does she live in town?"

"Oh no. Her place is out of town a bit. It sits on this ridge. Beautiful view, six bedrooms, three fireplaces. It's amazing."

"Wood-burning fireplaces?"

"Yep. I don't have a fireplace in my house, so using hers was a real treat. I'd start singing while she was getting it going."

"Did it create much ash or soot?"

"I don't remember. Maybe some, but that's a small price to pay for such great atmosphere. Besides, I didn't have to clean it up."

The senator smiled. "While you were in Jackson or Laramie, did you have a chance to meet some locals?"

"Not so much. We stayed at Millie's mostly. But one night, we did go to the Cowboy Bar and sat in the saddles. That was a blast. I did talk to some folks then when they asked for my autograph."

"Generally, how would you describe the people you saw while you were in Wyoming—at the concert, in the bar, on the streets?"

"Oh, they're real nice people. You know, regular-type people."

"Would you say normal, everyday *Americans*?"

"Oh yeah. Red, white, and blue all the way."

Senator Shelton glanced at Doolin, the committee chair, to register the last point and then resumed. "Speaking of homes, I recently read a lifestyle-magazine article about your place in Malibu. How is it possible to keep a four-thousand-square-foot home free from sand?"

"Five thousand square feet, Senator. And it's not easy if you're always going to the beach, but I usually hang out at my swimming pool."

"I'm guessing yours is not the only house with a swimming pool."

"Just about everyone in Malibu has a pool."

"And in the surrounding areas: Santa Monica, Beverly Hills, Pacific Palisades?"

"Yeah."

"How much rain do you get annually in LA?"

"I have no idea."

"But it's generally a sunny, dry climate, wouldn't you say?"

"That's why everyone wants to live in Southern California."

"Out of curiosity, how much water do you use in a given month?"

"I couldn't tell you. Morris, my house manager, takes care of my expenses."

"You've been very patient with my questions, Ms. Extravaganza. Thank you. I'd just like to summarize your efforts with Great Outdoors America before I move on to discussions with Mr. Devine. Would you say your involvement is limited to animal protection?"

"Oh no! We're actively involved in all types of conservation efforts. Protecting animals and their habitat is a major part, but we care about all environmental issues. We only have this one planet, so we have to protect our entire world and use our resources wisely: the land, the water, the air, and all the living creatures."

"Indeed! Thank you again, Ms. Extravaganza."

Hector Devine bristled in his seat while the senator exploited the singing diva's naivety. When his turn for interrogation arose, he cast a penetrating glare of pure disdain the senator's way. Not with words, but instead with narrowed eyes and a tightened jaw, the CEO of Great Outdoors America communicated an unmistakable message: "Try playing me like that, bitch, and I'll bury you."

Shelton recognized the new adversarial challenge yet began the dialogue in the same way she had with Extravaganza.

"Mr. Devine, like my other colleagues, I thank you for taking the time to educate us about Great Outdoors America, its ongoing efforts, and how they relate to the proposed effort to convert Wyoming, my home, from a state into a lesser political entity."

Devine offered an unsmiling nod and then mirrored his inquisitor in tenor. "Senator Shelton, like I said to your other esteemed colleagues, it is my pleasure to share the mission and passion of Great Outdoors America. However, I must correct your implication that my organization has an interest in the political stake of Wyoming. We do not. Our aim is to advance the preservation of our natural world whenever possible, wherever possible."

"I see. And to that aim, you are proposing that Wyoming be relegated to a region where human activity is minimized?"

"If not eliminated completely."

"If not eliminated completely," the senator echoed.

"Yes, well, that would be the ideal, but realistically, there would be some human interaction with the area."

"So you are advocating the removal of cities?"

"To the extent possible, yes."

"The elimination of farms and ranches?"

"Again, to the extent possible."

"The cessation of any mining activity?"

"Absolutely."

"Tourism?"

"That's negotiable, but it needs to be strictly managed."

"Pardon my ignorance, but what exactly is the benefit from all this hardship you want to place on the citizens of Wyoming?"

"You are so myopic in your thinking, Senator. The human race benefits. It benefits because we've taken steps to allow a small piece of our natural world to flourish. You're fixated on the citizens of Wyoming, who are at most one-half million people. There are eight billion humans on our planet. Asking a small percentage to endure some inconvenience in exchange for cleaner air, water, and a more balanced ecosystem is the deal of the century. Rarely on this earth do we get an opportunity to return such a large expanse of land back to its natural state."

"And the decision is a no-brainer if you aren't one of the few forced to make the sacrifices. If you want to play a numbers game, Mr. Devine, tell me, would you be willing to sacrifice the life of one healthy child if it meant saving the lives of twenty senior citizens?"

"That's ridiculous and completely irrelevant to this issue! No one's advocating any killing. We're only asking people to move, and mass migrations have taken place many times throughout history. Europeans migrated to America, and Americans living in the East trekked westward to California and Oregon."

"Those were voluntary decisions on the parts of the migrants."

"So what?"

"So maybe better examples are the Trail of Tears or the Bataan Death March. You know—involuntary expeditions."

Hector threw his body back into his seat and folded his arms. "That's real rich of you to throw out the Trail of Tears: a white lady citing Native American suffering."

"Can't we learn from our mistakes? And by the way, what ever happened to life, liberty, and the pursuit of happiness? Forcing people to leave their homes for political reasons doesn't seem to meet those tenets."

"Listen to yourself, Senator! Your ignorance is deafening. People have been rooted out of their homes due to politics since civilization began. Cuba, Vietnam, Hong Kong. Those are just some recent examples."

"It's funny, don't you think, that your 'recent examples' are all of the communist persuasion? Are you sympathetic to the communist cause, sir?"

A less disciplined man would have taken the bait and teed off on his assailant. Instead, Devine sidestepped it. He poured some water from a pitcher into his cup and drank. Then, with a wry smile, he answered.

"Like I mentioned earlier, our motivation for Wyoming's reclamation is not political. We view it as a double win for humanity and the planet. First, we stop activities that are damaging the planet: fossil-fuel extraction, raising methane-producing cattle and sheep, and the senseless killing of endangered species. Second, we facilitate a return to nature before man's intrusion. We allow wolves and grizzlies, predators indigenous to this region, to reclaim their territory. We permit bison herds to repopulate to their natural equilibrium. We rejoice in maintaining an area whose water and land are pristine."

The senator's blank stare and open mouth revealed the crippling effect of her opponent's blow. Devine's cogent remarks left her grasping for any sort of meaningful comeback. His succinct argument swayed anyone sitting in the gallery who'd previously been undecided.

Trying to recover, Shelton asked, "Converting Wyoming to wilderness won't solve the world's problems. It will barely have any effect. There are far greater transgressions around the globe causing substantially more damage: overpopulation in Asia and Africa, the destruction of rain forests, the decimation of ocean fishing. Why aren't you pursuing those with the same vigor?"

"We are pursuing those, but our influence is limited. Converting Wyoming is a tangible action we can achieve."

With elbows on the table, the senator allowed her outstretched fingers to support her head as she looked down at her notes. Highlighted in orange, her eyes caught two phrases: *Max the Moose and man's best friend*. She remembered an idea from a few days earlier.

"Mr. Devine, much of your pleading today has been for the protection and betterment of animals. Is that a fair statement?"

"Yes."

"And you, personally, have a deep love for animals?"

"Of course."

"Do you, by chance, own a dog?"

"Yes. Two. I have a black lab and a mutt who's a rescue."

"Lucky dog."

Extravaganza piped up. "I own two dogs, too, Senator. They're little shih tzus, and their names are Crunchy and Flakes. I named 'em that 'cause I was shooting a commercial for a breakfast cereal when I got 'em."

Extravaganza's interruption surprised Shelton, but she adjusted and brought the cheerful singer into the conversation. "How interesting! And I bet you spoil those little rascals rotten."

"You know I do," the singer answered gaily.

"And you'd protect them come hell or high water."

"They're family. In fact, I like them more than a lot of people I know." Extravaganza turned her body and looked back at the audience in the gallery. "Y'all know what I'm talking about."

Roughly half the heads in the gallery bobbed in enthusiastic agreement. Even Devine participated in the affirmation. After the heated exchange between the CEO and the senator, the audience was anxious for some tension relief, and here it was.

Shelton watched this sudden turn of events. She fed into the room's mood. "You know, if a person had to choose between saving a dog or Marcos Tuttle from drowning, I'm pretty sure I know which one would get picked."

Upon hearing that scenario, the crowd in the room howled in laughter. Marcos Tuttle played quarterback for the Dallas Cowboys, the archenemy of Washington's football team. The fog of stress that had been so dense only a few minutes earlier had dissipated. Senator Shelton allowed the residual jocularity to run its course. Then she resumed.

"But I wonder, what if we replaced Marcos with a homeless person? What about a stranger? A child? A neighbor? Even if that neighbor lives in another state?" She paused and permitted the silence to work its effect. "I have a dog, too, and I love him to pieces. But he's a dog! If I'm forced to choose between an animal and a human being, it's no contest! Seems to me that on our march toward greater compassion for our brothers and sisters, we've taken a wrong turn. We need to think long and hard about getting back on track."

She picked up her note cards and tapped them into alignment. Then, she turned her attention to the committee chairperson. "Senator Doolin, my time has expired. Thank you."

CHAPTER 8
HAPPY HOLIDAYS

IN DAYS FOLLOWING the fireworks between Senator Shelton and Hector Devine, media reporting varied by region. In Washington, DC, news outlets printed stories on page seven in the Politics section. One story portrayed Devine as a world-saving visionary, and another touted Wyoming's reversion back to its natural status as a great work of progressive civics.

Meanwhile in Wyoming, the tumultuous event registered as front-page news. What had begun as an uneasy rumor among citizens of the Equality State now exploded into the only matter anyone wanted to discuss. The push to eliminate Wyoming was real. Shelton's confrontation with the famous environmentalist served as the opening salvo in a desperate fight for their homeland.

From his new studio apartment in Washington, Grayson rested against the bed's headboard and massaged his feet. He listened to an update coming from a hospital room in Casper.

"Grayson," Tammy Woodley said. "I'm going to put you on the speaker." A pause. "Can you hear me?"

"Yeah, Mom."

"Please help me talk some sense into your dad. Now he's got an infection."

"Grayson," Daryl Woodley called, "what in the hell is going on back there? A return to nature! Are they out of their mind?"

"You broke your leg on Wednesday?" Grayson asked.

"Dad didn't break his leg," cried a third voice from the hospital—Grayson's younger sister, Cindy. "He fell on top of a wooden stake. Part of it split off and went through his leg. It's so gross!"

Tammy chimed in. "He didn't go to the doctor right away, like I told him, and now it's infected. The smart aleck gets to spend a week in the hospital."

"What happened exactly?" Grayson asked.

"Ah, hell. I was doing some fix-up on the garden side of the house. I reached out to grab some pliers off a window ledge and overextended. Landed on a pole bean stake," Daryl explained.

"Why am I just now hearing about this?"

"Well, son, it sounds like you might be a little busy these days in Washington."

His dad was right. After Cheyenne's strategy session in the governor's office eight weeks ago, Grayson had accompanied Claude back to DC. Because Grayson would be staying in Washington for an extended period, he had moved out of the hotel and into a furnished apartment.

That time span away from home felt like an eternity: eight weeks of late nights and phantom weekends, eight weeks in a strange bed, eight weeks with little sunshine. For a Wyoming native, the last entry on that list was perhaps the most difficult to endure. Gray days and a politically bleak outlook now weighed heavily on his countenance.

A lonesome Thanksgiving had come and gone. Grayson was anxious to reunite with his family during Christmas. Given the groundswell of environmental support for a repurposing of

Wyoming land, he wondered how many future Christmases at the Woodley ranch were left. His dad's predicament gave him one more reason to get home this year.

"I need to okay it with Claude, but I think I can fly back early, next weekend maybe. Help out a bit."

"Grayson, I don't need another damned babysitter. I've already got your mom and sister squawking over me day and night. We need you back there to shake some sense into those knuckleheads."

"Zach and Libby will be back from their trip Sunday," Tammy added. "Your brother's got a handle on things. Not that we wouldn't love to see you."

Grayson resigned himself to a few more nights in Washington. "What's the reaction to the 'go natural' push?"

"It's what you'd expect," Daryl answered. "People from Evanston to Gillette are shocked, including me."

Grayson had discussed the statehood situation several times with his dad and knew he was worried. Daryl's livelihood was at stake. "Well, talking a big game and playing one are two different things. Hector Devine's vision is too radical. The states won't ratify it."

"Well, let's hope so," Daryl said. "Then again, a year ago, this situation wasn't even a discussion item."

✦

A week later, Grayson's chances of spending Christmas at his family's ranch outside of Douglas dwindled to zero. Usually, the end-of-year holiday period was a dead zone at the Capitol, but the ever-changing proposals and responses to the Twenty-eighth Amendment made any yuletide planning futile. Claude guessed they might be able squeeze in a four or five-day break if nothing new came up. However, when Grayson factored in the necessary travel time—flights and a long car ride from Denver—he couldn't justify the holiday airfare premiums for such a short stay.

In the vanity mirror situated over an eggshell-colored sink, Grayson inspected his goatee as he wiped the last dab of shaving cream from his face. It had filled in nicely. He inflated his cheeks and then allowed the air to squeak through his lips while he considered his mood. A dreary face with sapphire-blue eyes stared back at him and offered little solace. *I got the blues.*

⪻

At eleven thirty that same morning, Grayson stepped into a hotel banquet room and searched for Senator Mendenhall. The senator waved and approached him at the check-in table.

"Hello, Grayson. Glad you could make it. We're sitting at different tables. Ask one of these nice ladies, and they'll tell you where your seat is."

"Thanks, Senator."

Mendenhall had extended a last-minute invitation for Grayson to join him at a luncheon. The gathering featured a multimedia presentation by a famous wildlife photographer. Politicians from both parties and key monetary donors committed to environmental causes filled the room.

Grayson canvassed the large venue and spotted his table. He took his seat next to Lanetta Spitz, a striking, older woman who maximized her attractiveness by making it appear as if she hadn't tried at all. She wore her blonde-tinted hair in a stylized mess of oblique bangs and torn ends long enough to pull behind her ears. Her jade drop earrings and matching necklace accentuated her broad smile. However, the absence of wrinkles in places they naturally belonged betrayed the cosmetic work performed to meet her vain standards.

After introductions but before the arrival of salads, Grayson communicated his temporary status in DC. Upon learning of his permanent residence in Wyoming, Lanetta gushed over her enchantment with the Rocky Mountain region.

"I love the majesty in that part of the country, the serene peaks, the gurgling waters," she cooed. "And the names out there are so inspiring. Once, I heard the most romantic name for a place: Crowheart Butte. Do you know it?"

Grayson smiled. *Of all the places in Wyoming, that one would not top my most romantic list.* He pictured the stand-alone, barren butte as he answered. "I do. Are you familiar with its story?"

"No. Please tell me."

"Well, two tribes, the Shoshone and the Crow, were competing for hunting territory in the Wind River Basin. One day, the Shoshone attacked the Crow, who were camped near this big butte with a flat top. The butte stood out from the surrounding landscape and could be seen for miles. The two tribes battled each other for days but neither side was winning, so Chief Washakie of the Shoshone challenged Chief Big Robber to an individual duel to decide the battle. Washakie killed Big Robber and then cut out his heart and put it on the end of his lance to display his victory."

"Oh my! That's ghastly. Not the love story I'd envisioned," Lanetta remarked in her proud Virginian drawl.

"No, it's not, but there are many, many romantic spots in the state."

As Grayson finished his tale, a waiter walked nearby, and Lanetta caught his attention with a hand wave. She requested some sugar substitute for her iced tea and then asked Grayson if he needed anything.

"Oh yes. May I get some more water?"

"*May I,*" Lanetta repeated with a light hand slap to her sternum. "A young gentleman with manners. Mr. Woodley, you are a rarity in today's world."

For Grayson, Lanetta's remarks brought his mom to mind. She constantly harped on the importance of saying "please" and "thank you." *Mom, you were right.*

Grayson continued his congenial conversation with Lanetta.

though it was interrupted several times by people, important people, going out of their way to stop and say hello. *This lady has clout. What's her story?*

When Grayson revealed his cancellation of holiday travel plans, Lanetta gently covered his hand with hers. "Then you must attend my holiday party. I insist."

∾

Grayson whistled a happy tune as he removed his coat and placed it on a hanger in Senator Shelton's office. The luncheon had given him an unexpected pick-me-up.

"What's up with you?" Claude asked. "You're not supposed to be happy."

Grayson told Claude about the lunch, his chance encounter with Lanetta, and the subsequent invitation to her holiday party. Upon overhearing the words "Lanetta Spitz" and "holiday party", Shelton rushed into the room.

"Did you just say you've been invited to Lanetta's party?"

"Yes, Senator."

She accepted Grayson's affirmation with a scowl. "I didn't get an invitation this year. I've gone the last five years. I think she dumped me like a bad habit."

"Well," Claude explained, "you did rough up her boy, Hector Devine. She's big into the environmental cause."

Grayson noticed the senator fidgeting with her wedding ring and knew she was clearly miffed. "I don't have to go to the party," he offered.

"Oh yes, you do," Claude insisted. "Lanetta throws a whopper of a party. It's one of Northern Virginia's most notable affairs. There'll be power players and plenty of gossip. You'll be our eyes and ears." He looked at the rebuffed senator for concurrence, and she reluctantly shrugged. He smiled at Grayson. "Network away, buddy. Go and do what you do best."

"So, what's the lowdown on the party hostess?" Grayson asked, and Claude briefed him.

Lanetta Spitz—formerly Lanetta Meyer, formerly Lanetta Bizet, and originally Lanetta Patterson—led a high-class life. Though zero for three in her quest to land a compatible husband, she boasted a perfect score in matrimonially uniting with the CEO of Wall Street's next high-flying company. Her divorce settlements had left her with hefty stock holdings in online commerce, biotechnology, and clean energy. Financial analysts were only half-joking when they admitted to tracking Lanetta's choice of dating companions as a means to pick the next stock about to skyrocket.

Lanetta maintained opulent residences in Kauai, San Francisco, and Manhattan; however, she considered her stone, colonial mansion in Great Falls, a ritzy community on the west side of the Potomac River, to be home. A Virginia girl by birth, she blended her Southern, genteel upbringing with an avocation for progressive causes. The generous donations she bestowed enabled recipients to overlook her many eccentricities.

In step with the season, snowflakes danced in the winter air as guests arrived at Lanetta's celebration. Tonight's event was the first of many parties she would host during the holidays, each for a particular group. This evening's attendees were an array of Democratic politicians and staffers with special consideration being given to those patriots working on the Twenty-eighth Amendment.

Grayson exited the rideshare vehicle and marveled at the gaily decorated mansion's exterior and manicured grounds surrounding it. Having now spent nearly six months in the nation's capital, he was slowly acclimating to the private monuments of wealth visible in and around the city. Even so, Lanetta's spread had him gawking in amazement.

As she did with her other guests, Lanetta cheerfully greeted Grayson at the door. He handed her a small jar of organic honey with a red ribbon wrapped around its collar.

"Made in Wyoming. Merry Christmas," Grayson said and smiled politely as she clasped his hands in hers, holding the grip long enough to make him a tad uncomfortable.

Once inside, Grayson roamed leisurely through the expansive main floor. Themed food setups varied from room to room. One contained a seafood spread, another a carving station of prime rib and ham, and a third offered classic hors d'oeuvres. In a side room on the home's west end, a decadent mountain of candy, cookies, and other sweet confections were arranged. Roving waiters passed out champagne and eggnogs, but an open bar was also available for those guests preferring a customized potable.

Grayson grabbed a champagne glass and surveyed the crowd. He recognized more people than he had expected and searched for a potential friend. Across the room, he spotted a tall, blond man facing away from him. When the man turned, he recognized Thomas Darling. Immediately, Grayson scanned for Leslie but came up empty. When he turned his attention back to Thomas, the reason for Leslie's absence became clear. Darling had his arm wrapped around some sweet young thing.

For the next hour, Grayson milled about, pausing occasionally to exchange season's tidings. He selected the seafood station for dinner and paid homage to Smitty by heaping a generous portion of spiced shrimp onto his plate. They were good but couldn't measure up to the Alaskan king crab claws. If this evening did nothing else, it at least spared him another night of takeout food in his lonely apartment.

Lanetta gathered the guests in the main hall to congratulate everyone on their contributions to environmental activism. Her only lament was Hector Devine's absence. He would have individually thanked each dedicated soul. She closed by wishing her dear friends the warmth of the season and a happy and healthy new year.

The crowd dispersed into the many rooms and resumed in merrymaking. Grayson made his way to the dessert room and was contemplating fudge versus pink divinity when a couple approached him. He recognized them from committee sessions he'd attended. A moment later, Theresa Cicci casually appeared at the room's entrance. He nodded at her and then turned to the couple.

"Hello, Grayson," the man said. "When I saw you in the hallway during the toast, I couldn't help but think how awkward you must feel this evening."

"We don't hate you," the woman added. "It's just that we find ourselves on different sides of this particular issue."

Grayson politely listened as the couple spoke but kept part of his attention on Cicci. She had advanced but remained apart from the group. Out of the corner of his eye, he caught her mocking the woman and mouthing some words.

Oh, we hate you. We really do. She punctuated her delivery with an impish smile and then turned to the dessert table, where she selected a sugar cookie.

Grayson redirected his attention to the couple. "We are indeed on different sides. I wasn't offended. Honestly, if I'm not overwhelmingly outnumbered, I feel out of place."

Lanetta entered the dessert room and beelined over to him. "I am so delighted you decided to come. You are a most welcome guest." Again, she secured his hand in hers. Turning slightly, she glanced at the couple and rolled out an arm in their direction. "All of you. It is such a pleasure."

Grayson watched Cicci take in Lanetta's show from afar. She caught him looking at her, turned, and strolled out of the room. *What's with her?*

Theresa Cicci had no direct influence in his life, but she did seem to wink in and out of it, riding along on her own little tangential vector. Her boss had assigned her to be on the Twenty-eighth Amendment team, but Grayson and she had seldom interacted. Okay—in fairness, he did beg a favor to sit in on the committee's brainstorming session a few weeks ago, but that was about it. Still, they did seem to run into each other more than expected. When they did, she always seemed primed to dish out a rash of grief in his direction. He wasn't going out of his way to make contact with her. Was she?

Grayson assured Lanetta she was the most gracious hostess he'd encountered while traveling. Then he grabbed a dessert plate, picked a variety of treats, and sauntered back to the great room. There he admired Lanetta's impeccably decorated, eight-foot Christmas tree. Many ornaments presented a coordinated theme of multiple stages in Santa's workshop. It reminded Grayson of his favorite ornaments at home. This recollection made him sentimental—and sad. He wasn't aware his face displayed the latter emotion until a recognizable voice startled him: Cicci's voice.

"Oh Cowboy, you look so glum. I think I'm going to cry."

Grayson smiled. "Didn't realize you were the teary type."

"Cheer up. It's Christmas." She sipped from her cocktail.

"Gin and tonic?"

"Not just gin. Tanqueray."

"Nothing less from Lanetta."

"Speaking of our hostess, I know just the remedy for your pitiful mood. Why don't you scoot over there and park yourself under the mistletoe? Lanetta will happily come dashing over and plant a big, sloppy one on your lips."

"Shut up!"

"Seriously. She's taken a shining to you, Cowboy."

Grayson tossed his head back and laughed. "Ms. Cicci, you are consistent—consistently annoying."

"Think I'm joking? Look around. You're the only enemy agent at this party."

Grayson remained silent, but his brain actively processed the guest list. She appeared to be right. He couldn't recall seeing any other guests from the Republican side of the aisle. *Any? Really?*

"Since she's now in the zillionaire's club," Cicci continued, "I think Lanetta's changed her courting priorities. Apparently, she's hot for the sweet and harmless type."

"Who said I'm harmless?"

She cackled. "You for real, Cowboy? You wouldn't be here if anyone considered you a threat."

Ouch. Instinctively, Grayson's body drew back. He turned sideways and looked around the room. "I'm tired of standing," he muttered and walked away.

He took a few steps and noticed an empty bay window. Complementing the remainder of the room, it was decorated with a holiday-green, custom-fit seat cushion. Grayson wasn't positively sure the cushion was meant for sitting, but sitting was what he wanted to do. Sitting and creating some empty space around him. He sat down and selected the next holiday morsel on his plate. The first bite lifted his spirits. He studied the half-eaten bourbon pecan tart and congratulated himself for having put two on his plate.

Cicci approached at a relaxed gait. "Those look good. Mind if I join you?"

Grayson shrugged.

She sat in the empty space next to him, crossed her legs, and rested the drink in her lap. "Sometimes I forget how sharp my elbows are. It's a habit, you know?"

"No worries."

Grayson reconsidered the apologetic figure sitting next to him. She smelled good—not a perfume-based aroma but instead something like a body powder. It was clean and fresh and simple. When she repositioned her legs, she inadvertently inched closer to him. The sides of their hips now touched. She smoothed her heather-gray, wool skirt, and Grayson glanced at her shapely calves. They were encased in maroon stockings that matched her sweater. These sensations of sight and touch and smell elicited a new regard for Ms. Cicci. Now, he associated her with a most unexpected trait—warmth.

"So, tell me: is there a Mr. Right for you under the mistletoe?"

Cicci took another drink and then ran her tongue over her top teeth while she formulated an answer. "A Mr. Right? Well, there are plenty of slimeballs, our political finest, who'd gladly accept me as their madam du jour. Many are at this party."

"The Thomas Darling types?"

"Ah, so you noticed, too?"

"Mm-hmm."

"Thomas is actually one of the tamer ones. But as for a Mr. Right? Apparently, I'm coated with a love-resistant Teflon. I've never had a relationship stick."

Grayson was surprised at her candor and more surprised she didn't seem sad. "Can I ask you a serious question?"

Cicci extended her arm and clutched the edge of the window frame. "My god, Cowboy! More serious than my heart's allegiance? I don't think I can hold up to this interrogation. Better give me that other bourbon thing."

"Not on your life," he said, laughing. *Score one for Cicci.*

She laughed, too.

"Why do you hate us?" Grayson asked.

"Us?"

"Me. Wyoming. Republicans."

"Now you've asked three serious questions," she joked.

Grayson waited.

"First, I don't hate you. Just the opposite: you amuse me. If I were earning a decent wage, I'd actually pay you for the entertainment value you provide. Second, I don't hate Wyoming. I don't love Wyoming, but if I'm given a limited number of poison darts to throw, I'm not wasting one on Wyoming. I'm not necessarily on board with the whole environmental throwback thing, but I do believe one requirement for statehood should be a minimum population level. Third, I do despise Republicans. I think they're a bunch of hypocritical bastards who profess unabashed moral integrity but then look the other way when their coffers and pet projects are getting filled by shitheads like Cran Fran."

"Fair point, but isn't that game played by both sides?" Grayson asked.

"Do you honestly think both sides are the same?"

"No. Your side's trying to destroy a state, and that's a big difference. A big difference."

A spontaneous singing of "Let It Snow! Let It Snow! Let It Snow!" filled the room, interrupting their discussion. Cicci joined in the merriment, and Grayson soon followed. Afterward, they quietly sat and watched the crowd intermingle. A long silence ensued, and for each of them, that was okay. Outside, snow continued to fall.

CHAPTER 9

NEW PLAYERS EMERGE

"I'M JUST TELLING you what I heard," Grayson explained. "Cicci said McKenzie is ready to roll it out as soon as Congress returns to Washington." He was briefing Senator Shelton and Claude about the latest bombshell in the Wyoming neutering saga. Toward the end of Lanetta's prior-night holiday party, Grayson had heard the news from Cicci. He remembered her admonishing jab when he had admitted ignorance on the topic: *Seriously, Cowboy! You haven't heard about it? Do you still receive your news by Pony Express?*

Congressional supporters of the Native American population intended to stake a claim to Wyoming's vast landscape. Led by Congresswoman, Blossom McKenzie, and activist, Hiram Dancing Grouse, the Native American contingent was about to pitch an alternative to the back-to-nature proposal. This new set of players advocated Wyoming's conversion into an independent Native American nation.

"This is news to me," Shelton said. "I'm not convinced it's

true, but if it is, there's going to be a bunch of mighty upset people. How does your friend know about it?"

Friend? Grayson didn't regard Cicci as a friend, but after brief consideration, he decided that description fit, albeit in a bizarre sort of way.

"I don't know exactly how she knows," he answered. "But she prides herself on being informed."

The senator frowned. "Her name is Cicci?"

"Yeah, Theresa Cicci."

"I don't know her. Claude, you know her?"

Claude answered. "Yeah, I think so. She's one of Edelman's."

"She's part of the Natural Resources working group," Grayson added.

Shelton mulled that over. "Competing factions for the spoils of Wyoming. I bet Democratic leadership is having a conniption. So much for fast-tracking the Twenty-eighth Amendment."

᷍

On a brilliant, sunny morning in early January, a medium-size crowd of ardent supporters braved the eighteen-degree temperature and huddled near the steps of the Capitol. They watched the speaker's breath stream and linger in the winter air as she pitched her plan for social redemption.

Hanging out in back, Grayson listened to the crowd's enthusiastic cheers. Wearing his favorite coat, a heavy, oil-impregnated Filson duster, he distinguished himself from the London Fog set. The garment reminded him of happier days when he had ridden the range on his folks' ranch. He tilted his felt Stetson to shade his eyes from the low-hanging sun.

Speaking with clarity and conviction, Congresswoman McKenzie dazzled her audience. She possessed striking physical qualities: straight, shiny black hair of shoulder length; nearly flawless cocoa-brown skin; and perfectly aligned teeth white enough to land her an advertising gig for a mouthwash company. Dressed this winter morning in a full-length coat of red wool with a matching beret, she proudly embraced her mixed-race heritage and never shied away from the limelight.

"Friends," she began, "like our beautiful sky this morning, a new day has dawned for the indigenous people of America. At last, we are witnessing an opportunity to begin mending past atrocities. As you know, the current state of Wyoming is undergoing a dissolution. In physical size, it is the ninth-largest state in the Union. We believe its vast and varied landscape provides a perfect setting to reunite Native American people with the land they love, to resume a symbiotic existence with Mother Earth, and to practice a self-determined lifestyle true to the culture of their ancestors. Tribes of the Great Plains will soon be able to fully restore a harmonious existence with nature after nearly two centuries of neglect."

Grayson watched signs bob up and down. A smattering of slogans written on posterboard and tacked to wooden stakes demanded justice for Native Americans.

"I am humbled to be the voice leading this quest in our nation's capital," the speaker continued. She paused until the applause diminished. "But I cannot do this alone. I would like to introduce you to my partner in this effort, a man of astounding vision. Please welcome Hiram Dancing Grouse."

A Lakota man of medium height with high cheekbones and black hair longer than the congresswoman's stepped to the podium. His stern expression never broke as he recognized the crowd's thunderous welcome with a single wave.

"Good morning, my brothers and sisters in spirit. When I began raising my voice against the White Man's oppression at Thanksgiving celebrations so many years ago, the gray sky would often cry frozen tears in sympathy for our plight. But today, the sun shines bright on our faces and our future. As the congresswoman has told you, the land that was once ours will soon be ours again. We will roam the grasslands and wade the streams with restored dignity. Wyoming will become a new nation for indigenous people. It will be populated by tribes of the Great Plains: the Arapaho, the Crow, the Shoshone, the Pawnee, the Kiowa, the Sioux, and many others."

In a surreal moment, Grayson watched the sun's rays illuminate Hiram's face. It was as if the heavens roared their approval for the activist's message of rebirth.

"But Wyoming will not be the end to our quest for justice," Hiram said. "We will continue to demand the return of our land in other regions. We will not relinquish our claim to the redwood forests of the Pacific, the canyonlands of the Southwest, or the Black Hills. We will not rest until all indigenous people resume control of their rightful lands. But until that time, our Native American brothers and sisters throughout the United States will be welcome in New Wyoming."

Grayson doubted "New Wyoming" would actually be the replacement name. Should the Native American land claim succeed, he suspected every tribe would attempt to stamp its own identity to this region.

Hiram continued. "During the journey to this monumental day, I have walked with others and, when necessary, I have walked alone. I have done so because I know the land. I believe in our people; I understand our culture. Yet I am as helpless as a child when it comes to comprehending laws and regulations in Washington. Fortunately, we have Congresswoman McKenzie on our side. She understands the books and procedures by which our dream will become reality. Congresswoman, I return the podium to you."

The congresswoman stepped to the lectern and grasped Hiram's hand with her own. She raised them in a display of triumphant solidarity.

"Thank you, Hiram. Ladies and gentlemen, this morning, we are formally launching our effort to return American soil back to our indigenous people. This effort will be called the Native American Land Exchange, or NALE for short. I will be working with my congressional colleagues to write the necessary language that will be included as part of the proposed Twenty-eighth Amendment. During this time, it is critical you contact your senators and representatives to make your voices heard. I thank you in advance for your support. Happy New Year, and let's get to work."

The rally concluded with boisterous applause and scattered war cries. Prompted by the cold, the crowd thinned quickly.

As Grayson made his way back to the senate building, he heard a familiar voice. He looked sideways and saw Senator Mendenhall smiling at him.

"Never a dull moment in this town," the portly statesman commented. "Wyoming's come a long way from its environmental tourism research."

While shaking Mendenhall's hand, Grayson laughed at the reference—a weak excuse for initially bringing him to Washington months ago. "Yep, Happy New Year, Senator."

When a lady pushing a wheelchair approached, the two men stepped aside and opened a path onto the sidewalk. The seated man with a broad nose and deep lines in his weathered face wore a baseball cap with the words, *Native Veteran Marine* written above its bill.

"Thank you for your service, sir," Grayson said, and the man responded with a nod. As the disabled man and his companion disappeared in the crowd, Grayson turned to Mendenhall. "So, you think this thing is gonna fly?"

Mendenhall adjusted his coat collar and presented a relaxed smile. "No. Not the way they envision it anyway. But McKenzie's a tiger, and they do have a wave of sympathy right now. So, they will influence the outcome. I think we might see some sort of trade-off; they get something in exchange for supporting the back-to-nature push."

"Like what?" Grayson asked.

"Like the Black Hills. Remember, Hiram Dancing Grouse is Lakota." Mendenhall wiped a wind-induced tear from his cheek and then mildly punched Grayson's shoulder. "South Dakota may soon need an environmental tourism program, too."

CHAPTER 10

BOUNDARIES

(Many Years from Now)

WITH A SATISFIED expression, Mr. Tang leaned back into the seat cushion. "So that's how Wyonation became more than just the state of Wyoming."

"That was the start. More would follow," Grayson answered. "The NALE effort planted the seed. It got people thinking about boundaries and what they mean."

"And the Native American contingent. Were they fully on board with the creation of their own nation?"

"Oh, some were, but not all." Grayson smiled at his contradictory answer. "In spirit, I believe many Indians romanticize about the old days and the notion of returning to that way of life. Their ancestors mastered a harmonious existence with nature. There's a lot to be said for that not-so-simple achievement." He noticed some residual crumbs on the table—courtesy of his visit to the complementary food station. He brushed them into his open hand and deposited them onto his used plate.

Mr. Tang waited until Grayson finished this mindless exercise. "But?"

"But, in practice, most folks weren't keen on going back to the old ways. There were exceptions, of course, but the simple fact was the world has moved on—even for the Indians. Like the rest of America, people had grown fond of modern conveniences. It's hard to give up indoor plumbing and take-out pizza once you've had 'em."

"Why would they have to sacrifice their existing lifestyle?" Mr. Tang asked. "Wasn't the issue really about self-governing?"

"Depends on who you ask. For people like Hector Devine and Barry Doolin, it was as much about the setting as anything. They envisioned a 1600s version of the West and expected the Indians to live accordingly."

In an "aha" moment, Mr. Tang's mouth opened as if he were about to speak, but his words were delayed. "Senator Doolin from back then and current Secretary of Interior Doolin are one and the same?"

"Yes."

"I never made that connection, but then we seldom deal with the Interior Department. Why did he leave his position as senator?"

"The president is a persuasive person," Grayson said. "And Doolin's always fantasized about the West. We call his affliction 'frontier envy.' He grew up in the Big Apple but envisions himself as the sheriff of Dodge City. Problem is, he has no real understanding of the situation in our part of the country. The other problem is he simply wants to wear the star on his chest. When trouble rides into town, he disappears. Did you happen to notice his absence this afternoon?"

"You disapprove?"

"I'm not a fan."

Mr. Tang sipped some Yuengling. "After all these years, I'm

still amazed at how emboldened Americans are to publicly criticize their superiors."

"A benefit of living in the land of the free."

"Hmm," Mr. Tang acknowledged. "I suppose."

Grayson studied his face intently but couldn't determine whether the Chinese official envied or disapproved of the practice. Besides his adoration for Yuengling and Alabama, Grayson struggled to establish any kind of read on his tablemate.

"Anyway," Grayson continued. "Blossom McKenzie's dream was dead from the start. She chose to ignore NALE's impractical aspects."

"Such as?"

"For starters, the idea of Indians fitting into a single mold is bonkers. Once you get past the general classification of Native American ethnicity, the commonality among them starts to disintegrate. Did you know there are more than five hundred federally recognized tribes in the US?"

"Really? I had no idea."

"Each has its own identity, its own history and culture."

Feeding off Grayson's explanation, Mr. Tang added, "Certainly, customs and lifestyles are dependent upon the region and the resources available. A tribe living on the coast would be very different from one on the plains."

"Exactly! Oh, that reminds me. I forgot to mention this earlier. Kinda funny. A few of the tribes beyond the Plains region took Hiram up on an offer to visit Wyoming. A big rendezvous was scheduled for mid-May that year. Hiram raised some money and coaxed the folks on the Wind River Reservation to host the festivities down in Casper. Unfortunately, he couldn't control the weather, and eleven inches of snow fell in a howling-ass blizzard. Buses of attendees got stuck on I-25. It was a disaster. The Seminole and Choctaw turned back without having made it to

Casper. Needless to say, after that, no tribe outside the Plains wanted to call Wyoming home."

"Interesting." Mr. Tang nodded. "But why couldn't the remaining tribes work it out? I would think they'd have much in common."

"Well," Grayson started, "they'd have to overcome a history of being rivals for hundreds of years. Tribes frequently battled one another for hunting territory. They raided each other's camps and stole horses."

"I would have thought one or two dominant tribes would ultimately win out," Mr. Tang mused.

"No, it wasn't like Europe where nations amassed giant armies to try and control the entire continent. The various tribes were concerned with having access to just enough territory to survive. For any particular region, you might have had several tribes control it, each at a different time," Grayson said as he rhythmically tapped the table with his fingers. "And that's the great challenge in 'awarding' land back to its rightful owner. What time period do you use? How far back do you go? Where do you start? Where do you stop? It's the same story around the world—the Middle East, for sure, and I'm guessing Asia, too."

Mr. Tang's face turned pensive. "I suppose it comes down to the party who can articulate the best case or be the most persuasive."

"Or who has the biggest club. More times than not, might makes right." Immediately, Grayson remembered how China had recently been wielding a giant stick. He could almost swear he was enjoined in a momentary mind meld with his new drinking buddy, sharing a nearly identical thought. However, he supposed in the Chinese diplomat's mind, America held the club.

Again, Mr. Tang's expression yielded nothing. "From your description, Hiram Dancing Grouse sounds like he was skilled in the persuasive arts."

"Not persuasive so much as persistent," Grayson answered.

"The entire Sioux nation was adamant about not relinquishing their claim to the Black Hills despite a court ruling awarding them over a billion dollars in compensation. Led by Hiram, they insisted the entire Black Hills be included in any political reconfiguration to create an Indian state."

"And they succeeded," Mr. Tang said. "The Black Hills are a part of Wyonation."

"True, but not in the way they hoped. Ultimately, NALE in its pure form was abandoned and incorporated into the larger reconfiguration. As it turned out, Indians weren't the only people to demand their own land for self-governing."

CHAPTER 11

SEEDS OF REBELLION

(Eighteen Years Earlier)

GRAYSON SWUNG OPEN the passenger door on Smitty's vintage Ford F-150 pickup and hopped onto the frozen pavement. They were running late to the public assembly and consequently relegated to a parking space two hundred yards from the Cheyenne Event Center's entrance. While Smitty griped about the cold's effect on his middle-aged joints, Grayson mentally tallied the vehicles they passed. More than half had the number 2 positioned to the left of Wyoming's famous bucking bronco on its license plate—those were Cheyenne residents. Another third belonged to the other Wyoming counties, and the remainder were out-of-state plates. Most of those hailed from Nebraska and Colorado, but North Dakota and Montana each registered a lone representative.

As they entered the facility, the duo was greeted with a whoosh of warm air and a low, buzzing murmur from the gathered crowd. Grayson quickly scanned the arena and estimated the nine-thousand-seat venue to be about one-third full. A coordinator from the event center walked across the floor and shook hands with both of them.

"Boy, am I glad to see you," the coordinator said. "I was starting to worry none of your group would show, though I can't say I'd blame you if you decided to back out."

"Sorry about that," Grayson answered. "We're improvising. Senator Shelton's flight was canceled due to weather, and Claude texted forty minutes ago. He's got stomach flu. We were briefing the Chamber of Commerce when we heard from Claude. Got here as quickly as we could."

"How did the chamber meeting go?" the coordinator asked.

"About like you'd expect. Lots of questions and anxiety," Grayson replied. "Probably similar to what we're about to encounter here."

"I don't know," the coordinator answered. "This group feels unruly."

"Smitty, you didn't see anyone holding rotten tomatoes when you came in?" Grayson asked.

"No tomatoes but a few hand grenades," Smitty joked.

"Not funny," Grayson said. He assessed the audience and guessed what their assorted roles in life might be: ranchers, roughnecks, single parents, business executives, fishing guides, and land developers. Their life pursuits varied like ice cream flavors, but tonight, they shared one common trait: a deep concern regarding the impending federal intrusion of their home.

Grayson drew in a deep breath to calm himself. He was an experienced speaker, but this was a big event, one thrown in his lap at the last minute. "Well, here goes nothing." He grabbed the wireless microphone and strode out to the center of the floor.

"All right. Let's get started," he said. "I'd like to thank everyone for coming out on a frosty night for this town hall meeting. My name is Grayson Woodley, and I am the public-relations lead for Wyoming's Office of Environment and Natural Resources.

Senator Shelton was hoping to be here, but unfortunately her flight out of Washington was canceled due to weather. For the past several months, I have been working with the senator and her staff in Washington to combat the passage of the proposed Twenty-eighth Amendment."

The crowd hissed at the amendment's mention.

Grayson felt perspiration bead around his neck. "I'm here tonight to sort out fact from rumor. I know you've heard all kinds of stories during the past few months. Some of them are accurate, and others are wild speculation. I have two goals this evening. First, I want to address your concerns to the best of my ability. Second, I want all of us to leave this building with a common understanding of what is taking place legislatively, key decision points in the process, and our best guess at a timeline."

The agitated crowd unleashed its frustration with a barrage of comments and questions.

"They can't make us move!"

"I have just as much right to my land as any Indian!"

"Who's going to pay for my house?"

"I'll shoot any cocksucker who tries to steal my property!"

Grayson's face reddened as he absorbed the blunt words. When he felt control of the meeting slipping away, he rebounded with an impassioned volley.

"Hey. Hey! *Hey!* Knock it off! *Knock it off!*"

The energy from his voice startled the crowd into a near silence. Still coasting on an adrenaline rush, he paused long enough to redirect the presentation into something semi-productive.

"You're upset. I get that. I'm upset, too. But being upset and venting out of control are not going to solve our problems. If we're to have any success in taking on this challenge to our statehood, we are going to have to understand the situation, be smart in our response, and, above all, be united in our efforts. Can we all act rationally? Please."

Using a technique he'd practiced in a few previous hostile-crowd situations, Grayson transformed the indistinguishable group mass into distinct individuals. One at a time, he selected five people from various seat sections, called them out by their gender and clothing description, requested they stand up, and then asked them directly if they would work with him in a calm and thoughtful manner. Each one responded affirmatively, and the remainder of the audience bought into the message.

Back in control, Grayson resumed his presentation. "The final language of the proposed Twenty-eighth Amendment is still being haggled over, but we do know whatever form it ultimately takes, Congress will pass it, and it will be forwarded to the states for ratification. Our best guess is states will begin conducting the ratification process in May or June. We think those states favoring the amendment's passage will move fast and complete their ratification by summer's end. States supporting us could drag their feet on the ratification effort, but if thirty-eight states vote yes, it won't matter."

"How many states want us out?" a voice blurted out in the crowd.

"Fair question," Grayson answered. "But to keep tonight orderly, if you have a question please stand, and I'll call on you."

An older gentleman wearing a green, flannel shirt and a Denver Broncos cap stood and repeated his question. "How many states want us out?"

Grayson raised his chin. "Thank you for the question, sir. We don't know for sure, but it's going to be close."

A woman's hand raised in the second row, and Grayson pointed in her direction. "Yes."

"Are we talking with other states to persuade them in our direction?"

"We can't hear in back!" an anonymous voice deep in the crowd bellowed.

Grayson responded. "The question was whether we are communicating with other states to side with us, and the answer is yes, we are actively talking to other states. Governor Linsey has taken the lead in this effort and has been communicating with other governors since late last year."

"You, sir." Grayson called upon the next person to speak, a barrel-chested man with thinning gray hair and weathered skin.

The stocky man sidestepped his way along the row until he reached the aisle. He walked down the arena stairs and over to Grayson's location on the floor. "May I use the microphone so everyone can hear me?"

Initially, Grayson stepped back in surprise. Then he handed the man the mike.

"Hello, my name is Rudy Essex. I farm a place just outside of Sidney. Here's my question: instead of fighting so hard to stay in the Union, have you considered breaking away from the country on your own terms? If you did, I know a lot of folks in the Nebraska panhandle who would like to join you."

There it was. The topic Wyoming officials had dared not speak now dispersed through the event center like a poisonous fog. Blood rushed to Grayson head, and his back knotted in a near spasm.

A moment passed while the crowd digested the farmer's comments, but soon conflicting noise buzzed throughout the crowd. Those in agreement with Rudy started a spontaneous round of clapping while dissenters vigorously voiced their opposition.

Once again, Grayson was on the verge of losing control; yet he was fast on his feet. He asked Rudy for the microphone, and to Grayson's relief, the Nebraska man complied without resistance. Instead of yelling into the mike, Grayson simply held his left hand high into the air and waited for the audience to silence themselves. It took a few moments, but his patience eventually won out.

"Mr. Essex raises an interesting point; one I know at least

some of you have also considered. Frankly, it's one I've heard whispered in the back halls of government buildings from time to time. However, we are still a legitimate state in the US, and I believe we stand a good chance of resisting the push to remove us."

Boos erupted from the crowd, and anger flew from the stands.

"Screw Washington! Let's split."

"Stop being a wuss, Woodley, and get ready to fight."

Get ready to fight? Did that guy mean a confrontation with the United States, or should Grayson prepare to punch his way out of the arena? The involuntary tightening in his back and shoulders suggested the latter. He struggled to retain control.

"People! Come on. One at a time, please." He spotted one cooperative person with a raised hand and rewarded her. "Madam, you in the white parka, please stand and give us your question."

A medium-sized lady with peroxide-blonde hair stood and began, "I agree with the Nebraska guy…"

"Can't hear you!" came a cry from high in the stands.

Grayson motioned for her to come and use the microphone and waited until she made her way to him.

"My name's Amy, and I said I agree with the Nebraska guy. This country isn't what it used be. The federal government has put its nose in every aspect of our life. I run a hair salon in Denver, and I'm choking on all the rules and forms they throw at me. They tax me ten different ways and then turn around and hand out money to all the bums and drug addicts who hang out on the streets and harass my customers. They even give them needles, for God's sake. I think we need to get back to people taking responsibility for their own lives. If that means going radical like starting a new country, so be it."

Again, thunderous applause intertwined with boos.

"Right on, lady! Right on!"

Badly in need of some moral support, Grayson found it in the form of an attentive lady. She was sitting in the third row with her hand raised when he waved her over to join him on the floor. As she positioned herself next to him, Grayson addressed the crowd.

"Ladies and gentlemen, I'd like you to welcome our very own Speaker of the Wyoming House of Representatives, Ms. Winnie Lopez. Madam Speaker, I yield the floor to you."

The Event Center echoed with conflicting noise, lukewarm applause clashing against hostile slurs. Grayson handed Lopez the microphone.

"Thank you, Mr. Woodley."

Despite the chaotic atmosphere, she greeted the audience with a politician's becoming smile—a sincere gesture but one mistrusted by a cynical working class. Combined with practical attire consisting of gray woolen slacks, nonslip boots, and a geometrically patterned cardigan sweater, the speaker conveyed both calm and confidence.

"We are living in interesting times. As of this moment, I honestly believe none of us know how Wyoming, our home, will look one year from now. We may still remain a state, or we might be something entirely different. However, while we don't know the outcome with certainty, it behooves us to pursue the course of action in our best interest. Right now, that means vigorously resisting the ratification of the Twenty-eighth Amendment. We have thrived as a state, and given the chance, we will continue to do so.

"And what if the bastards kick us out and say we have to relinquish our land?" another voice cried.

The legislator didn't answer immediately. Instead, she carefully removed her glasses and softly bit on the temple tip. Then, speaking in the general direction from where the question had emanated, she replied. "Well, we'll weigh our options at that time, but I can assure you we will exhaust all legal avenues before we comply with any mandate to surrender our property."

The crowd again responded with rude hoots and gestures.

Out of hopelessness, the color drained from Grayson's face. The circus continued late into the evening.

⤚

Three hours later in a dimly lit bar, a cue ball cracked against its targets in the backroom. On this Tuesday night, the venue catered to a predictably sparse crowd. At one end, Grayson and Smitty fumbled with their whiskeys.

"Well," Grayson said, "that was a public abortion."

With sympathetic eyes and a measured voice, Smitty responded, "Tough night for sure."

"Ya think? I feel like absolutely nothing was accomplished. People are all over the place."

"I think tonight had some value," Smitty offered. "We got a true read on the level of passion out there. Folks are fired up. If need be, they're ready to fight."

"Oh, great. A few ranchers taking on the United States Army. That will surely end well."

"I think it's bigger than that," Smitty pressed. "Based on what I saw tonight, if push comes to shove, I think most of the state will actively resist a takeover."

"How? With a militia? Sabotage? Economic sanctions?"

Smitty shrugged.

Grayson stared at the usually easy-going career civil servant, but Smitty didn't yield. Finally, Grayson broke down and offered a weak smile. He grabbed his whiskey and raised his glass. "Here's to new found knowledge and state spirit."

"Hear! Hear!"

After downing his glass, Smitty added to his assessment, "We also learned another thing. If there is a rebellion, it'll be bigger than just Wyoming."

CHAPTER 12

THREE'S COMPANY

(Many Years from Now)

GRAYSON WATCHED CICCI dab a tinge of perspiration from her forehead as she ambled her way through the standing crowd at Gerry Manders. He took satisfaction in knowing Washington, DC, locals were also affected by this evening's heat. He stood, waved to get her attention, and broke into a wry smile. She spotted him, smiled back, and moved in his direction. When she was almost to the table, she stopped suddenly. Her smile disappeared as she recognized the man sitting with Grayson.

"You made it," Grayson said as he rose from his seat and motioned for her to sit next to him. "I was beginning to think I'd have to wait for your Christmas card to hear from you again. Oh, that reminds me. I'm still waiting for your card from last year—and the year before that."

"Don't hold your breath, Cowboy." She glared at both men. "Am I interrupting something?"

"Not at all," Grayson responded. He noticed Mr. Tang had also stood and suddenly realized why Cicci seemed put off. "Theresa Cicci, this is Mr. Tang. You might remember him from this afternoon's meeting, but I bet you didn't know he goes by LeRoy when he's off the clock."

"I know who he is," she said. "I didn't realize this afternoon's session had been continued."

Mr. Tang offered a toothy grin as he extended his hand toward Cicci. "Ah, Ms. Cicci. It is a pleasure to meet you outside the formalities of official business. Happily, we are now engaged in relaxation. Please join us."

Reluctantly, Cicci completed the handshake and took the seat next to Grayson.

"Finish all your calls?" he asked.

"Yes," Cicci replied. Her eyes remained on Mr. Tang.

Billy, the waiter, swung by the table. "Welcome to Gerry Manders. What can I bring you?"

"Tanqueray and tonic," Cicci replied.

"That's my girl," Grayson chirped, prompting Cicci to roll her eyes and look away.

"Anyone else?" Billy asked.

"Another Yuengling, please," Mr. Tang answered. "Grayson?"

"Sure. Same as the lady," Grayson said. He turned to Cicci. "Care for a carrot stick?"

"No," she replied tersely and glanced long enough at Mr. Tang to communicate there would be no idle chatter while he was present.

Mr. Tang acknowledged the silent message by standing. "Please excuse me. The beer is taking effect. May I bring you something from the buffet when I return?"

Cicci declined with a hand wave. Grayson and she watched the Chinese diplomat leave the table and pick his way through the crowd. When he was no longer visible, Cicci whipped her head toward Grayson and punched him in the arm.

"Cowboy! What the hell? Since when did you start consorting with the enemy?"

"Hey! Ow!" He rubbed his violated limb.

"Seriously, what is going on?"

"Nothing's going on," he said while massaging his arm. "He showed up while I was waiting for you."

"Quite a coincidence, don't you think?"

"Yes," Grayson agreed. "Seems a little strange, but it's not like we've been swapping clandestine information. He told me about coming to America and going to college in Alabama, and we've talked a little about how Wyonation came to be."

"Mm-hmm. Just a couple of chums pounding drinks and recollecting the good ol' days. Are you really that naive? He's after something."

"Maybe, but I don't know that for a fact. Theresa, I'm not that gullible," Grayson growled, resenting her scolding.

Billy's drink delivery halted the argument. Grayson hoisted his gin glass toward Cicci. "It's been a while, Miss Cicci. Here's to the old days."

Cicci clinked her glass against his, and they each sipped the nectar of sophisticates. Grayson readied himself for a second toast. "Here's to Stella."

"Give me a break," she moaned.

Mr. Tang returned with a new appetizer plate and sat. He motioned toward the mushroom-filled fried pastries and offered to share. He cut one of the triangular pieces in two and consumed the first half.

"These remind me of a fabulous food I once tasted in Africa," Mr. Tang said. "They were fried pastries like these. I believe they were called sambusas. The filling consisted of onions, vegetables, and some type of meat—goat, perhaps. But it was the sauce that made them special. It was a pepper sauce, quite spicy and very delicious."

"Where in Africa?" Grayson queried.

"Djibouti."

Despite being partway into his third cocktail, Grayson's sense of suspicion remained operable and now flashed an alert. *Djibouti. Not your typical African tourist destination like Egypt, Kenya, or South Africa.* He skimmed through his knowledge of the country. It was a small nation on the African horn, sitting strategically at the point where the Red Sea met the Indian Ocean's Gulf of Aden. Because it represented a potential shipping choke point, the location carried immense trade and military importance. Both China and the United States maintained an active presence there, but in recent years, the former had grown in stature while the latter shrank. Djibouti provided yet another embarrassing example of the US being out maneuvered by its Asian rival.

"How long were you there?" Grayson asked.

"Oh, probably three months."

"That's a lot of time for sightseeing."

Mr. Tang smiled as Grayson pumped for information. "As I'm sure you've experienced in your own careers, diplomatic work demands much time, but I try to enjoy life's simple pleasures when possible."

Grayson accepted the deflection in stride. Still, he wondered. *First, Himalayan India, now Djibouti. I wonder where else this guy's left his diplomatic fingerprints?*

"So, Ms. Cicci, please forgive me, as I've forgotten. Were you at this afternoon's meeting on behalf of the State or Interior Department?" Mr. Tang asked.

"Interior."

"I see." Mr. Tang continued. "May I ask in what capacity?"

"I'm involved with resource management oversight."

"Yes, yes," Mr. Tang agreed. He smiled and continued. "I

imagine it must be amazing to interact with a brand-new, geographical entity, one that lies entirely inside your borders."

"Mostly, it's a pain in the ass." She glanced at Grayson, who accepted the dig with a grin.

"We love you, too, my dear," he said.

"I can appreciate your frustration," Mr. Tang said. "I think it can be hard to embrace unorthodox practices. Especially those running counter to one's basic values."

"What practices and values are you referring to?" Grayson asked with a raised pitch in his voice.

"Forgive me, my friend. I don't mean to offend you or revisit this afternoon's arguments. I was simply interested in learning how Ms. Cicci dealt with two conflicting societies—the United States, where capital punishment has been fully rescinded, and Wyonation, where a person can be shot for hunting out of season."

Cicci put down her drink and stared at Mr. Tang, clearly annoyed. "I reconcile the conflict, as you describe it, by accepting the fact that as a sovereign entity, Wyonation calls the shots within its own borders. I may not like those calls, but hell, there are a lot of things in this world I don't like. For example, I don't much care for the human-rights violations practiced by your government on your own people."

Grayson lauded her blunt response. *Touché! After all these years, she still suffers no fools.* He watched Mr. Tang's normally stoic posture crack. His back grew rigid and his jaw clenched. Grayson suspected his agitation was aimed in two directions. Part of it, obviously, was directed at Cicci, but the remainder was pointed internally for recklessly overreaching in his dialogue. Mr. Tang was a skilled diplomat, but he wasn't perfect. Maybe the beer was having an effect.

Whatever control Mr. Tang had lost, he soon regained. The worldly man pulled a cloth from the inside pocket of his tailored jacket, grabbed the spectacles from his face, and wiped the lenses.

He smiled tersely. "Yes, Ms. Cicci, you are correct in noting the limitations of outsiders concerning domestic policy. Still, the pro-active use of lethal force as a deterrent fascinates me."

Cicci harumphed.

Mr. Tang addressed Grayson. "During the briefing I recall you mentioning something about a situation or event necessitat-ing the severe no-poaching enforcement. What happened?"

The question returned Grayson to a difficult time in his life. His expression took on a somber tint. "In a nutshell, Wyonation's game population, particularly the big game, was getting decimated by poachers. This happened a few years after Wyonation's creation."

"I hate the term, 'poachers,'" Cicci blurted out. "It's so mis-leading. People were trying to feed their families."

"I'm not entirely unsympathetic to the plight of those folks, but the violations spun out of control. It was completely chaotic, an ecological calamity in the making. We had to act."

"I don't quite follow," Mr. Tang said.

Grayson ran his fingers against his jawline and felt the stubble of a five-o'clock shadow. "You remember the bovine brucellosis epidemic, right?"

Mr. Tang nodded.

"One-third of the North American cattle population died directly from it or had to be put down. Beef was no longer avail-able for dinner, even for the wealthy. Pork and poultry prices went through roof."

"But as I remember, Americans made an amazing conversion to a plant-based diet at that time," Mr. Tang said.

"Yes, they did!" Cicci crowed triumphantly. "The country's resilience during the crisis was one of our finest moments."

"Yes, they did," Grayson echoed. "Many people bought into the new nutrition model." He paused. "Many, but not all. A sig-nificant portion was still intent on keeping meat in their diet, and so they looked to the wildlife in Wyonation as an alternative source. Not only was meat available there, but if hunted illegally, it was available at little to no cost. The problem was that wild game came nowhere close to replacing the thirty-plus percent loss in cattle."

Cicci shook her head. "I thought by that time the bison herds had grown back to the desired population."

"The bison herds were recovering nicely," Grayson clarified, "but they were still well short of our desired numbers. Even if they'd been at full population, we couldn't replace all the lost cattle. Theresa, we lost almost forty million animals in the US and Canada combined."

"And so, you enacted an aggressive campaign to secure your wealth," Mr. Tang concluded. "That must have been an extraordinary undertaking to protect such an extensive border."

"It was. I briefed you on some of the technology implemented, but it also sucked up a ton of manpower."

"Amazing," Mr. Tang acknowledged. "Tell me, how did the officials in Washington react when you presented your justification for lethal force? I'm guessing they strongly objected."

"To the contrary," Grayson answered, "they were very supportive. In fact, their cooperation was instrumental in the program's overall success. They aided us in keeping their people on their side of the border so we wouldn't have to take action. They also realized what was happening to our animal population. We didn't agree on much, but one of the founding principles for Wyonation's existence was sustainable natural-resource management. Slaughtering animal species out of existence definitely isn't a sustainable practice." He stopped talking long enough to take a swig from his gin glass and then continued. "Oh, and for the record, taking action for self-preservation never requires justification."

If Grayson's last remark affected Mr. Tang, his countenance failed to show it. He leaned back in his seat with folded arms and a pensive expression on his face. "I can understand the policy, given the predicament, but I'm surprised the extreme measures weren't repealed once the crisis had passed."

Grayson didn't answer immediately. He cast his eyes toward nothing in particular while he thought. Finally, he said, "Our proactive deterrence policies remain ongoing for two reasons. First, we don't know when another crisis of that sort might happen, so we need to be prepared. Second, we like the message it sends. It lets everyone know how highly we regard our wildlife. It shows the lengths we're willing to go to protect not only them, but all our natural resources. By and large, visitors to Wyonation have heard that message. Those situations like Mr. Lin's are unfortunate when they happen, but they're rare in occurrence."

Mr. Tang showed no signs of acceptance nor objection. Instead, he retrieved another mushroom pastry from his plate and washed it down with his amber-colored beer. He swiveled his attention back to Cicci.

"Ms. Cicci, you seem so knowledgeable about Wyonation's history. Does your involvement extend back to its origins?"

Before she could answer, Grayson chimed in. "Actually, Ms. Cicci played an active role in the saga of Wyonation's formation."

"Impressive," Mr. Tang nodded. "I can only imagine how useful an ally she must have been."

Grayson laughed. "Well, not quite. We were adversaries almost the entire time." He studied his longtime acquaintance and then added, "But there were some occasions when we were on the same side. For a while, we were teammates—close teammates." He punctuated the last two words with a flirtatious wink.

The gesture surprised Cicci, and she reacted in a manner unusual for her. She blushed.

CHAPTER 13
YOU WANNA BET

(Seventeen Years Earlier)

"ALL RIGHT," CICCI slurred. "Which of you cowards is willing to back up your bullshit cause with some hard cash?" She stood over the small group of Republican staffers seated at a long table. They'd congregated at Code Red, another post-work hangout frequented by the Hill's younger set.

Grayson shot her an annoyed glance. The others ignored the drunken volley and carried on with their own conversations.

Cicci continued to pester them. "I'm serious, damn it! A hundred bucks says the Twenty-eighth Amendment gets passed before Congress leaves on Friday."

Grayson had heard enough. Embracing defeat was already tough. He didn't need an overbearing antagonist to rub his nose in it. He pushed away from the table and stood.

For the past two weeks, his normally witty adversary had morphed into a foul-mouthed, mean-spirited bitch. Cicci's eyes now seeped with dull bitterness. The transformation had occurred out of seemingly nowhere, and it puzzled him. When he began walking toward the restroom, she chased after him.

"Hey, Cowboy! Off to fondle that microscopic prick of yours? Where's that sappy devotion to your high-plains homeland?"

Her persistent jabs had finally worked their way under his skin, and he wheeled about. "Sucks, doesn't it? I can fondle at will, and you can only dream about it."

"You wish," Cicci retorted. "You're as limp as your loyalty."

The malicious dig enraged Grayson. "You're so damn sure of yourself, fine, I'll bet!" A twisted thought popped into his brain, and he smirked. "If the Twenty-eighth Amendment passes by Friday night, I'll pay you the hundred dollars. But…"

She smiled victoriously. "But what?"

"But if I win, I don't want cash." He adjusted his belt buckle and lifted an eyebrow. "Because you're so interested in my personal habits, I'll let you do the honors."

It took a moment, but Cicci's expression transformed from satisfaction to comprehension and then to disbelief. "You want a hand job?" She blanched.

Grayson watched her look down and tug her jacket edges as her feet shifted uneasily. He had knocked her off her high horse, and they both knew it. Unfortunately for Grayson, the satisfaction extracted with the surprise wager was fleeting. Cicci had just goaded him into making a losing bet. Everyone estimated the amendment's passage to be a virtual lock. His lapse in good judgement was about to cost him one hundred dollars.

Cicci bounced back and issued her acceptance with an over-the-top smugness. "Is that how you want to play, Cowboy? You're going to lose. I'll be happy to take your Benjamin."

"I call him Willy."

"Asshole!"

Grayson ducked as a wicker basket containing breadsticks

and saltine crackers whizzed over his head and smashed into the nearby wall.

A male bartender rushed to the scene and wagged his finger in Cicci's face. He bellowed in his deep, stern voice. "We do not throw things in here! Do you understand?"

Flush in the face, Cicci surrendered and said, "I'm sorry." While the crowd watched, she grabbed her handbag from a nearby table, paid her tab at the bar, and stumbled toward the door. Before exiting, she turned and looked at Grayson. "A hundred dollars, Cowboy."

⁓

Later that evening, Grayson leaned into a teal throw pillow on a worn sofa—the centerpiece of his second-floor, studio apartment in DC. He mentally juggled an assorted set of regrets. He regretted making the foolish bet and the ensuing ruckus. Most of all, he regretted the inevitable failure of his mission to Washington. The constitutional amendment to dissolve Wyoming as a state sat on the brink of passage. On his phone's screen, he scanned the latest version of the proposed action.

Amendment XXVIII

SECTION 1. A territory being considered for admittance to the Union must have a population greater than or equal to one-seven hundredth of the current United States population.

SECTION 2. Every existing state in the Union must continue to maintain a population equal to at least one-seven hundredth of the Union's current total population.

SECTION 3. Failure of an existing state to meet the population requirement in Section 2 will result in its loss of statehood, and the geographic area of that state will be declared a natural range region (NRR).

SECTION 4. Each NRR shall be governed in accordance with the NRR rules established by Congress. A governing body shall be created from NRR residents to manage the internal affairs of the NRR. No less than fifty percent of this governing body shall be federally registered Native Americans who reside in the NRR.

SECTION 5. Residents of an NRR who were American citizens prior to the creation of that NRR or who were born into that NRR will be regarded as American citizens upon leaving the NRR and residing elsewhere in the United States.

SECTION 6. Congress will be empowered with discretion in 1) determining how a former state will transition into and function as an NRR; 2) managing the external affairs of that NRR; 3) settling disputes between the NRR and the government of the United States, individual state(s), or other NRR(s); and 4) deciding how the current population of the United States shall be determined.

Grayson sighed as he realized the end product from months of intense debate, negotiation, and bickering consisted of just a few paragraphs. He recalled the initial cut of the proposed amendment and now tallied the key additions made to this iteration; there were four items.

First, a replacement term, natural range region or NRR, had been chosen to identify the land area belonging to a dissolved state. This term distinguished the land area as being different than a US territory, thereby allowing the folks in Washington, DC, a means for establishing a different set of rules by which an

NRR would operate. Also, the term itself conveyed an image of untouched land.

Reluctantly, Grayson admired the cleverness in distinguishing an NRR from a territory. It stood out as a deft political play. Unlike US territories, which could petition for statehood, the declaration of a new NRR would be a one-way journey. Politicians responsible for Wyoming's demise would be writing the NRR rules to ensure that once Wyoming was dissolved as a state, it couldn't apply for readmission—even if its population exceeded the one-seven hundredth minimum.

Second, Congress would sit firmly in the driver's seat regarding NRR governance. It was being empowered to make the rules for the NRR, formulate the state-to-NRR transition plan, and manage all the NRR's external affairs, including the handling of disputes with other states.

Next, the amendment permitted individuals to regain and exercise their rights as American citizens should they leave the NRR and move to another state in the US. No waiting period would be required.

The final addition to the amendment served as the deal maker for the Native American cause. At long last, Native American interests would actually be embedded into the Constitution. The Twenty-eighth Amendment required at least fifty percent of an NRR's governing body to be individuals belonging to a federally recognized tribe.

The issue had been hotly disputed for weeks. Native American activists wanted the NRR to be governed exclusively by indigenous people; however, many Washington, DC, insiders and the environmental contingent disagreed. They advocated a need to maintain some connection to the rest of the country. They were insistent on giving the Interior Department authority to coordinate and manage NRR affairs. Also, those same insiders balked at putting too much specificity—such as the exact makeup of the governing NRR body—into the Constitution. Instead, they wanted to spell out the governing details through legislation.

The Native Americans stood firm in their request. They demanded the Constitution recognize their right to govern these new lands. Having been duped for centuries by the White Man and his false treaties, they wanted their rights secured by the highest authority. Ultimately, a compromise had been reached, and now the proposed amendment was set for congressional vote and approval.

On Saturday morning, the bright sun radiated throughout Grayson's apartment as he relaxed in bed with one foot outside the confines of his sheet and comforter. On his phone, he reread the lead story from the morning's news. Enlightened with this new information, he rested the phone at his side and began to laugh. He laughed and laughed, and then he laughed some more.

At the eleventh hour on Friday, the Twenty-eighth Amendment vote had been postponed. It wasn't dead—just hijacked. Congressional representatives from Washington, Oregon, and Northern California had united to exercise a classic political power play. They had decided their support for the amendment carried a price: nine hundred million dollars, to be exact. This amount represented funding for a proof-of-concept study concerning a proposed high-speed rail line from San Jose, California to Bellingham, Washington. The majority of their colleagues regarded the project as a boondoggle, but the rogue element from the Pacific Northwest had now flexed its muscle by threatening to vote against the amendment if their request was denied.

The action wasn't a surprise. Federal monetary spigots were flowing freely, and everyone was reaching for their perceived share. The legislators making the latest demand pointed to South Dakota's sweetheart deal as justification for their own request.

As part of the grand plan to appease Native American demands and secure the Twenty-eighth Amendment's passage, the state of South Dakota and private landowners were in line to share a revenue stream equaling seven hundred million dollars per year for the next twenty years (fourteen billion dollars total). In exchange, these recipients would collectively relinquish two million acres of land in the southwest corner of South Dakota, much of it being in the Black Hills. The South Dakota carve-out would be combined with Wyoming to create the nation's first natural range region.

Grayson realized the posturing on Capitol Hill was simply a burp in the march toward Wyoming's elimination. Ultimately, the congressional majority would patch together a political fix, pass the amendment, and forward it to the individual states for ratification. Still, the delay meant he won his wager with Cicci. In a year of dismal outcomes, he had scored one small victory—one he intended to savor for as long as possible.

⁓

During the next week, Grayson and every other able body on Senator Shelton's staff scrambled to coax pro-Wyoming votes from any congressperson or senator still sitting on the fence. One day, Grayson rounded a corner in the Cannon House Office Building and spotted Cicci midway down a corridor. Upon receiving his not-so-subtle, triumphant gaze, she ducked into an office.

Later that week, they crossed paths again, but Grayson was called away before they could engage in a post-bet discussion. Still, her awkward behavior revealed she'd been stewing uneasily with her self-inflicted predicament. He was ecstatic.

In the stifling July heat on the following Wednesday, all political maneuvers and countermeasures concerning the Twenty-eighth Amendment ceased. The US Senate overwhelmingly passed it. Combined with similar results in the House of Representatives, the proposed amendment was now headed to the fifty states for ratification.

That afternoon, Mickey Corbin, a congressional staffer who'd worked on the Hill so long his colleagues referred to him as lifer, called an impromptu meeting. Those he summoned were the foot soldiers responsible for the research, wrangling, and rewrites associated with the amendment campaign. During the late nights too numerous to remember, they had forged a fraternity. Those working on the same side of the aisle had established an inseparable bond brought about by the quest for a common cause. However, staffers from both sides shared a second bond, one of respect and empathy for colleagues working in the legislative profession. Though the meeting's majority were the victors, a handful of attendees came from the losing side, Grayson being one.

Soon after Grayson entered the conference room, Nellie Campbell, a Democratic staffer, approached him. She hailed from Iowa or Indiana or Illinois, one of the *I* states. He couldn't remember which.

"Why hello, Grayson. I'm so glad you came. You're a good sport."

"Keeping the communication channels open," he said. On the inside, pangs of failure ricocheted in his gut.

"Mmm," Nellie acknowledged while fiddling with her earring. "Speaking of communication channels, and pardon my intrusion, but is something going on between Theresa Cicci and you?"

Grayson kept his surprise under control. "Why? Did she say something?"

"No, not directly. It's just that your name came up a few days ago, and she started wigging out. That's not like her."

Grayson shrugged.

Nellie waited for additional details, but none came. Finally, she said, "I don't know if you're aware, but Theresa's gone through a rough few weeks." As Nellie leaned in and began whispering something in his ear, Grayson looked across the room and saw Cicci watching them.

Meanwhile, others began popping corks and distributing plastic glasses filled with cheap champagne. Corbin stepped onto a small, two-step elevated stage located in one corner. He rang a little red bell—symbolic of his unofficial authority—and called for silence.

"First, I want to confirm a rumor going through the building today. It's true. You all get the night off."

Rousing cheers erupted.

"But don't get used to it. Double shifts start tomorrow."

Boos replaced the cheering.

Corbin smiled. "Seriously, go home, take a breath. It's been a long slog. You deserve it." He waited for the clapping to end and resumed. "I have to be honest. When I invited everyone from both sides here, I did so as a courtesy. But I'm grateful to see that some of our friends who opposed this effort took me up on the offer. It speaks to your character and gives me hope for a chance to unify as we move forward."

"Hear! Hear!" chanted scattered voices in the room.

Corbin nodded. "Now that the Twenty-eighth Amendment has been passed, I hope everyone behaves in a way that allows us to come together as a country. For those on the winning side, it means staying humble. No need to gloat. For my friends on the other side, I hope you'll take comfort in knowing our country reached a decision in accordance with the process laid out by our forefathers. The American system works."

The room roared with loud applause.

Corbin continued. "All that being said, if I have harmed someone during this effort, I ask your forgiveness. Also, I think sometimes we get carried away with this 'I owe you, you owe me' business. For the record, I forgive any debts or favors owed to me."

Grayson surveyed the room and assessed the reactions to Corbin's personal pledge. Some appeared to be genuinely moved, while others reacted as if he were touched in the head. Grayson turned back to Corbin, and their eyes locked.

"Finally," Corbin said, "I'd like to recognize one special person. Grayson Woodley, get on up here."

Grayson stood stunned among the crowd until a few people moved aside to create a clearing to the stage. Nellie gently nudged him forward, and Grayson edged toward Corbin. The older man greeted him with a firm handshake.

"Grayson," Corbin began, "we appreciate the fact you took time away from your occupation as a… as a… dang! What's that slang expression for cowboy? A sheep buster?"

Grayson smiled. "A goat roper."

He clasped Grayson's shoulder and laughed. "Yeah, that's it! A goat roper. Anyway, we're glad you left the dusty trail to come and work with us city slickers."

The younger man detested Corbin's over-the-top attempt at reconciliation but played along. "Glad I could help."

Corbin's big smile then transitioned into an earnest gaze of appreciation. "In all seriousness, you're a class act. You came here as an outsider with no formal title—or authority, for that matter—and you just jumped in, and you made sure the case for Wyoming was heard. Obviously, we differ on this issue, but I realize no one in this room will be impacted more by this amendment than you. Just know, when it's time for you to resettle, you have a future here."

The crowd cheered, "Go, Grayson!"

Corbin continued. "And if not DC, then some state will be lucky to have you."

Grayson grew warm around his collar. "I appreciate the praise, Mr. Corbin, but I don't think I did anything more than anyone else in this room." He took a deep breath. "As for resettling, I don't plan on moving anywhere, and I think you'll find that to be the case for most folks in Wyoming."

Grayson's remarks rushed through the room like a chilling wisp of wind.

"I mean, you have to understand. Next to family, a fella's home is the most important thing in his world. Think about that when you close your eyes in your own bed tonight, and I bet you'll agree. This story's far from over."

Some in the white-collar congregation cast their eyes to the floor; others stood with mouths agape.

Grayson soaked in the reaction. He looked at the faces and recognized each as an individual he had come to know, Cicci being one. "Listen, in the end, we're all Americans. I'm grateful to you for allowing me to be part of the process, and I agree with Mr. Corbin about forgiveness. If I offended you somewhere along the way, I'm sorry." He put his hands in his pockets and served up a kind of sweet, little-boy smile. "Oh, and I, too, waive any debts owed to me." Looking directly at Cicci, he finished with, "Whatever they may be." He'd had his fun. Time to move on.

Cicci smiled back in relief, but the expression on her face quickly degraded into a frown.

With her swizzle stick, Theresa Cicci manipulated the ice cubes in her nearly finished cocktail. The wall clock indicated a new day would begin in ten minutes. The stool next to hers was empty, as were most of the other seats surrounding the mahogany bar. She assessed the final results of a game she enjoyed playing when she went out alone. The game was simple: compare the number of drinks she'd downed against the number of times a guy had hit on her. Tonight's score was five to two in favor of the drinks. Not a banner evening, she concluded. It wasn't so long ago when male advances exceeded alcohol consumption by a multiple of ten. To add insult to injury, both of tonight's suitors were jacked on cocaine, par for this month's course.

In the annals of her life, the past several weeks registered near the bottom. Was it unreasonable of her to expect a promotion to legislative director and its associated prestige? Hell, no! She had busted her ass for months, met every deadline, prepped her superiors so they didn't look like idiots, and kept the amendment legislation focused and on track.

Yet Congresswoman Edelman, her boss, had failed to come through. Instead, she had hired the cousin of a key donor back in Minnesota. The little turd—yes, she had met him and harbored no doubt the term fit—barely worked in DC, and that had happened years ago. Recently, he'd been spending his time back in Saint Paul bouncing from one political appointment to another. It was bad enough the guy lacked the requisite skill set and experience for the director's role, but worse, he was a guy. What had happened to the women-helping-women theme reverberating throughout the enlightened nation? If the lesson hadn't been etched in her brain before, it certainly was now: it's not what you know, it's who you know, and then it's not even who you know if someone else has more dough.

Well, to hell with Edelman! Cicci had established some credentials and contacts of her own. Maybe she would make the switch to some federal agency. The hours were shorter and the pay just as good. Still, this disappointment stung. She'd poured her soul into this job and had been rewarded with a feeling of rejection.

Her current salvation was believing her rocky self-esteem couldn't deteriorate any further, but even that notion had been shattered this afternoon. The handsome gentleman from Wyoming had seen to that when he committed the most egregious of transgressions: he dismissed her. He dismissed her out of pity.

Days later, Grayson smacked the steering wheel in delight when he saw an available parking spot just a block from Gerry Manders. He marveled as Claude's electric sedan automatically executed its parallel-parking routine. He glanced at the clock. *Hell yeah! Five minutes early.* He had driven Claude to the airport, and as compensation, his boss had allowed him to borrow the car for the week.

Before heading to Cheyenne, Claude had tasked Grayson with several assignments. The first task—and the reason Grayson now strolled into his favorite bar—was to meet with Claude's Florida counterpart and walk through the talking points against the ratification of the Twenty-eighth Amendment. Grayson peered into the establishment and located his meeting partner. He also saw Cicci sitting at a table with some of her colleagues. If she had seen him, she didn't acknowledge it.

Grayson and his Florida contact shared chicken wings and guzzled Potomac Autumn lager while they reviewed Grayson's notes. The meeting lasted about ninety minutes, and during that period, Grayson saw Cicci eyeing him a few times. However, she looked away whenever she caught him looking back.

At the meeting's conclusion, Grayson shook hands with his dinner partner, who then excused himself. Afterward, Grayson ambled to the bar and began chatting with one of his waiter acquaintances. He wanted to confirm a baseball rumor about the Washington Nationals and their purported acquisition of a new shortstop. While receiving the low down, Grayson glanced over to Cicci's table. She was gone.

When Grayson finally left Gerry Manders, he was greeted by the darkness of night and a rocking thunderstorm. He cursed himself for not having an umbrella yet again. Anticipating rain simply wasn't part of his DNA. He weighed his options and decided he could make the one-block journey without too much damage. He was wrong. By the time he reached the car, the deluge had soaked his body, and his shoes were waterlogged from stepping through a minefield of puddles. As he dug into his pocket for the car remote, footsteps splashed behind him. He wheeled about.

A flash of lightning illuminated the sky and highlighted Cicci in the downpour, her normally curly, brown hair plastered against her face and forehead. Water streamed down her cheeks and spilled off her nose. Her sheer white blouse clung to her shoulders with the outline of her bra now visible. The unexpected temptation aroused Grayson to the core. *Whoa!*

Without a word, Cicci stepped into him, cupped his face with both hands, and placed her lips on his. Startled, Grayson pushed his hands against her arms to break the kiss. She halted long enough for him to read her expression. Its intensity radiated a type of beauty he'd never seen. She leaned in and kissed him again. He didn't resist. The pace and energy of her kissing made her intent clear. She wasn't pleading for affection. She was insisting upon it.

Thunder clapped again as they settled into a deep embrace. Their torsos fused, and Grayson felt her soft breasts press against his chest. He cinched his arm tighter around her lower back, and she moaned softly. They kissed with open mouths and unrestrained passion. Grayson tasted the essence of Cicci, a combination of flavored lip gloss, gin, and rain.

The downpour increased in fury as Grayson fumbled for the rear door handle. Without breaking the embrace, he unlatched it and began to pull the door open. Using a series of awkward duckling steps, he waddled Cicci toward the opening. Suddenly, she spun him around and pushed him into the back seat. Surprised by the unexpected maneuver, Grayson peered into her face and detected a wicked, unmistakable liveliness in her eyes. It wasn't a sinister look, but it was wicked just the same—wicked good. She continued pushing him into the middle of the back seat as she crawled in. Then, with a devilish smile, she unzipped his pants.

"I don't welch on my bets."

CHAPTER 14

HOME ON THE RANGE

GRAYSON RAISED THE post hole digger and jammed it into earth, mercifully softened by a recent rainstorm. He pulled apart the handles, scooping dirt between the blades, and deposited the soil off to the side. Despite the gentle breeze, sweat beaded on his forehead. Perspiration stained his long-sleeve, plaid shirt both around the neck and under his arms. He removed a work glove to examine the palm of his hand.

"Shit, I'm getting a blister," Grayson complained to his father and brother. More than a year had passed since the three of them had stood together on the edge of the four-thousand-acre Woodley ranch, yet their presence on the land felt as natural as the sagebrush surrounding them.

"Don't tell me my little brother turned into a candy ass during his time back East." Zach Woodley carried a coil of barbed wire as he returned from the weathered, white pickup parked just off the rutted trail. Like Grayson, Zach possessed a pair of deep-set, blue eyes, yet his hair was auburn in color, a trait from their mother. Zach had also grown a full beard since Grayson had seen him last.

"Ya got a Band-Aid, smartass?" Grayson asked.

"Why would I? I'm not the one with the blister."

Daryl Woodley interjected, "There's a first aid kit in the truck."

"I don't know, Dad," Zach mused. "Maybe Grayson would be more useful fluffing pillows back at the house."

Grayson walked to the pickup and tended to his wound. He wasn't about to give Zach the satisfaction of knowing he'd scored big points in their verbal joust, but internally Grayson was taking his brother's words to heart. How soft had he become during his stay in the nation's capital? The thought annoyed him more than the blister on his hand.

When the afternoon's project was finished, the white pickup and its three passengers—four counting Ringo, the border collie—chugged for home. They drove into the yard where the Woodley's spacious, ranch-style house stood. Tammy Woodley greeted them. She held a cordless grass trimmer by its red handle.

"How's it look?" she asked as the men hopped out of the truck.

Grayson admired the manicured patch of grass in front of the house. "Looks good, Mom."

Tammy nodded. "Hey, I made a pie crust earlier but haven't added the filling. Would you like apple or cherry?"

In a bang-bang response, Zach and Grayson shouted conflicting answers: "Cherry!" "Apple!"

Tammy folded her arms. "You know how this gets settled."

The brothers grinned and drew closer for a game of rock-paper-scissors. After each used a series of false starts as psychological combat, Grayson yelled triumphantly when his hand of paper covered Zach's rock. Unfortunately for Grayson, he'd chosen the blistered hand. As Zach retracted his fist, the older brother dug his knuckles into Grayson's palm.

"Ouch! You rotten bastard!"

"Office wimps shouldn't be eating dessert anyway," Zach sulked as he trailed off toward the house.

Two hours later, Grayson sat with his entire family around the dining table. They feasted on a delicious meal of pork tenderloin, mashed potatoes, and fresh vegetables. The smell of homemade dinner rolls on the table and apple pie baking in the kitchen wafted among the gathering.

Libby Woodley, Zach's wife of seven years, broke away from supervising their two toddlers long enough to direct the conversation Grayson's way. "So, tell us, Mr. Big Shot. What's it like rubbing elbows with all those senators?"

"Actually, they're pretty grimy," Grayson joked. "I have to take lots of showers."

"Mmm, I'll bet. Have you got yourself a honey?" Libby asked.

Cicci's image dashed through Grayson's head. The back-seat wager payoff—with interest—had ignited a torrid, pent-up passion between them. Two weeks of pulsating, back-scratching love making had ensued in multiple locations—some unique. His return to Wyoming, two days ago, was the first interruption to their affair. Still, he didn't think "honey" was an apt classification for her. Not yet, anyway. "No," was all he said.

"What about friends with benefits?" queried an adolescent voice belonging to Cindy Woodley.

Daryl coughed and threw his hands in the air. "Whose child is this?"

The question from Grayson's kid sister, who was fourteen years his junior, broke him up. He missed his spunky little shadow, and wow, how she'd changed in the past few years. Cindy had grown three inches taller, sprouted some breasts, and cultivated a hysteria at the sight of the slightest hint of acne.

At age fifteen, Grayson had experienced true love for the first time. However, unlike most boys his age, his object of affection was a baby. Cindy had entered the Woodleys' life as a ten-month-old, foster child. Soon, the entire family had become smitten with her, but none more so than Grayson. Their emotional bond was unbreakable. Months later, the family legally adopted her as one of their own.

"The question still stands," Zach declared. "Spill it."

With his spoon, Grayson flicked a pea toward his brother.

"Penalty!" Tammy shouted and pointed at her son. "You, sir, have earned clean-up duty."

As the family's boisterous exchanges continued through dessert and beyond, Grayson realized how much he missed home. He missed the radiant, blue skies and expansive panoramas of mountains and buttes. Most of all, he missed his loved ones. Tonight's interactions were even more touching than he recalled.

Eventually, Zach's crew departed for their own home in Douglas. Cindy retreated to her social media world, and Tammy retired for the evening. In the living room, Grayson and his dad relaxed with whiskeys on the rocks as the local news began. During the first commercial break, Daryl pushed out of the lounger and stretched.

"How's the leg feeling?" Grayson asked.

"Better than my back. I have to be careful not to sit for too long."

Grayson watched his father battle his ailments without complaining. The man had survived the demanding physical rigors of ranch life for more than thirty years. He was not only tough; he was smart, too. Daryl possessed keen skills as a businessman. He was shrewd but fair. As the older man settled back into his chair, Grayson posed a question weighing on his mind.

"I don't remember you ever drinking gin. Did you?"

"Nope."

"Why not?"

Daryl turned his attention away from the TV and to his son. "Because God created bourbon," he answered with a perfect deadpan delivery,

Grayson smiled. "I should get an assist for that setup."

Daryl nodded and then became pensive. "So, tell me. What are the geniuses in Washington planning to do with us?"

Grayson rolled his head back and stared at the ceiling. "Well, that's an interesting question. Basically, they're going to incentivize you to leave."

"How so?"

"They're pushing a four-year transition period to get most of the people out of Wyoming, but they want folks to start moving immediately. They plan to pay market value for individual properties, and if you agree to move in the first two years, they'll add a fifteen percent premium. If you wait until year three, the premium is only five percent, and if you hold out until the end, you get no premium. They're also wanting to incentivize businesses in the rest of the US to hire Wyoming transplants. I'm not exactly sure how."

"Who determines market value? Are we going to get the same per acre amount as South Dakota? How much are they getting for the Black Hills?"

"Fourteen billion over twenty years," Grayson said, "and we should be so lucky. In the minds of Congress, the Black Hills and Wyoming are two different circumstances. The money being dangled at South Dakota is a bribe; for Wyoming, they have the Twenty-eighth Amendment to bludgeon us."

"What if I decide not to go?" Daryl asked.

"Well, they're not going to make it easy for you to stay. They're laying out what types of industry will be allowed and who gets to operate it. Unfortunately, your occupation as a rancher is in their crosshairs. They want to phase out sheep and cattle ranching over the next decade. Production limits will be set each year on a declining basis. As ranchers sell out, their properties will be converted to open range for bison and other game."

"What about crops? Are they going to let me grow any grain?"

"It looks like dryland farming might get a pass, but they want to clamp down on irrigation. You know, save the water for their downstream constituents."

Daryl hissed, "So you're telling me my only possible future in agriculture is to raise wheat?"

"Well, yeah, I guess," Grayson answered. "That's what they're pushing, but on the bright side, there will be opportunities to mentor."

"Mentor? Mentor who, for Christ's sake?"

"Congress is intent upon creating opportunities for Indians to own and operate businesses, and they're going to provide funding to support that initiative."

"Wait a minute," Daryl protested. "The Feds are purchasing the Black Hills, buying out all the ranchers in Wyoming, and bankrolling the Indians. Where in the hell are they getting all this money?"

Grayson answered in a sarcastic tone, "Progressives have created this new economic notion called Modern Monetary Theory. Basically, they contend government can increase the debt pretty much at will without any negative consequences."

"Oh, there'll be consequences. In the long run, someone's going to have to pay."

"You know what they say to that? 'In the long run, we'll all be dead.'"

Daryl clicked his tongue. "Typical answer. You were saying about these government payouts?"

"Yeah. They plan on providing monetary grants to registered tribal members so they can purchase existing stores, services, ranches, or whatever. However, everyone understands there will be a learning curve, so they plan on hiring mentors who are experienced in managing money and running businesses to show the new owners the ropes."

"I'm confused. I thought you said the Feds were planning to buy and shut down ranches."

Grayson hesitated.

"Well?"

"They are," Grayson said, scrambling to find the right words. "The Feds want to convert ranches to open rangeland, but they're talking about making an exception for Indians. If the plan is to help them thrive under this new arrangement, then we need to identify situations where they have a chance to realize some early success. They have a decent amount of experience in agriculture and hospitality."

"We? Whose side are you on, Grayson?" A crazy rage stirred in Daryl's eyes. It reminded the younger Woodley of an angry bull.

"I'm on yours, Dad," Grayson said, blood rushing to his head with his own growing anger. "I'm against this whole state confiscation thing, but if it happens, helping out the Indians is the one good thing I can see coming out of it. If that includes rigging the game a little in their favor, I don't care. God knows they're due a few breaks."

Daryl pushed a stack of magazines off the end table. "You're telling me I'm supposed to give my ranch to some son of a bitch I don't know and then hang around to teach the bastard how to run it?"

His dad's frustration resonated with Grayson, but he couldn't offer any consolation.

"Now listen here," Daryl continued. "I went to school with Arapaho and Sioux kids. We played basketball together. I've hunted with Simon Bitterroot on the rez, and he's fished our stream. I've done business with Indians all my life. I understand their plight and am sympathetic. But the US Government is the last entity who should be advocating solutions. Hell, they spent a hundred years taking the Indians' land and sending them where they didn't want to go. Then they felt guilty about it for the next hundred years, so they created a culture of government dependency. Now they think they can change that culture with a few bucks and the flip of a switch? Ain't gonna happen! Not in this generation—or the next."

Grayson sympathized, "I hear ya, but…"

"My granddad settled this ranch and passed it on to my dad, who passed it on to me. I'll be damned if I'm going to let a self-righteous set of numbskulls living two thousand miles away tell me how to live my life. If they want to kick us out as a state, so be it, but they're not going to dick with my lifestyle. This ranch will most likely pass on to your brother—or you, if he doesn't want it—but I'm starting to think Zach was right. You've changed, and not for the better."

His dad's last comment stung Grayson worse than a thousand blisters.

CHAPTER 15

IRONY

THE NEXT MORNING, gravel scrunched beneath the tires as Tammy's bronze SUV pulled into the parking lot. It joined a cluster of vehicles in front of the unassuming restaurant. In the extensive vacant space across the road from the diner, a motorhome towing a sedan was parked alongside two eighteen-wheelers. Situated on the Old Highway and a mile from the interstate exit, the diner's location was suboptimal for luring cross-country travelers. However, its reputation for gargantuan breakfast burritos and to-die-for cinnamon rolls drew in a faithful stream of locals and even a few out-of-towners.

A meadowlark's song hailed Grayson as he stepped out of the SUV's passenger side and into the summer's early-morning sun. Along the barbed-wire fence, he searched for signs of the avian singer but saw nothing. Two antelope grazed on tufts of wild grass about fifty yards beyond the fence. Like so many other momentary glimpses afforded to him the past few days, this snapshot invigorated his spirit and restored him with a badly needed sense of grounding.

Grayson rounded the vehicle's front end on his way to the entrance. A sign written in large block letters and adorned with hand-painted, four-leaf clovers sat in the diner's window. *Lucky's Breakfast Inn. Open daily. 6 a.m. to 8 p.m.*

"Mom, why hasn't Bonnie ever changed the name of this place? They serve all three meals."

Tammy shut the driver's-side door without locking it—a common practice in Douglas. "She's superstitious. Afraid it would doom the place." With a giggle, she added, "But then, I guess she could call it Bad Lucky's."

Grayson groaned. He held the door open for his mom, and they entered the modest but orderly eatery. Welcoming aromas of fried bacon and bread yeast greeted them. A familiar voice from a scurrying figure sang out, "Pick any open spot."

Tammy pointed to a table alongside the knotty-pine paneled wall, and the mother-son duo seated themselves. Grayson had suggested dining out this morning, not as a slight to his mom's cooking—which was consistently exceptional—but because he wanted some one-on-one time with her.

Soon a twig of a woman appeared with a plastic carafe of coffee. "Hi, Tammy. Hey, Grayson. Long time, no see."

Grayson took note of the middle-aged waitress. Her pixie hairstyle with its contrasting colors, a butterscotch dye job with purple streaks, made a statement. "Howdy, Bonnie. You're looking rad these days. I like it."

"I'm one hip chick, hon. Coffee for the both of you?"

Grayson and Tammy nodded.

Bonnie filled two mugs with the steaming brew. "You still working in Cheyenne?"

"Yeah, I'm based there, but lately, I've spent a lot of time in DC."

"Mmm. Like it?"

"It's an interesting place. I spend most of my time working."

"Don't I know the feeling," Bonnie said. "Know what you want, babe?"

"I'll take a cinnamon roll."

"Tammy?"

"Same. Oh, and I'd like two to go, please."

"Got it," Bonnie acknowledged before dashing away to her next table.

"You take good care of Cindy and Dad," Grayson observed.

"Try to," Tammy answered.

"When did he leave this morning?"

"Just after four. He couldn't sleep." Tammy's affectionate gaze softened. "He felt bad about your argument last night. I hope you know he thinks the world of you. He's a proud papa."

"But a frustrated rancher. I get it." Grayson smiled to ensure her the disagreement was yesterday's news. Changing subjects, he said, "Wow! I can't believe how much Cin has changed. She's a whole new person."

"You wanna take her with you?" Tammy asked half-jokingly.

"She's a little feisty," Grayson agreed, "but any more than Zach and I when we were teens?"

"Let's just say I'm out of practice, and girls are tough. Two alpha females under one roof are a recipe for trouble."

A new voice intervened: "Is that who I think it is? How's it going, partner?"

Grayson looked up and spied Vic Moody standing over him. The man's becoming smile filled the lower half of his square face. Grayson stood and shared a firm handshake.

"Hello, Vic. How are you?"

"Fine, fine. It's good to see you, Grayson." The man, who was roughly Tammy's age, wore a tan camel-hair sport coat; a light-blue, open-collar shirt; and charcoal-colored slacks. His gold-and-blue lapel pin read *Douglas Chamber of Commerce*. "You home for a little R&R, or did you come back for reinforcements?"

"We sure could use your smooth-talking power of persuasion," Grayson said. "It's been tough sledding."

"So I've heard," Vic answered with a supportive nod. Then he turned to Tammy. "Hello, Mrs. Woodley. Enjoying some time with your boy?"

"You know it." She beckoned toward an empty chair. "Care to join us for breakfast?"

"I don't want to impose," Vic said.

"No bother at all," Tammy assured him.

"At least have some coffee," Grayson added.

Vic slid into an open chair. "Where's that cantankerous husband of yours?" he asked as he waved to Bonnie with an empty cup.

"He had some business in Lusk this morning. Hoping to seal the deal on a used tractor."

"I pity the seller. Daryl's a tough negotiator." Vic thanked Bonnie as she filled his cup. "So, Grayson, what's your read on the chances of getting the Twenty-eighth Amendment ratified?" he asked while reaching for a packet of sugar.

Grayson chewed on his lip in contemplation. "Honestly, it's too close to call, but there's a realistic shot things will go our way. I'll say fifty-one percent in our favor just because I'm an optimist."

"I understand they're already laying out plans for the great exodus."

"Yeah, Dad and I were discussing that last night," Grayson replied while giving Tammy a careful sideways glance.

"It's kind of funny," Vic continued. "At our last chamber meeting, we were brainstorming ideas for next year's tourism campaign. Raylene Baker—Tammy, you know Raylene and her quick sense of humor—well, she pipes up. She says that instead of 'Wyoming—Vacationland,' we should be saying, 'Wyoming—Vacating Land.'"

"Raylene's a hoot," Tammy agreed.

"Yeah, yeah she is." Vic answered. "Here's another thing.

Kinda funny, too. Only this time, not funny like 'Ha, ha,' but funny like the world's a real interesting place. I'm up in Casper last week for the statewide meeting of chamber presidents. We meet quarterly. I'm checking in with Ralphie Arnold, Casper's prez, and I…"

"You call Mr. Arnold, Ralphie?" Grayson asked incredulously. "He played defensive end for the Pokes. He could crush you like a grape."

"Oh yeah. Just to yank his chain. He hates it."

"Boys," Tammy muttered, shaking her head.

"So anyway, I ask *Mr. Arnold* about the latest population trends in Natrona County. When I'd talked to him previously, the story was pretty bleak because of drilling shutdowns and that county's dependence on energy. Given the cold reception Wyoming's getting back in Washington, I expected to hear more of the same, but his answer surprised me. He said the population has leveled off. Basically, those who were only here for the work have already left. The established families are staying put."

"Seems reasonable," Grayson said. "Nothing too weird about that."

"True," Vic answered. "But here's the weird part. Ralphie—er, *Mr. Arnold*—said the number of inquiries from out-of-staters has spiked. He said the queries range from requests for general information about the state to detailed questions about schools and property taxes. These people aren't planning a vacation. They're considering a move."

"Wow! That is strange," Grayson agreed. "Just out of the blue?"

Vic flashed his effusive smile. "After the first wave of inquiries, Ralphie, er, *Mr. A*—ah, to hell with it. He's Ralphie to me. Ralphie had his folks ask callers what prompted their curiosity. The majority said, 'I believe in the Hands-Off movement,' or 'I want to be part of the Hands-Off cause.' Or, better yet, 'I want to live the Hands-Off lifestyle.'"

"I've never heard of a Hands-Off movement," Tammy said with raised eyebrows.

"I've heard it mentioned, but no one in Senator Shelton's group took it seriously," Grayson answered.

"I hadn't heard of it, either," Vic admitted, "so I did some research. It turns out a lady from Dayton, Ohio, by the name of Cornelia Witherspoon has established quite a faithful following in the digital world. She puts out a podcast series called *CW's March of Reason*, and she has half a million followers. Apparently, she's one of the top conservative influencers in the country."

"What's an influencer?" Tammy asked.

"What's an influencer?" Vic mocked. "Tammy, quit being an old fud and get with the times."

"An influencer is someone who has a large audience on social media like Twitter or Facebook. It's another word for *trendsetter*," Grayson explained.

"Oh, sorry for my ignorance," Tammy spat. "Some of us still work in the physical world."

Vic responded with his signature grin. "Just teasing, Tammy. Just teasing."

"What's the Hands-Off story?" Grayson asked.

Vic refocused. "Yeah, so Cornelia's schtick has been to champion the Libertarian, limited-government cause through her podcasts. She blasts government overreach at every possible opportunity, and apparently, she does so in a way that's witty and resonating, because her audience numbers are exploding."

"And naturally, Wyoming's proposed dissolution falls right into her wheelhouse," Grayson tacked on.

"Yep," Vic said. "And when the idea to grant Indians autonomy in this new land was presented, she jumped on it as a Hands-Off blueprint for returning governmental control to localities. Her main objection to the federal proposal is that it's limited to Native Americans. She's advocating Wyoming residency be available to any American seeking this alternative lifestyle, not just the Indians."

Tammy said, "I'm not sure I follow. This lady from Ohio wants to open up the new Wyoming to all the Western romantics in the US? Are these people wannabe cowboys or tree huggers?"

"Cowboys, I suppose," Vic answered. "Maybe some naturalists, too. Maybe neither, but they're definitely free-spirit types. I think the common thread is a desire for self-rule. They're tired of government intervention in so many facets of their life."

"Interesting," Grayson mused. "When we held a town-hall meeting in Cheyenne last winter, there was a guy from the Nebraska panhandle who wanted to align with Wyoming, essentially creating a larger area of autonomy. Have you heard anything like that?"

"No, but this Hands-Off concept has just come to our attention," Vic said.

Tammy steepled her fingers. "I'm just thinking out loud here, but my guess is most people interested in this movement would prefer to expand the practice of self-rule to the places where they currently live. Folks generally like it where they are. If they had their way, I could envision special pockets throughout the country free from federal regulation."

"Never going to happen," Vic countered. "Remember how this whole thing got started. Dems control the federal government, and nationally, they're the majority of the population. They've no interest in relinquishing political control to various pockets of territory. Wyoming is a special circumstance, and one that ultimately strengthens their electoral hand."

Grayson polished off his last bite of cinnamon pastry and licked the white frosting from his fork. "For sure. We're struggling just to get twelve other states to side with us on the ratification fight. There's no chance a block of Texas or Alabama is going to be carved out for autonomous rule, but I wonder about a place like Western Nebraska. The fact that it's adjacent to Wyoming, similar in landscape, and sparsely populated makes it a feasible expansion. Congress bent to the will of the Indians and added the Black Hills. Don't you think the Nebraska situation is possible?"

Vic shrugged. "Well, I doubt any more land will be added to Wyoming, but I guess it's possible. Then again, I never expected all these inquiries about moving here."

"How ironic would it be if the state actually increased in population after getting kicked out on the pretense of not having enough people?" Tammy asked.

"Pretty damn ironic," Vic agreed. "I guess the unknowns are how much these people value the Hands-Off life and what are they willing to do to make it happen."

"That's only one side of it," Grayson added. "We still haven't seen the final version of NRR regulations. The Hands-Off and Nebraska folks should be careful what they wish for. They could actually end up with fewer freedoms."

CHAPTER 16

AN UNCOMFORTABLE QUESTION

(Many Years from Now)

AS GRAYSON RECOUNTED stories about his long career in Wyonation's Department of Treasures, Cicci sat back in her seat with folded arms and yawned. Conversely, Mr. Tang leaned forward with his eyes keenly fixated on the speaker.

"Yeah, that was probably the roughest winter we had," Grayson said, now twenty minutes into answering Mr. Tang's continuous prompts. "I think the mortality rate for yearlings in the deer population approached ninety percent."

"Fascinating!" Mr. Tang cried. "Despite all the modern technology, we are still at the mercy of nature's whims."

While Grayson nodded in agreement, Cicci twirled the swizzle stick in her drink. A text notification chirped on her phone, disrupting the conversation at the table. She grabbed the device and studied its screen. An annoyed frown spread across her face. "Damn!" She glanced at her companions. "I'm sorry. I need to make a call." Cicci hastily stood and headed toward the entrance door. The men tracked her path until she disappeared out the exit.

"Work?" Mr. Tang asked.

Grayson shrugged. "Maybe. I don't know." The break gave him an opportunity to pivot the conversation. *My turn to ask a question.* "Speaking of work, I was wondering, how did you enter the diplomatic core? I thought your father wanted you to pursue a technical field."

Mr. Tang's face brightened. "Oh, he did, and I did. I earned an engineering degree at Alabama and planned to work in manufacturing, the US, if possible; back home if not. However, a family friend who worked in government services took notice of my English-language skills. He referred me to the Office of International Relations. They encouraged me to join their team."

Encouraged how? A gun to the head? The threat of imprisonment? "Nice," Grayson said. "And the allure of world travel had to be an enticing perk."

"It has been a fulfilling career," Mr. Tang said.

"Do you ever miss the technical discipline of engineering?"

"No. Engineers are problem solvers. The engineering skill set is applicable to numerous pursuits. Did you know more Fortune 500 CEOs have an engineering background than any other?"

"I'd heard that."

"Engineering trained me to see the big picture, to understand how all the pieces fit," Mr. Tang boasted with a distinct glimmer in his eye. "It's important to know how all the pieces fit. Don't you agree?"

Grayson felt a chill snake down his spine. *He's telling me something! What is it?*

Mr. Tang sipped his beer. "Have you always been with the Treasures Department?"

"Yes. Did you know I was the first Wyonation Director of Treasures? In fact, labeling our natural resources as treasures was my idea. Given that land and wildlife preservation drove The Birth, it made sense."

"The Birth?"

"Yeah. It's a phrase Wyonationals gave to the moment of our creation."

"I see," Mr. Tang said, drawing back his shoulders. "What was your mood in that moment? Jubilation?"

The question sobered Grayson. "Hardly jubilation. We were forced to change."

"What about the Native Americans?" Mr. Tang prompted. "Weren't they jubilant?"

"Some, maybe. They're skeptical people, so most took a wait-and-see stance." The question continued to gnaw at Grayson.

Mr. Tang waited, hands in his lap.

"I guess the general feeling was acceptance. Resignation, maybe. The important point was we survived," Grayson concluded.

"Yes," Mr. Tang agreed. "And you became a lead figure in your reconfigured homeland."

"For a while. I served in the director's capacity for five years. I was fortunate to be in the right place at the right time and helped shape a brand-new government. Few people can say they've had that experience. Not bad for a rancher's son."

"Why only five years? Did you ascend to a higher role?"

Grayson chuckled softly. "No, quite the opposite. I demoted myself to a district protector."

Mr. Tang raised his eyebrows.

"After five years, most of the creative work had been completed. The job turned into an administrative chore, and I was bored. Like I mentioned in this afternoon's briefing, 'protector' is the name we created for our folks out in the field. I missed working outdoors, so I left the director's role to the aspiring political types."

"Of which there's no shortage," Mr. Tang offered.

"You got that right."

"And your family? Did you return home?"

"No," Grayson said. "I grew up on a Central Wyoming ranch. My folks still ran it, but the unspoken reality was that it would eventually pass to my older brother."

"I understand the privilege of the first-born son—a custom throughout the world."

"Oh, don't get me wrong. I didn't mind. Zach deserved it. He stuck around while I went to college and then on to state employment. He put in the time, and honestly, he's twice the rancher I am."

"But you were able to live nearby?"

Grayson laughed again. "Nearby is a relative term. Folks in Wyoming think any place within a four-hour drive is nearby. A protector position opened up in the Spearfish District, so I jumped on it. Ideally, I wanted to work out of Jackson, but so did everyone else. No vacancies there. Landing a spot in the Black Hills was a decent consolation prize."

"How long have you been a protector?"

"Up until recently. Now I serve as the district director in Spearfish." Grayson sighed. "An accident necessitated the change."

"What happened?" Mr. Tang asked.

"I was patrolling some rugged country on an ATV—sort of a four-wheel motorcycle. Anyway, I'm navigating it along this narrow mini-ridge when a rabbit pops out of the brush. Damn thing caught me off guard, and I reacted by steering hard right. Two wheels go off the edge, and I hold on while the machine does one and a half rolls. Sometime during the tumble, my leg gets caught and breaks at both the ankle and mid-shin. The upper break was a compound fracture. My memory's fuzzy, but at some point, I called in for help because some other protectors rescued me—but not until the next morning. I spent that night out there during a frickin' rainstorm thinking this was the end."

"How awful!" Mr. Tang exclaimed. "I can't imagine the agony you endured."

The ache in Grayson's hip and lower appendage pulsated as the memory manifested. "It was a bitch," he agreed.

"How long was your recovery?"

"Still going on. It turns out I had wrenched my hip pretty good, too. Some muscle tore away from the bone. After surgery, I spent five months at home in a wheelchair and another three on crutches."

"I'm sorry for your misfortune," Mr. Tang said.

"During my downtime, I got fat and drank more than usual—which is saying something. Those bad habits didn't go away after I returned to work. It was gently suggested that I move back to the office full time. They offered the district directorship to me, and here I am."

A sparkle of light reflected off of Cicci's gin glass and caught Grayson's attention. He gazed at the door but found no evidence of her return. "I wonder how long she's going to be?" He spoke aloud but had intended the question for himself.

Mr. Tang shrugged.

Playfully, Grayson winked at him and asked, "You think she may have ditched us with the bill?"

Playful wasn't Mr. Tang's style. "No. I'm sure Ms. Cicci is an honorable person."

Grayson put his elbow on the table and allowed his chin to settle into his palm. He smiled slightly at his failed attempt to be funny. "She is," he agreed.

Mr. Tang sat back and folded his arms. "You have led an adventurous life, my friend."

Briefly, Grayson glanced at him before looking off into the room. "Yeah, I suppose."

Mr. Tang tilted his head. "May I ask you a personal question?"

If Grayson's attention hadn't been fully devoted to the Chinese diplomat, it was now. "Sure, you can ask. No promises as to how I'll answer."

Mr. Tang nodded. "I was wondering—during your career, was there ever an occasion where you had to kill a man?"

CHAPTER 17

JUST A SIDE TRIP

(Seventeen Years Earlier)

GRAYSON BEEPED THE remote of his metallic silver Toyota 4Runner. He loaded Cicci's suitcase and his duffel into the back. He motioned for his companion, who was dressed in a baby-blue-striped romper with white sandals, to hop in the passenger seat and kept his eyes riveted on her while she climbed in. He noticed goose bumps on her tantalizing thighs, courtesy of the refreshingly brisk Cheyenne breeze.

"Brrr. That wind's chilly," she said.

"Autumn's not far away."

"Thanks again for breakfast," she said, buckling her seatbelt. "It was delicious. You actually do have some worth."

"Did you like the green chili? I mixed in some elk sausage. I think it goes great with eggs."

"Super yummy, not too spicy." She reached across the console and smoothed his shirt collar. "You've got a little wrinkle."

Grayson seized on her proximity and planted a quick kiss on her lips. "Ah, and now you've got some cowboy on your mouth."

Cicci licked her lips. "Super yummy, not too spicy."

He drew back, observing her sunny disposition. From the moment he'd picked her up in Denver yesterday afternoon, she had seemed more relaxed—bubbly and carefree.

"Wagon ho!" Cicci yelled. "Isn't that what they say in the frontier when it's time to move out?"

"It's wagons ho," Grayson corrected. "Several rigs make up the wagon train. "A cowboy yells, 'Wagon ho!' when he's seeking a prostitute."

Cicci slapped him in the chest. "You are filthy and disgusting. I don't know why I let myself be seen with you," she said, trying to suppress a smile.

"Like that old song says, it's more fun to laugh with sinners than cry with saints." He glanced at her, and another change in her appearance hit home. "You're letting your hair grow out. Looks good."

"I'm glad you came around to noticing, Cowboy. It only took you a day."

"It's not as curly."

"Yeah, but that's not my doing. There's no humidity here."

"And as far as I'm concerned, that's a good thing."

He pulled the 4Runner away from the curb and maneuvered through the streets of Cheyenne enroute to the interstate. Along the way, they passed some fairgrounds with a large set of grandstands.

"Cheyenne Frontier Days," Cicci read as they passed the fairgrounds marquee. "Is that a big deal around here?"

Grayson couldn't believe his ears. "You've never heard of Cheyenne Frontier Days? It's huge. The rodeo's called The Daddy of 'em All."

"I've heard of it, but I never knew what it was. I never thought about it, really."

"You have fairs in Minnesota, right?"

"Oh yeah. The Minnesota State Fair in Saint Paul is enormous. It takes place just before Labor Day. I think it's the biggest fair in the country."

"And you have a rodeo at the same time?"

Cicci shook her head. "No. No rodeo. You can walk around and see livestock, and there are a bunch of concerts with different entertainers each night."

"Same for us. Every night, there's a rodeo and then a concert. Big names, too. Mostly country and western singers. Frontier Days are over for this year. Ended a few weeks ago."

"Did you go?"

With pursed lips, Grayson turned to his passenger. "No. Not this year. I've been a little busy."

"I meant ever."

"Oh yeah. I've been several times. Downtown streets shut down at night, and there's a rockin' party. It's summer's main event for Southern Wyoming."

"Mmm," Cicci acknowledged. As the road bent away from the fairgrounds, she cast a final look. "Maybe I'm too much of a city girl, but I just don't get rodeos."

"What don't you get?"

"I don't know. It just seems like a show where people come to watch animals get tortured. Kind of like what the Romans did in the Colosseum."

"Oh, c'mon!" Grayson blurted out. "Animals are not getting tortured."

"They sure are! Horses are getting kicked in the ribs, and those poor little calves get their legs jerked out from under them. It's mean."

"Theresa. *Theresa!* The events in rodeos are skills contests.

They're everyday skills cowboys use on the ranch. Bronc riding is the technique people have been using to break horses for thousands of years, and those poor little calves get roped because sometimes the little shits run off from the herd and you have to bring 'em back."

"Isn't that what herding dogs are for?"

"Dogs are great if you have one around, but sometimes you don't."

"And what about bulls? Don't tell me anybody actually rides a bull when doing their chores on the farm."

Grayson grinned. "Okay, fair point. Bull riding is more of a manly dare kind of thing, but they're not being tortured." He remembered some of his own painful tumbles. "It was probably my worst event."

Her jaw dropped when his last words sunk in. "Worst event? What are you saying?"

"Didn't I tell you? I rodeoed back in high school."

Cicci stared at him. "Really? Hmm."

"Yep. I was pretty good, too—except for bull riding."

"Well, that explains a lot. All those falls you must have taken on your noggin shaped the dopey fella you've become."

Grayson cackled. "I'm telling you, Miss Cicci, if you could've seen me bulldoggin' them steers, you'd be jumping my bones like a mountain lion in heat." He considered what he'd just said and added, "I mean, more than you already are."

"I swear to God. I am going to beat you to death and leave you on the side of the road." She harumphed. "Bulldogging. That's the one where you throw the cow to the ground by breaking its neck?"

"They're steers, not cows, and we don't break their necks. We grab their horns and twist their necks a bit so we can take them to the ground. The key is to get them off balance and then use your own body weight as leverage."

"Oh, twisting their necks. That's so much more humane. I thank you, the ASPCA thanks you, and I'm sure the steers thank you."

Grayson ran a hand through his dark-brown hair and adjusted his sunglasses. "Whew! You're relentless. I mean that as compliment."

Cicci rolled her eyes.

"Hey, could you get me a water? They're in the cooler behind my seat."

She complied by passing a water bottle to him and grabbed a second one for herself. She tilted back her head and took a long swallow.

While Cicci quietly gazed out the passenger-side window, Grayson surveyed the countryside. They had left Cheyenne's city limits and were now headed east on Interstate 80. Along the highway, tall stalks of ripened grass waved as golden tufts. In the distance, curated fields with neat rows of churned soil intermingled with vast swaths of virgin prairie.

As they drew closer to the Nebraska border, Cicci turned to him. "Cowboy, I don't mean to hurt your feelings, but I'm looking around here, and all I see is a whole lot of nothing. No trees, barren land. I'm puzzled why you're putting up such a tough fight for this worthless space."

He accepted her observations in stride. He'd heard this assessment from outsiders many times before. "If you think this is bad, wait until we drive through Shoshoni."

"It gets worse?"

"Baby, the ground before you is an oasis compared with other parts of Wyoming."

"You're not enhancing your case for resisting the Twenty-eighth Amendment."

"Well, I don't know. The place grows on you over time. Besides, it's home."

"And why did I let you talk me into coming here?"

"Because you wanted to see the free-spirit lifestyle firsthand. Give it a few days. You'll catch the vibe. And I'm going to show you the Tetons and Yellowstone, quite possibly the most spectacular places on Earth."

"Okay, you've earned a wee bit of credibility," Cicci said and emphasized it by pinching a tiny slice of air between her thumb and forefinger.

Switching gears, Grayson said, "Hey, I'm sorry about the change in plans. I really appreciate your understanding on this side trip. It'll just take a couple of days."

"Well, Cowboy, you are one lucky dude because my schedule just happens to be open for the next few weeks."

"Yeah, so bring me up to date. That's quite a change." He glanced at her and again was surprised at her almost carefree behavior. *What happened to the high-strung version of Cicci?*

She clapped her hands. "Well, I think I was destined for this change because everything has fallen into place so easily. I'd barely given Nancy my notice when Arnie Schafer reaches out from Interior. I'm not sure who told him, but he mentioned he heard a rumor about me leaving Edelman's team. He makes this big pitch on the spot. He tells me how valuable my experience in working with the Twenty-eighth Amendment would be to the transition effort being placed in Interior's lap. He made me feel special."

"That's great, Theresa."

"Wait. It gets better," Cicci said while clutching his shoulder. "Arnie says he can bring me in at a GS-12 level, definitely more coin than I was getting paid as a staffer. So just before I'm ready to say yes, I get a different call from Melody Perkins. She's in Interior, too, but manages a different section. She wants me in her group and says she has a GS-13 spot open."

"Score!" Grayson shouted. "But not so many hand motions

in the storytelling. You're getting a little spastic, and it's distracting my driving."

"Shut up! You're so annoying."

Grayson laughed. "Back to the story."

"No."

"No?"

"You have to apologize first."

"For what?"

"For being a snot and mocking my enthusiasm."

His next laugh came straight from the belly. "Okay, okay. I am sorry for mocking your enthusiasm."

"And being a snot."

"I don't think I was a snot."

"You were."

He chuckled again. "And for being a snot."

"And you have to kiss me."

"Just a quick one." Grayson turned and pecked her lips. "More to come later. Now back to the story."

"Okay, so you think I would have jumped on Melody's offer, right? But something about Arnie struck a chord. He was so sincere in wanting me on his team, and truth be told, I thought helping to establish a new homeland for the Native Americans would be pretty cool. So I called Arnie and explained Melody's offer. I asked if he could match the GS-13 spot, and he said he'd see if that was possible. The next day, he calls back, and, voilà!, I have a senior analyst position waiting for me in Washington."

"That's awesome! What did Edelman say when you told her?"

"That bitch! She tried laying this guilt trip on me about loyalty to the team, and so I deftly reminded her about how she blew off her whole staff to bring in an incapable outsider just to gain some political points."

"Good for you."

"I was upset right afterward, but by the time I made it home, I felt like the weight of the world had been lifted."

An exit sign reminded Grayson of their travel progress. At eighty miles per hour, the 4Runner had reached Kimball, Nebraska, in less than an hour. There, they turned north onto Nebraska State Highway 71. An occasional butte interrupted the prairie's monotony.

"I'm going to shock you with my next remarkable observation, but Nebraska looks a helluva lot like Wyoming," Cicci said.

"How astute. You should have lived in nineteenth-century London. You would have given Sherlock Holmes a run for his money."

"My loss—and the world's," she replied. "How much farther to Scottsbluff?"

"Not far."

"Did you say Claude was coming, too?"

"Yep. He's meeting us up there."

"Tell me again, what's there?"

"A gathering of Hands-Off followers. You heard of 'em?"

"Yes, actually. I saw a story on the news. They're a bunch of crazy, off-the-grid types who want their own country. I didn't think anyone was taking them seriously. Please tell me you're not."

"I wouldn't categorize them as off-the-grid types, but they are very interested in independent living, and they've taken a keen interest in Wyoming's proposed change in status. The first I heard of them was a few weeks ago. It's a grassroots movement that's picking up steam. Claude thought it would be prudent to get a read on them. I agree."

"What exactly do you hope to learn?"

Grayson didn't answer the question immediately. Instead, he formed his mouth into an O shape and tapped his cheek with his index finger, thus making a hollow, percussion sound.

"Now what are you doing? Summoning the supernatural?"

"I'm thinking." He turned toward her and double pumped his eyebrows.

"Give me a break."

"Here's what I want to learn: Who are these guys? Where do they come from? How large are their numbers? Are they organized? If so, who are their leaders? Do they have an end goal, and if so, do they have any sort of coherent plan to get there? Yeah, that'll do for starters."

"Do you think they're on your side?"

"That is the great unknown, Miss Cicci. On the surface, one would think they are allies, given their desire for a self-sufficient lifestyle. However, they may be overly zealous in that pursuit, perhaps even fanatical, in which case they would want to see Wyoming booted as a state. That, my dear, goes against our current quest to defeat the ratification effort."

"*Whoa!*" Cicci cried. "Whoa, whoa, whoa. Did you just say you think the ratification decision is still in play? That ship has sailed. It's a done deal."

"The hell you say! That decision is very much unsettled. We only need a dozen other states to side with us."

"Cowboy, we are deep into transition planning back in DC. I can't believe you are so naive."

"You and your cronies are way too optimistic. I like our chances—a lot."

"Okay, name the states in your camp."

"Wyoming. That's one. Idaho. That's two. Montana, three; Nebraska, four; North Dakota, five; Utah, six."

"You won't get South Dakota."

"That's because you bastards bought 'em off."

"Keep going."

"Nevada, seven"

"Oh, come on, Grayson. Not a chance. They've swung Democratic."

"I disagree. Their water shortage is serious. No water, no people. Their legislators are just starting to realize how vulnerable they are."

"You're still at six."

"Hmm. Arizona is a maybe. Texas, seven; Oklahoma, no because they love the Native American solution. Kansas, eight. Arkansas, nine. Missouri, maybe. Mississippi, ten. Alabama, eleven. Florida, maybe. Tennessee, maybe. Kentucky, maybe. South Carolina, twelve, and West Virginia makes thirteen."

Cicci's jaw dropped in astonishment, and she shook her head. "In your dreams, Cowboy. You. Oh, you are so blind."

As the 4Runner drew near a livestock truck, Grayson tapped the brakes. He turned to her and said, "We'll see. Wanna make another bet?"

❧

Four hours later, Claude Mullin joined Grayson and Cicci on the patio of Goshen Pints and Pretzels, a brewpub in downtown Torrington, Wyoming.

"Have you ordered?" Claude asked.

"Just beers," Grayson answered. "Their sandwiches look pretty good. I saw a couple go by." He grabbed a handful of pretzels from the complimentary bowl and popped one into his mouth.

While Claude ordered a hazy IPA, Grayson casually tallied the establishments sitting on the intersection's other three corners—a drugstore, a clothing emporium, and a professional building. "This is nice," he said.

Claude nodded in agreement. Then he addressed Cicci. "So, Grayson tells me you're out here for a grand tour of Wyoming."

"That's the pitch he's given me," she answered.

"By the way, should I call you Theresa or Cicci?" Claude asked.

"Well, my friends call me Theresa, but this guy," she said while pointing her thumb at Grayson and pursing her lips in annoyance.

"Say no more, Theresa."

Grayson ignored their exchange. "I'm going to show her the Tetons and Yellowstone after we finish here."

"Indeed," Claude said.

"This little side trip has changed my original plan. I've been thinking about our new route. Fort Laramie is on the way. You'll get a bonus attraction, Miss Cicci."

"Remind me why I want to see it," she said with a frown of skepticism.

"It was a major stop on the Oregon Trail," Grayson said. "Lots of history."

"It's definitely worthwhile," Claude agreed. "My family's history is tied to that place."

"No foolin'?" Grayson asked.

"Uh-huh. My ancestors from four or five generations back passed through Fort Laramie on their journey west. Kellen Mullin and his wife, Elizabeth, were there in 1858. Elizabeth caught fever and died at the fort. Kellen settled a place farther up the North Platte with his five children. Eventually, he remarried and had two more kids. Kellen also outlasted the second wife. When he died, they buried him alongside Elizabeth."

"Interesting," Grayson said, shooing a fly from his arm. When he glanced up, he noticed Claude's lower lip quivering.

"My boy's buried there, too," Claude said in a broken whisper.

Grayson's mouth gaped open. "You never told me you were married."

"I wasn't. I mean, we were going to. The pregnancy was a complete shock, and I was traveling a ton. We agreed to wait on the wedding ceremony until after Jane gave birth; she didn't want to look huge in her wedding gown." With his index finger, Claude wiped away a tear.

"You okay, Boss?" Grayson asked, and Cicci promptly kicked him under the table.

"He was born with a defective heart, but he was a fighter. Fought hard for five days, but…" Claude said, choking on his words. "But it just wasn't in the cards."

Cicci's eyes moistened.

"Afterward, we tried to stay together—for a while—but seeing each other just reminded us of him. We decided to go our separate ways."

An uncomfortable silence passed before Claude changed subjects. "Is your room okay?"

"Yeah," Grayson said.

"I still can't believe every room was sold out in Scottsbluff," Claude remarked. "The clerk at our motel said they're almost full here, too."

"All because of the Hands-Off rally?" Cicci asked.

"She thought so."

"Hmm. So what's the plan?" Grayson asked.

Claude took a pretzel from the basket. "I don't think it makes sense to drive the thirty miles back tonight. I talked with a few people there while I waited for you, and they said nothing formal is going on this evening. Apparently, a farmer east of Scottsbluff has agreed to lend his place for a rally at 10 a.m. tomorrow. He even opened up some fallow fields and brought in port-a-potties for out-of-town campers. They've lined up a few speakers, including a local county commissioner, some state representatives—oh, and Cornelia Witherspoon."

"What exactly are they trying to accomplish?" Grayson asked.

"Depends on who you ask," Claude said, in between bites. "The local Nebraskans want Western Nebraska to secede."

"That's old news," Grayson replied. "They've wanted to break away and join Wyoming—at least in its current version—for decades."

"Really? I've never heard that," said Cicci.

"It's true," Claude verified.

Grayson continued his hand combat with the fly. "Cornelia Witherspoon certainly isn't traveling here to push that cause."

"No, she's not," Claude agreed. "I'm guessing the out-of-state contingent, of which no one yet has a handle on their numbers, wants something more grand in scale. I've been listening to Cornelia's podcasts, and she's advocating complete separation from the US of A. She's not interested in reshaping a couple of states; she wants a brand-new country. However, her emphasis has been on *what* this new country should entail, some sort of limited-government, self-sustaining operation. She's never talked specifically about *where* this alternate nation would be located. Now—this is complete conjecture on my part—but my guess is that upon hearing about the upcoming rally, she's thinking Western Nebraska could be ground zero."

"Not Wyoming?" Cicci asked.

"No, not Wyoming. Here's why. Again, I'm thinking out loud. The proposed change to Wyoming is being pushed by the folks in Washington. Wyoming has never asked to exit. We're still battling to defeat the ratification."

Grayson turned toward Cicci and blew her a raspberry. "A battle we're going to win." Then, turning back to Claude, he said, "Cicci's been dissing our chances for victory."

Claude made a balancing gesture with his outstretched, upturned palms. "It's close."

She nodded.

Claude continued. "Cornelia has no sway in Congress, so the only way Wyoming fits into the equation is if the state initiates some type of rebellion."

"Wouldn't that be a distinct possibility if the ratification succeeds?" Cicci asked. "From what Grayson says, there's already whispering going on about resisting any mandated change."

"Nothing official has ever been considered," Claude snapped.

"But certainly it has on the streets and in the coffee shops,"

Grayson argued. "Cicci's right. Not everyone, but a fair chunk of the populace could revolt."

Claude's face reddened, and air whooshed through his nasal passages, increasing in pace and sound. To Grayson, it appeared as if he had suddenly been cornered by a bogeyman he refused to acknowledge.

Grayson went on. "If we were to lose the ratification fight—which we're not—what would our state leaders do?"

"They'd better suck it up and comply," said Cicci emphatically.

"Even if that goes against the will of their constituents?" Grayson countered. "Say Wyoming loses the political battle but refuses to accept its new role. Instead, it goes rogue, and a lot of people from a lot of other places flock to their aid. What happens then?"

Claude's respiration had returned to normal, but his face revealed grim death. "Chaos," he said.

CHAPTER 18

IN THE MIDDLE OF THE NIGHT

THE LACE CURTAINS in the motel window billowed as a light rush of cool air crept through the screen and into the room. Outside, crickets chirped in rhythmic song. Grayson savored these late-night gifts of summer. He lay awake with one hand folded behind his head and the other around Cicci's warm body. At this moment, life was spectacular. However, time couldn't be frozen, and tomorrow with its uncertainties would be calling in a few hours.

This realization altered his mood. He worried about the upcoming rally. An irrational sense of dread churned in his stomach.

That sense of dread was soon disrupted by physical discomfort. The arm lying under Cicci was going numb, so Grayson tried to pull it out without waking her. His attempt failed, and with a quarter turn, she nuzzled her face into his side.

"Are you thinking again, Cowboy?" she asked dreamily. "I smell smoke. Mmm."

She stroked his midsection upward from the navel to the

breast bone with the back of her fingers. At the top, she reversed direction, with the palm side now making contact. Before she reached his pelvic area, her hand went limp and slid off to the side. Soft, steady breathing confirmed she had fallen back into slumber.

Grayson exhaled in relief. The past two nights of exuberant wango tango had done wonders for his spirit, but he needed a breather. Just as they had established themselves as worthy adversaries in political debate, they also demonstrated sexual compatibility in all aspects save one. Cicci possessed superior stamina, leaving Grayson's carcass physically spent. So much so—at least in his mind—the mythical notion of "death by coitus" had now entered the realm of possibilities.

He softly brushed her cheek with a finger and carefully studied her features. Her muscles lacked the toned cut of an athletic-club junky, but she was a beauty just the same. She owned all the classic feminine features: dark hair contrasting with creamy-white skin, full bosoms, and an eye-pleasing hip-to-waist ratio. Her contours defined succulence, and he felt glad to share the night with her.

As she stirred and pulled the sheet over her shoulder, Grayson wanted to know more about his lover. Who had she been in high school? Who would she be at sixty-four?

Were the past few weeks simply a fling or something more? He didn't know. Hell, he didn't even know if he qualified as her exclusive. If they did try to make a go of it, where would that be? She didn't seem to be a Western lady. Could he be an Eastern man? While a distant train whistled its way through the lonesome Wyoming night, Grayson closed his eyes and fell asleep with a single word on his mind.

Cicci.

CHAPTER 19

SCOTTSBLUFF

AFTER A QUICK breakfast of eggs, toast, and coffee, Grayson, Cicci, and Claude hopped into the 4Runner. All three were dressed in long-sleeve cotton shirts and blue jeans. The men were clad in cowboy boots, while Cicci left her ankles exposed in a pair of white Keds.

"Wagons ho!" she shouted from the backseat. "Did I get that right, Cowboy?"

"Yes, ma'am, you did, but today you'd better call me Grayson. If you say, 'Cowboy,' when we're out at this rally, twenty guys are going to answer."

"Well, maybe I'm in the market for another cowboy or two. Hell, by the end of today, I may be calling you, Cowboy Number Five."

Claude grinned at her over his shoulder. "How many days have you two been in the car together?"

"Day three. Seems like thirty," she answered.

"Hey, isn't that from a musical?" Grayson asked.

"Well, you'd need to switch days to years, but that's pretty close, Cowboy," Cicci said, clapping her hands in applause. "Where did this jolt of culture come from?"

"My musical repertoire extends well beyond ballads of broken hearts and empty beer cans," Grayson asserted. "I don't think you appreciate the depth of my sophistication."

Claude spoke up. "Something's getting deep in here, but it's not sophistication."

"You can say that again," Cicci agreed.

"Doubters," Grayson said. "I don't need this type of negativity."

"Did you happen to apply your mind toward anything useful overnight?" Claude asked.

"My mind?" Grayson snipped. He arched when Cicci kneed the back of his seat.

"I don't want to know," Claude said, putting his hands over his ears.

"Actually, I did think about Nebraska as a possible ground zero."

"And?"

"It won't happen," Grayson said. "Virtually all of that land is privately owned. Those farmers aren't interested in sharing their lands with Cornelia Witherspoon and company. I think at most, today's event is just going to be a feel-good rally for the Hands-Off people, a chance to blow off some steam."

The 4Runner cruised into Scottsbluff, a slower-than-usual ride due to the high level of auto and foot traffic on its streets. An invisible energy permeated the town. They joined a caravan of vehicles heading toward the rally. Ten miles later, they reached the farmer's field already packed with cars. A teenage boy playing traffic cop waved them on to an overflow field a thousand yards farther.

Grayson monitored Cicci's demeanor as they made their way

toward a makeshift stage. She uttered some choice phrases as she sidestepped cow pies and flicked grasshoppers off her clothes. Unlike last night's refreshing climate, this morning's temperature was already eighty degrees and climbing. He wondered if by day's end he would be ruing his decision to have dragged her along.

"It always makes my heart glad to see free enterprise in action," Claude said, referring to a couple of booths on their left. At the first one, four children were selling homemade lemonade and iced tea. Grayson guessed at least one of the purveyors belonged to the host farmer's brood. The second enterprise consisted of several tables packed with baseball caps and T-shirts in multiple styles and colors. All the garments featured the Hands-Off slogan printed across the front.

"You selling any beer?" a man asked while passing by the children's table.

"We wanted to, but Mom wouldn't let us," came the reply.

At the Hands-Off stand, Grayson stopped and doled out twenty dollars for a gray cap with blue lettering. He handed it to Cicci.

"Here's a weapon for your war with the bugs."

She frowned but instantly put it to use as a fly swatter.

"Testing one, two, three," came an amplified voice over a loudspeaker.

A man holding a wireless microphone gave a thumbs-up to another guy crouching by a nest of electrical cords.

Quite a production going on. Grayson's shoulder brushed against Claude.

"Remember," Claude said, "we're not here to make any speeches. The more we keep our Wyoming identity under wraps, the better."

"Right," Grayson agreed. "Does Wyoming have any formal representation here?"

"No. I spoke to the governor last night, and Wyoming's official position is nonrecognition. No endorsement of the Hands-Off movement whatsoever."

Soon the procession of prearranged speakers began. Though their words varied, each followed a similar pattern. They rallied the masses by launching an emotional call to action, yet, they were vague on specifics. When Cornelia Witherspoon spoke, Grayson caught Claude's triumphant wink. His previous day's conjecture had been right on the mark. She encouraged a secession from the Union and advocated for Western Nebraska—Scottsbluff specifically—to be ground zero.

As he watched in amazement, Grayson assessed the crowd. People were fully absorbed by the emotional rush of revolutionary rhetoric. It served as a drug to stimulate their desire for some type of self-imagined Shangri-La. He knew the high for half the audience would only be temporary. For attendees outside the region, Scottsbluff signified the promised land, territory waiting to be settled. For locals, that land was already theirs. They simply wanted to change the rules by which they were governed. They had no intention of making room for outsiders.

At the conclusion of Cornelia's appeal, she introduced the next speaker, one who hadn't been advertised. "My fellow freedom lovers, I am delighted to welcome our next speaker. He is a man of great stature, exemplary vision, and unrelenting devotion to the cause of individual liberty. Hailing from the great state of Wyoming, please give it up for Congressman Cranmer Francis."

Grayson and Claude looked at each other in dumbfounded awe. "*Former* congressman," Claude whispered. "This can't be happening."

Cran Fran limped to the microphone wearing his signature outfit: an embroidered white shirt, bolo tie, and a gray Stetson. Once a man of robust size, the now frail specter engaging the crowd had physically withered in proportion to his depleted political stature. Still, dying didn't mean dead, and the man recently disgraced by a scandal of his own making now smiled and waved at this receptive audience.

"My fellow patriots. My fellow Americans. And by Americans, I mean true Americans, not the prima donnas who take a knee during "The Star Spangled Banner," not the cowards who punish our police and reward criminals, and not the intolerant elitists who insist on squashing our right to free speech."

What had begun as a lukewarm reception for the old geezer escalated into rousing cheers and whistles. "Should we do something?" Grayson asked Claude, but the latter shook his head.

Cran Fran continued. "I'm not here to give a long-winded speech. It's hot, I'm old, and we're all thirsty."

Sporadic bursts of laughter emanated from the crowd.

"I want to leave you with one simple message. As you embark upon your quest—a quest to reestablish a nation that values hard work, personal responsibility, and individual liberty—take comfort in knowing the citizens of Wyoming will stand with you. Wyoming has been unfairly persecuted. Soon we will be removed as a state, but that redesignation will not dampen our free spirit. If the asses in Washington don't want us, that's fine. We will go our own way, but we will do so on our terms. We look forward to joining with our Nebraska brethren in creating a land where parents can raise children in peace, prosperity, and freedom."

With a thunderous roar of applause surrounding them, Grayson watched Claude remove his sunglasses and rub the bridge of his nose. Wyoming was getting sucked in as an unwillingly player in the Hands-Off bedlam.

⋙

On the ride back to Scottsbluff, Grayson and company suffered through snarled highway traffic. Most rally attendees were relocating to participate in a solidarity march through the Nebraska panhandle's largest town. The Sheriff's Office of Scotts Bluff

County had underestimated the interest in the Hands-Off frenzy and were badly undermanned for traffic management.

"Can you crank the AC any higher?" Cicci asked, clearly irritated. "I'm roasting back here."

"It's on high," Grayson answered.

"Let's switch places," Claude suggested. "The next time we stop."

"No, we're almost back to Scottsbluff," Cicci said. Then, with a large dollop of sarcasm, she added, "Can this adventure possibly get any better?" Her rhetorical question received an unexpected answer when a waft of dead-skunk odor overwhelmed the cabin. "Isn't that special? Par for the course."

At the east edge of town, the drive deteriorated further. A large caravan of incoming traffic from the south was merging with the rally crowd. Grayson tapped the steering wheel as other cars honked impatiently, barely rolling in the congestion. After ten minutes in the snail-like procession, Grayson finally found a parking space eight blocks from the main street.

The heat's heavy atmosphere nearly pressed the trio into the pavement as they exited the 4Runner. They merged into a cluster of pedestrians headed toward downtown—some decked out in Hands-Off gear, others not. As they approached the main street, Grayson heard the chants of competing factions long before he actually saw people yelling back and forth.

A hodgepodge of activists had journeyed to Scottsbluff from Denver, Boulder, Fort Collins, and Greeley. Their primary purpose was to confront the Hands-Off movement. This collection of protesters included assorted groups: individuals genuinely concerned about Native American land rights, pro-ratification advocates, idealistic college students true to the leftist cause, and random delinquents who simply wanted to raise hell.

On the parade avenue, an eerie contrast between the two groups made Grayson shudder. One quick glance at Claude's face convinced him that his boss shared his sensation of bad juju. As they continued walking, Grayson felt tapping on his shoulder. He turned and saw Cicci caked in dust. She was not a happy camper.

"I'm going to that café over there," she said, pointing to a sign in the middle of the block. "You coming?"

"Can you wait a few minutes?" Grayson asked. "I want to check out this parade."

"No, Cowboy! I can't. I've got a rippin' headache, I'm about to suffer heat stroke, and I haven't eaten since breakfast."

A guilty pang struck Grayson as he realized he'd ignored his out-of-town guest.

"You two grab a table," Claude said. "I'll keep looking around."

Grayson looked at Cicci, then at Claude, then back to Cicci. "I'll see you at the café. We won't be long."

Daggers flew from her eyes. She said nothing as she wheeled about and headed down the block.

"Let's move down!" Claude yelled.

Grayson nodded. They crossed a side street and found an open space a few blocks later.

The counter protesters had brought signs, bullhorns, and other miscellaneous props to advance their position. Grayson read two poster boards being waved across the street. The first read *Keep Your Hands off Our Region. Go Home, Losers*, while the latter stated, *The Plains Belong to Native Americans*. Suddenly, a shirtless man with long, greasy hair darted in between two sign holders. He had tucked part of an oversize American flag into the back of his jeans and allowed the remainder to drape down the back of his legs and drag onto the ground. Maniacally, he ran down the street in a serpentine pattern while shouting something incoherent.

The Hands-Off crowd carried signs, too. American flags intermingled with signs reading *Hands Off* or *A New Land for Old Freedoms*. However, they were caught off guard by the presence of the counter protesters. As they paraded down the street, many seemed unnerved by the sideline heckling. Others engaged in volleys of verbal slurs. F-bombs sailed in both directions. Grayson couldn't help but notice the surreal irony on display. Aspiring secessionists proudly waved Old Glory while a supposed pro-government supporter desecrated the Red, White, and Blue.

The Hands-Off disciples marched past them, heading for a nearby city park. Hecklers hustled along the sidewalk, keeping pace with the parade. As the afternoon grew hotter, anger burgeoned along the avenue.

"What else do you want to see?" Grayson asked Claude.

Claude eyed the surroundings. "Nothing," he said. "It's nuts."

They began walking back toward the café when a voice cried out, "Claude! Claude Mullin!"

Grayson spotted the caller but didn't recognize him. Claude did.

"Go on," he said to Grayson. "I won't be far behind."

Anxious to reconnect with Cicci, Grayson picked up the pace. Before he reached the café, he spied her sitting on a porch bench under a striped awning. She was chewing on a candy bar with a can of cola at her side.

"Hey," he said as he reached her. "Why aren't you at the café?"

"Couldn't get in. Too busy," she answered. She raised the cola can. "Had to settle for this."

"Looks good. Where'd you get it?"

"They've got a machine inside that store," she said, turning to the establishment behind her. "Where's Claude?"

"He stopped to talk to someone he knew. He'll be here soon. Then we'll get outta here and find some real food," Grayson said. "I'm gonna grab a soda."

Grayson entered the store and selected a carbonated, orange beverage. When he stepped back out, two men were hovering over Cicci.

A large, lumpy fellow with a spider tattoo on his left triceps nudged his thinner companion. "Now here's a fine-looking woman. Too bad she's a Hands-Off bitch."

Cicci scowled, annoyed by the unwanted disturbance. "Parade went that way, fellas. Take a hike."

"Feisty little vixen," the smaller man said. He wore a grimy white T-shirt with the caption *Sometimes Antisocial, Always Antifascist* on its front.

"Easy there, fellas," Grayson intervened. "She's not bothering anyone." He broke into a conciliatory smile and held up his soda. "The heat's brutal. Want something to drink? I'll buy."

"No," the big guy said. "But you can suck my dick."

"You Hands-Off fuckers need to crawl back into the hole you came out of and die!" the other man erupted.

"We're not part of Hands Off!" Cicci yelled. She turned toward Grayson, her eyes pleading for support. Immediately, he recognized the cause of the misunderstanding. The cap on her head, purchased earlier that day, said it all. But it was too late.

Cicci stood and started toward Grayson, but the big man grabbed her shoulder. "Where do you think you're going?" he asked.

She slapped his hand away and tried to slide by, but he clawed at her collar, ripping her shirt.

"Stop it!" She caught his pinkie finger and yanked it backward, ripping the ligament.

He wailed in agony, then retaliated with a punch to the face, busting her nose with his giant fist. "Twat!"

Cicci reeled backward a few steps and buckled to her knees. Blood spurted from her nostrils.

Grayson dropped his soda can and lunged forward. He planted his forearm into the big man's chest, driving him away from Cicci. As the guy struggled to rebalance, Grayson cased his opponent. He was three inches taller and at least fifty pounds heavier. For a brief instant, it appeared like the man might quit. "Step away, Chief."

The big man wasn't about to take orders. He reared back, stepped toward Grayson, and swung a wild roundhouse. Grayson ducked the telegraphed punch and countered by thrusting the heel of his hand underneath the man's chin. The blow's force drove the man's lower jaw upward, causing him to bite through his tongue. Blood filled his mouth, and he spat a gob of red foulness onto Grayson's face.

As Grayson wiped away the goo, the big man's friend ambushed him with a sucker punch to the back of his head. Grayson tried to stand but was driven back down with a vicious shot to the kidney. He curled into a protective ball while the cheap-shot artist attacked with knees and fists. When the small man paused for a quick breath, Grayson pushed to his hands and knees. The man stepped forward to resume the attack, but Grayson was ready. With explosive force, he pushed himself backward and swung his elbow deep into the assailant's groin. A whoosh of agony came from above.

The big man broke an empty beer bottle against a support post while Grayson staggered to his feet. He dodged the man's jab at his belly but stepped beyond the elevated walkway, wincing in pain when his ankle twisted on impact. While Grayson pushed himself back onto the walkway, the big man thrust again. Grayson raised his forearm, and the jagged glass weapon gashed into his flesh.

The two men embraced in hand-to-hand combat. Grayson's larger adversary hugged him with his left his arm while stabbing at him with his right. Grayson freed an arm and stuck his finger into the man's eye. The opponent relaxed his grip and dropped the bottle, leaving Grayson the advantage.

Reacting with his bulldogging skills, Grayson grasped the top of the big man's head with one hand and gripped his chin with the other. He applied a quick push-pull motion to get the man off-balance. Then, he flung his own body backward off the walkway, bringing the man with him. As they sailed through the air, Grayson wrenched the man's neck with as much torque as he could muster. The struggle ended with a loud, sickening *pop*.

The hard landing on the pavement dazed Grayson. His eyes blinked in a frazzled stupor. He heard Claude's voice and looked up on the walkway just in time to see the skinny guy jump into Claude's space. With his fist, the wiry figure stuck a blade of glimmering metal into Claude's throat. Onlookers tackled the small man and pulled him away from his victim. Grayson struggled to maintain focus. Then he saw Claude, gargling his own blood and gasping his final breath. His friend's eyes bulged in disbelief.

CHAPTER 20

WHAT IF?

GRAYSON ADJUSTED THE tourniquet just above his elbow before stepping into the police car. He pressed his blood-soaked handkerchief against the jagged wound on his forearm, then canvassed the crowd in search of Cicci. She sat on the curb, her face and shirt streaked with blood. Two women stood over her. One had her hand on Cicci's shoulder while the other fished for something in an oversize purse.

"Officer, do you see that lady on the curb?" Grayson asked.

The policeman nodded.

"Could you radio someone to check on her? I think her nose is busted."

"It looks like she's being cared for by those ladies. Man, we've got a shit show on our hands. Yours isn't the only altercation happening. Treating a broken nose is a ways down the list."

Grayson said nothing but watched Cicci as the vehicle pulled out on its way to the emergency room. He remembered his last image of Claude and began to retch.

"Hey! You okay, buddy? You've lost a lot of blood. Hang in there. We'll be at the hospital in five minutes."

Upon arrival at the ER, a doctor stitched Grayson's laceration, but examination of his other injuries—a throbbing headache and a swollen ankle—was delayed. Patients with gunshot wounds superseded his position in the tiny, overwhelmed hospital queue.

During his wait, Cicci texted: *How are you?*

Grayson: *I'll survive. How are you?*

Cicci: *Not great. Nose is broken. Nurse at the hospital gave me an ice pack and some ibuprofen. Told me to see a doctor tomorrow.*

Grayson: *Are you at the hospital?*

Cicci: *No. They threw me out. Swamped with other patients. No space. I'm sitting on a bench across the street.*

The police officer who had driven Grayson to the hospital poked his head into the room. "You doing okay?"

"Yeah, they want to check me for a concussion but said it would be a while before they could get to me."

"It's crazy around here," the officer replied. "Two separate shooting incidents at the city park. One dead, three injured—besides the two at your scene. Listen, I need to ask some questions and get a statement regarding this afternoon. You feel like talking while you're waiting for the doc?"

"Fine." Grayson rubbed his eyes and felt the dried, grimy sweat pasted on his face. *I must look like a disaster.* "I'm guessing this might take a while."

"Probably."

"Give me a second to text my friend. Let her know she shouldn't wait for me."

"Is that the lady from the curb?"

"Yes."

"I'd like to talk to her as well."

⁘

It was almost 5 a.m. when Grayson steered the 4Runner into the parking lot at their Torrington motel. On the somber ride back, few words had been spoken, but frequent sobbing had occurred inside the Toyota's cabin.

Grayson sat in semidarkness on the king-sized bed and waited for his turn in the bathroom. He replayed earlier conversations from two of the most difficult calls he had made in his life. The first was to Senator Shelton. Her phone had been buzzing throughout the evening regarding the melee in Nebraska, but he was the one to deliver the personally devasting news. Her chief of staff had been killed. Given the emotional toughness required of a politician, Grayson knew she would keep it together. Still, she said yes when he offered to contact Claude's sister.

The second call was more tortured. According to Claude, he and his sister, Caroline, hadn't been close. Yet when Grayson contacted her, she had just hung up with the Scottsbluff Police. She cried uncontrollably, tears virtually pouring through Grayson's phone. He listened to almost fifteen minutes of indecipherable burbling while seeking guidance regarding Claude's remains.

Light from the bathroom vanity spread across the bed when Cicci opened the door. Her nose had swollen considerably, and deep-purple bruises had formed under both eyes. She passed by Grayson without a word while delicately towel-drying her hair. She pulled a small bottle from her suitcase.

"Can I do anything for you?" he asked, guilt evident in his voice.

"No," Cicci replied as she stood rubbing lotion on her hands.

"I told the detective I'd check in with him sometime, but we don't need to get over there until afternoon. We've earned a few hours of sleep. I want to see the coroner first about Claude. I need to get an estimate about how long the autopsy will take."

"How long do you think you'll have to stick around?" Cicci asked. She walked to the opposite side of the bed and folded back the sheet and comforter.

"You mean tomorrow?"

"I mean in total."

"I don't know. Hopefully, no later than Tuesday. It depends on the autopsy. I also need to get Claude's car home somehow." He began to crack as he watched Cicci brush her hair. "Theresa, I am so sorry. I never imagined something like this would—"

"I'm going home tomorrow," she interrupted. "You have enough to worry about."

Grayson stood in protest. "Please, don't do that," but when he scrutinized her face, he understood the decision was nonnegotiable.

"I'll check my options when we wake up."

"Seriously, please don't go."

"Grayson! No!" Cicci wrapped herself in the sheet and hugged the edge with her back toward him. She wept into the pillow.

Grayson gripped the bathroom doorframe to stop his hand from trembling. He stared vacantly across the room, astonished by how much his world had changed in a day.

At a small café a block from the motel, Grayson sipped coffee while he read the morning's stories from his phone. Across America, a headline read, **THREE PEOPLE DEAD AT SECESSIONIST RALLY**. Subtitles varied but included: **Wyoming Representative Incites Masses to Revolt** and **Hands-Off Protesters Overwhelm Small Nebraska Town with Lawless Behavior**.

Besides the two men killed in Grayson's altercation, a third man perished one block away from the city park. After breaking a store window with a club, he was shot by the proprietor. Numerous other fights resulting in hospitalizations were also noted. National politicians and federal authorities were already calling on local law enforcement officials to throw the book at the instigators.

Reading about a possible prosecution made Grayson feel a little uneasy. However, after last night's police interview, the officer told him three eyewitnesses corroborated his claim of self-defense. He wasn't sure how the various gunmen would fare legally, but he'd heard the shopkeeper was one of Scottsbluff's finest citizens. As for the pathetic little fuck who had murdered Claude, Grayson hoped he would be burned at the stake.

Grayson replayed his own encounter with near death. His guts heaved, and he pushed his breakfast plate away. He struggled to recall details of the big man's face, but the guy's pungent body odor lingered. Most of all, he remembered the Hands-Off accusation.

Could he have better handled the situation? Of course. What if he'd joined Cicci in denying the accusation? What if he'd taken out the guy's knee with a precise kick? What if they hadn't gone to the rally in the first place? What if? Now, he would live with a dead man's blood on his hands every day for the rest of his life. He left the coffee shop with a caffeinated buzz and a stack of regrets.

Cicci stood next to the 4Runner as Grayson hobbled back to the motel.

"Good breakfast?" she asked as he lifted her suitcase into the back seat.

"Pancakes," he answered. "Did you eat anything?"

"I still have half a sandwich and an apple from last night."

"How's the nose?"

"Hurts like hell," she said. "Even with the painkillers."

He drove her seven blocks to a small car rental outfit. Grayson walked behind his vehicle and retrieved her suitcase. He lowered the luggage to the ground and softly clasped Cicci's arm. She avoided eye contact as she redeployed her hand to extend the luggage handle. Then, she leaned in and placed a quick kiss on his cheek.

"We'll talk," she said. She turned quickly and dashed into the building.

CHAPTER 21

THE HAMMER DROPS

MONTHS AFTER THE Scottsbluff debacle, an unprecedented level of fierce weather strangled Cheyenne and most of Eastern Wyoming. For the third time in five weeks, all highways in and out of Wyoming's capital had been closed for at least four consecutive days due to blizzard conditions. The few calm periods barely provided enough time to restock supermarket shelves, and a high-clearance vehicle was required to reach those stores. On city side streets, deep-rutted channels precluded residents with sedans from travel. Many who tried abandoned their automobiles in futility.

Grayson peered out his frost-etched apartment window. Below, a frisky black Labrador plowed through the pristine blanket of white precipitation. Occasionally, it paused to root its snout into the fluffy substance. Over time, Grayson noticed the dog's rest periods becoming more frequent. The snow's depth taxed even the most athletic of creatures. Still, the lab continued to play until its owner from across the street called it back into the house.

Grayson appreciated the outdoor distraction. Since the severe weather's onset, he had spent more days at home than in the office and was beginning to suffer from cabin fever. Video games consumed much of his time, but for him, TV diversions were limited. He wasn't the binge-watching type, and live programming seemed to be solely devoted to the Twenty-eighth Amendment's assured ratification, a topic and a set of memories he was trying to forget.

He walked into the galley-style kitchen and spotted a used shot glass alongside a half-empty whiskey bottle next to the sink. Drinking was another way he passed the time, but that habit caused his bitterness to fester. When alone, his mood grew dark like the long winter nights.

He contemplated returning to the office. It was silly, really. There wasn't much to do. He hadn't put in more than five quality work days since returning from a period of mental health leave. In theory, he should have easily moved off the Twenty-eighth Amendment fight and back into his old role with the governor's Office of Environment and Natural Resources, but how does a person perform future planning for a state with no future?

No, returning was more about commiseration, coping with his recent failures and disappointments. Shared misery with coworkers might actually improve his emotional health. To say Scottsbluff sealed the deal for the Twenty-eighth Amendment's ratification was a gross understatement. Shocked by the extreme violence—the media, and in turn, most of the nation—blamed Hands-Off and Wyoming radicals. Some considered the two groups interchangeable. Because the Hands-Off movement was only a loose collection of ideologues, punishment was limited to condemnation of their cause. Neither Cornelia Witherspoon nor any Western Nebraska speakers were charged with crimes.

Wyoming was a different story. The state was politically vulnerable. It could, and it would be disciplined despite Governor Linsey's, Senator Shelton's, and other Wyoming officials' cries of innocence. At no time, they argued, had the state recognized or endorsed the Hands-Off movement. Cran Fran's appearance at the rally was his own doing, and the two Wyoming citizens involved in one of the fatal altercations had simply been observers when they were ambushed by thugs.

Their pleadings fell on deaf ears. There were too many Wyoming fingerprints at the crime scene. Critics pointed out that Claude and Grayson weren't just Wyoming citizens; they were key players in Wyoming's resistance effort. Why had they been at the rally? Even officials from other states sympathetic to Wyoming's plight couldn't ignore the circumstantial details. It looked bad. It *was* bad.

Within days, backing for Wyoming's effort to remain a state soured. Three weeks later, forty-two states declared support for the ratification. The Twenty-eighth Amendment would be signed into law before spring began.

The state's humiliation didn't stop with the ratification. Though changes to the amendment itself were not politically feasible, the rules for transitioning Wyoming into a natural range region and for overseeing that NRR were still being crafted. Hard-liners back in Washington, DC, now flexed their political muscle. With public sentiment in their favor, they reneged on the land-premium sweeteners proposed in the draft version of the transition plan. Now land would be purchased from Wyoming residents at a value decided by the federal government with no additional premium. Further, the relocation time period for Wyoming citizens would drop from four to three years. After that three-year period, the only commercial agricultural enterprises would be owned and operated by Native Americans.

Grayson rinsed the shot glass and placed it and the whiskey bottle back into the cupboard. While wiping down the counter, he lifted a wooden candy dish—a remnant from his days in middle-school shop class. He remembered how Cicci had admired his handiwork. She had laughed when he had suggested it was the M&M'S, not the dish, that had caught her eye. He missed her laugh.

That horrific episode in Nebraska had knocked Grayson for an emotional loop, but it had totally ravaged Cicci's psyche. At first, they had spoken almost daily and shared their sadness. Over time, resentment set in. Cicci blamed him for the crook in her nose and frequent nightmares. He accepted responsibility. Grayson offered to visit DC during the holidays, but she shut him down. Now they spoke infrequently. He hadn't heard her voice in a month. It was time to change that.

"Good afternoon, madam," he said when she answered. "As a public service, we are giving away anti-choking devices to all the Minnesota Vikings fans for future use. I believe you are eligible."

A long pause ensued. "Well, at least we made it to the Super Bowl. I forget, how did your team of little horsies do?"

"We had to settle for style points."

"Uh-huh."

"How are you doing?"

Another long pause passed. "I'm okay. Work's been busy. That's good."

"Yeah," Grayson agreed. "We couldn't help but notice out here. Your side's been sharpening the guillotine blade."

Her tone softened. "I know. Grayson, I'm sorry. Doolin and company are out for blood. It's really unnecessary."

"They're putting us in a tough spot."

"I understand. I'm hoping the vitriol eases up over time. Maybe some low-interest loans can be offered to your folks after they relocate."

Grayson chafed at her remark. "No, you don't understand. Your side is assuming unconditional surrender while plenty of our folks say the battle's just starting. We're talking about principled people who don't think they're getting a fair shake. They're not just going to lie down and take it."

"The law is on our side!" was Cicci's terse comeback. "A constitutional amendment has been passed! What are they going to do? Commit sedition?"

"Yes!" Grayson realized his response was too strong and adjusted his tone. "Maybe. It would make Scottsbluff look like a cake walk." He pictured her dark eyes burning in rage. "Theresa, look. The ratification is one thing, but stripping property and identity from decent citizens, that's a direct slap in the face."

"They're willing to risk their lives?"

"They will go the distance."

More uncomfortable silence followed. "Grayson, I don't think we should talk anymore."

CHAPTER 22
GENUINE DENIABILITY

SMITTY GRINNED WHILE balancing three hotcakes on his spatula. A gathering of children stood with their eyes riveted on the man wearing the chef's hat. He and his kitchen utensil were engaged in an impromptu performance of food acrobatics.

"Do it again! Do it again!" the youngsters cried.

For theatrical effect, Smitty rolled his shoulders, moving the pancake-laden spatula from side to side. Abruptly, he stopped moving and summoned the most serious of facial expressions.

"Quiet! Quiet, please. I need your complete silence."

A hush fell over his section of the large exhibit hall. Smitty closed his eyes and drew in a deep breath. Then, with a careful lowering of the spatula followed by a quick snap of the wrist, he sent the pancakes airborne. In near-perfect alignment, each griddled buttermilk cake made one and a half rotations and landed solidly on the awaiting kitchen tool. Children and grownups alike roared in approval.

Smitty set the utensil on a table, removed his outlandish white hat, and bowed as deeply as his pot belly would permit. He stood tall and patted another cooking volunteer on the shoulder. "I just earned a coffee break. Carry on."

From the bacon station, Grayson raised his hands high and clapped. "Bravo! Bravo!"

"It's all in the wrists," Smitty said smugly.

Today was a good day. One badly needed by Grayson. Volunteering at the annual Saint Patrick's Day Pancake Breakfast was just the tonic to cure his weeks-long bout of self-loathing. The event, put on by the Wyoming State Employees Federation, was headed for a record turnout. He appreciated being on a winning team for a change.

Was it the comradery or the rising temperatures lifting his spirits? Both, he decided. On this mid-March morning, Cheyenne residents had finally caught a weather break with bright sun and a forecast high of fifty-eight degrees. Grayson, Smitty, and their coworkers emerged from winter's isolation to bond in altruism. By filling the bellies of revelers wearing the green, the employee's federation would raise more than thirty thousand dollars for the children's ward of the Laramie County Hospital. By 10:30 a.m., twenty-eight hundred breakfasts of green pancakes had been served.

Amid the aromas of hot coffee and fried bacon, Grayson felt at ease as he watched Smitty bask in glory. The pancake break-fast was his baby. What Smitty lacked in work conviction during the standard week, he counterbalanced with stellar organizational efforts for philanthropic events. The National Kidney Foundation and Special Olympics also tapped his skill set annually.

By noon, virtually all the takedown and cleanup work was finished. Only a handful of the sixty volunteers remained. One of those still on duty was Hogan Linsey—Wyoming Governor Hogan Linsey.

"Why's he still here?" Grayson asked as he passed Smitty on his way to the dumpster.

"Don't know. It's not an election year," Smitty answered with a smile.

When Grayson reentered the exhibit hall, Smitty was standing with the governor. They had corralled the remaining items—paper supplies, two rented grills, and an event banner—into one corner of the room.

"Grayson, you and I can move this stuff back to my house in two trips," Smitty calculated.

"I'll help," the governor said. "I have my pickup. Let's load it, too, and be done in one?"

"Sounds like a plan," Grayson said. "Smitty, grab the other end of this grill."

✌

Grayson and Linsey dusted off their pants and jackets as they stepped out of Smitty's storage shed.

"Another pancake breakfast in the books," Smitty said with twinkling eyes.

"Good job, gents," Linsey said. "I'd forgotten how much effort goes into this event. I've worked up a thirst."

"What's your pleasure?" Smitty asked. "I've got water, Pepsi, maybe some lemonade."

"I was thinking of something in line with today's theme. You got any green beer?"

"No, but how about a Guinness? Come on in." Smitty led the trio through the back door.

"Where's the family?" Linsey asked.

"Mary drove Rachel to Wheatland for a volleyball tournament, and Preston, he's somewhere."

"We could have used him at the breakfast," Linsey said.

"Yeah, well I think it's his mission in life never to be seen around me," Smitty replied coldly. "You know teenagers."

Changing the subject, Grayson asked, "How's Rachel's ankle?"

"Better. She sprained it a few weeks ago." Smitty pulled three bottles from the refrigerator and handed one each to the governor and Grayson. "To the Irish!"

"To the Irish!" responded the guests, clinking their bottles.

The group indulged in long, satisfying swallows. Then Linsey raised his bottle again. "To Claude!"

A dagger of distress pierced Grayson when he heard the name of his deceased colleague, but he recovered in time to toast, "To Claude!"

Linsey wiped the liquid remnants from his mouth. "Did you know Claude and I were roommates at UW?"

"Claude said you were," Grayson answered.

"Oh man, he was a lightweight when it came to drinking." Linsey laughed. "We'd be over at a friend's apartment, and he would pass out after three beers. Smitty, you knew him when he still had his big Brillo 'fro, right?"

Smitty nodded.

"Well, after he zonked, the rest of us would peel the labels off beer bottles. Then we'd roll them up like cigarettes and stick them in Claude's hair. So one night, we've probably planted a dozen of these things, and he wakes up all grumpy but doesn't realize all this stuff is sticking out of his head. When it's time to go, he insists on driving because he's had the fewest beers, which I'm sure was true."

Grayson began messing with his own beer label, sentimentally recalling his former associate's face.

"Four of us, including Claude, hop into the car and head back to campus. Claude is oblivious to what's going on, and the rest of us are trying not to pee our pants. Claude pulls up to a traffic light, but there's a police car in the left lane. One of the cops looks over and sees Claude with all this shit sticking out of his head and motions him to pull over. So Claude's saying, 'Be cool, be cool.'"

The governor took another swig of beer. As Linsey reminisced about his college life, Grayson could almost swear his worry lines vanished from his forehead.

"The officer walks up and asks, 'Have you been drinking?' and Claude says, 'Just a couple, but that was two hours ago.' The cop pulls a label out of his hair and unrolls it. Then he says, 'Oh, it looks like more than two. Please step out of the car.' For the first time, Claude sees himself in the mirror and starts to freak. He's screaming at us, and the cops order everybody out of the car. They cuff Claude, we all get breathalyzed, but the only one who passes is Claude. But now the cops are pissed, so they write him a ticket for disturbing the peace. Claude was miffed at me for a long time."

"Great story," Grayson said.

"Yeah," Linsey mused. "I miss him. I miss him as a friend, and I miss him as an advisor." The governor downed the remainder of his beer. "Fellas, I'm in a pickle."

"I don't envy you," Smitty said.

"I'm about to get squeezed. The Feds will be demanding my cooperation for the transition while my constituents are preparing to fight tooth and nail against any confiscation of their property. I have a duty to represent the folks who elected me, but I also don't want to see people getting hurt, possibly killed, on either side."

"We're going to challenge the transition plan in court, right?" Grayson asked.

"Of course, but our case is dead on arrival. The Twenty-eighth Amendment clearly gives Congress the power to execute the transition as they see fit. The rational for eminent domain was carefully laid out during ratification."

"True," Grayson said. "But eminent domain requires fair compensation for property. We can argue that angle."

Linsey shrugged. "We might ultimately cut a better financial deal, and a court challenge might buy us another three to six months, but in the end, I'm worried about a violent transition."

"Why would the legal process be so short?" Smitty asked.

"Washington is prepared for our challenge. The courts will fast-track it. You can count on that."

Grayson grabbed a toothpick from the decorative Devils Tower holder. He chewed on it a moment before asking the question weighing on his mind. "So why are you telling us?"

The governor's smile made Grayson shiver. He had witnessed that look all too often in Washington—the overdone display of teeth, the calculating eyes. It was an acquired trait, the mark of an established politician.

"Because I want to explore the possibility of resolving this matter in another way—maybe an unconventional way," Linsey answered.

Alarm sirens blared inside Grayson's head. "What are you thinking?"

"During this whole dissolution process, we've played by the rules," Linsey began. "We've lost at every step. We've lost because, in this game, Congress has all the cards."

"Tell me about it," Grayson said. "I spent more than a year back there getting beaten up. You're preaching to the choir."

"Yeah," Linsey agreed, "but since this Scottsbluff thing, their attitude has changed. I can accept the new amendment; it's legitimate. But now, they've gone from being philosophical to becoming punitive, Doolin in particular. It's not enough to disband Wyoming. He's demanding we pay a penance. It's not fair to our folks, and it pisses me off."

"But what can we do?" Smitty asked.

"I don't know exactly," Linsey said, interlocking his hands behind his head. "Somehow, we have to change the way the game's being played. For once, I'd like to rattle their cage, cut them down a notch."

"What did you mean by unconventional?" Grayson asked.

The hair on his arms raised as Linsey responded with a chilling stare. "I'm thinking we need to play rougher on a personal level. Learn what it is that scares them and use it as leverage. Maybe dig up some dirt about an embarrassing situation. Everybody has a past." He unlocked his hands and placed them upon the table. "That was my initial thought. Maybe you two will come up with different ideas."

"Extortion?" Grayson blanched.

"I call it hard ball," Linsey continued. "I actually bounced this idea by Claude last summer. At the time, he was convinced we could stop the ratification, so we didn't pursue it. Now we're no longer a state, and Claude's gone."

"How does the governor's office execute that type of mission?" Smitty asked.

"It doesn't. This kind of operation could never be run out of the governor's office. That's why I'm talking to you here in your house rather than at the Capitol."

Grayson wondered if his eyes were as big as Smitty's.

"Are you suggesting we do something illegal?" Smitty whispered.

"I'm asking the two of you to consider helping Wyoming in its most dire hour. Claude believed in your abilities, as do I. Maybe there's something you can do to put some winning cards in our hand for a change. Maybe there isn't. I'm just asking you to give it some serious thought. You have the advantage of operating under the radar. I don't."

Smitty spoke with an uncharacteristic sternness. "I'm forty-nine years old, and I've got a family, so I'll ask again. Are you asking us to break the law?"

Grayson leaned forward on the chair's edge. *Is Wyoming's top dog orchestrating a patriotic Hail Mary? Is he setting us up to take the fall should his desperate ploy fail? Is the answer yes to both questions?*

"Smitty," the governor began, "the livelihood and perhaps the lives of thousands of people, our people, are at stake. If by some miracle you are able to fix this shitty mess, I think the public will forgive you if some legal boundaries were skirted along the way."

"If we do come up with some ideas, how should we coordinate with you?" Grayson asked.

"You won't," Linsey answered. "I need to stay out of the loop. What you'd be doing is purely unofficial. I need to be genuine if I'm forced to deny any involvement."

Genuine deniability. How convenient.

CHAPTER 23

WE CAN'T WIN

DURING THE REMAINDER of the weekend, Grayson wrestled with the dilemma shared by Linsey. The heavily one-sided dominance of the United States over Wyoming made the famed biblical confrontation between David and Goliath look like a relatively even matchup. He considered Wyoming's potential conflict from several angles. The battle for American hearts and minds was already lost. Scottsbluff had sealed that contest. Despite Wyoming's public denouncement of the Hands-Off movement, the country's majority viewed the state as a collection of reckless agitators. Should any physical skirmish occur, Grayson had no doubt Wyoming would be blamed for the bloodshed. Martyrdom wasn't an option.

If a direct military confrontation was to happen, how would his state fare? Wyoming would lose. They were outmanned and outgunned, and it wasn't even close. Even guerilla-style tactics offered little advantage on the high, open plains.

Grayson rubbed the back of his neck to ease some anxiety. He glanced out his apartment window and caught the last brilliant rays of a western sunset—an event taking place fifteen minutes later than the previous week. The days were growing longer, one positive note to an otherwise gloomy outlook.

Resuming his analysis, if Wyoming couldn't effectively resist by force, could it take economic action to pressure the US? Ten years ago, the answer would have been maybe. As the country's top coal producer and one of the top-ten producers of oil and natural gas, Wyoming played a major role in the nation's energy equation. A production embargo back then would have put a severe crimp in everyday life. However, with the rapid transition to renewable energy sources, Wyoming's esteem as an energy supplier had dwindled. The state still produced electricity, mostly from wind, in excess of its needs, but withholding that surplus wouldn't be enough to bring the US to its knees.

The same argument held true for other goods. Sheep and cattle numbers each represented less than ten percent of the national total. Though Wyoming was the leader in uranium reserves, most of that mineral was imported from other countries.

Overall, Wyoming provided less than one percent of the nation's gross domestic product. Unless bentonite, the absorbent clay found in kitty litter, was declared vital to national security, Wyoming simply had no economic leverage.

The ringing of his phone interrupted his analysis. He smiled when the caller's ID appeared.

"Hello, Dad."

"Hello, Grayson. I'm ten minutes out of town. You had dinner?"

"Not yet. You want to stop by? I could whip up some of my famous macaroni and cheese."

"I was thinking more like steaks at The Lasso. Meet me there?"

"Twisted my arm. See you soon."

᷐

Grayson pulled into a parking spot alongside Daryl Woodley's old white pickup. The Lasso, a Cheyenne institution, had served railroad barons and cattlemen more than a century ago. Now past its prime in popularity, the antiquated restaurant decorated in dark wood and soft lighting mostly drew the over-fifty crowd. Regardless of age, customers savored the sizzling New York strips and mouth-watering prime rib served with an Idaho spud.

In the waiting area, Grayson shook his dad's powerful rancher's hand while sharing a hug. "I didn't know you were traveling this weekend. Not that I'm surprised."

"Just a daytrip down to Sterling," Daryl answered. "I hated to go and leave your brother alone, this being calving season and all. But it's been the first break in this crazy damn winter."

Grayson knew the importance and unpredictability of calving season. "What was so urgent in Sterling?" The absence of an immediate answer and the tortured look on Daryl's face alerted him to trouble. His dad's shoulders drooped as if some enormous invisible weight was pulling them down.

Finally, Daryl said, "I needed to talk to some folks. Now that the ratification is official, we are starting to pursue some contingencies. We're selling half our cattle to a couple of outfits in Colorado."

"Why so sudden?" Grayson asked. "Even under the revised timelines, you still get three years to settle your affairs."

"We're hedging our positions. The closer we get to the deadline, the more buyers are going to squeeze us. It's already starting to happen. I was only able to get eighty-nine cents on the dollar for the animals I sold today."

A nauseating uneasiness churned in Grayson stomach. "So why didn't you tell them to stuff it and move on to the next buyer? You're established as a top-grade livestock producer."

Daryl drew in a deep breath. "Earlier this week, we received a joint letter from the Departments of the Interior and Agriculture notifying us we had been selected as one of five ranches in the state for a pilot project. They are testing an accelerated transfer of ownership program to qualifying Indians—in our case, members of the Eastern Shoshone tribe. A full property transfer is to be completed in six months."

The news stunned Grayson to the point of being light-headed. A deluge of questions filled his mind. "Did you say five ranches were chosen? Out of the thousands of possibilities, how did you get so lucky?" When he saw Daryl clenching his jaw, he answered his own question. "This was no accident. They picked you on purpose—because of me and what happened in Scottsbluff."

"We don't know that for sure."

"Bullshit!" Grayson shouted. "Goddamn them! They are the biggest set of vindictive bastards I've ever known."

"Either way," Daryl said, "the clock's ticking. So far, our situation's not public knowledge. That's why I acted today."

Among the father and two brothers, Grayson was the least likely of the Woodley men to be labeled hot-headed, but right now, he burned in rage. His thoughts were reduced to a set of jumbled fragments. "I'm surprised they didn't freeze your assets."

"An oversight on their part," Daryl answered. "I'm sure it won't last, but I talked to our attorney, who said today's sale is legal."

Grayson nodded. "What does Zach think about all this? I bet he's ready to stomp someone's guts out."

"He is, but what good would that do?"

Grayson studied his dad's face. He looked tired. More than just tired: tired and sad. What was the right word? *Despondent? Defeated?* It disturbed him.

"We're going to fight this, aren't we, Dad?"

Daryl licked his lips. "I don't know, son."

Those weren't the words he had expected to hear from the most principled man on the planet. Grayson could see Daryl reading his mind.

"If it were just Mom and me, we'd stand our ground till the

very end and go out in a blaze of glory. We've lived the better part of our lives, good lives. But, when I think of Zach and Cindy and you, I'm torn. Part of me says that if I don't fight for my convictions, I'm not much of a person. Then the father in me looks at his kids and realizes you still have most of your lives to look forward to. Is the ranch worth dying for? Maybe a different life can still be a great life. Who knows? The world has changed so much."

Angry tears welled in Grayson's eyes, and he turned away. He sipped some water while regaining his composure. The waiter's delivery of garlic bread bought him additional time to collect himself. He grabbed a slice from the basket.

"I don't know the answer, Dad, but we're not the only ones agonizing over this problem. Yesterday, the governor sat down with Smitty and me for a heart-to-heart."

"Oh?" Daryl said with raised eyebrows. "What's Linsey thinking?"

"He's frustrated. He feels like Congress is walking all over him despite cooperating during this entire ordeal."

"They *are* walking all over him. They're walking over all of us."

"Yeah, well, now he's getting desperate and grabbing at straws. He suggested maybe we should stop playing nice. Maybe that's how we can win this game."

Daryl tilted his head. "That's pretty vague. Did he mention any specifics?"

Grayson looked around to make sure no one else was in listening distance. "He suggested gathering dirty laundry on key figures and leaning on them."

"Blackmail?"

"Here's the kicker: he's asking Smitty and me to muddy our hands. He says that as governor, he can't be involved."

"Typical politician," Daryl said with a caustic snort. "Stay away from that asshole, Grayson. He's dangerous and delusional. Besides, there's no winning this game. It's over. We've lost."

"I hear you." Grayson said. "But I'm not ready to give up, not yet. We deserve a say in our future. If we could get Washington to agree, I'd consider that a win. The problem is I've spent the last day looking for ways to exert some influence and have come up empty. Like Linsey said, as it stands, they hold all the cards."

Daryl ran his fingers through his thinning hair. "Well, the governor was right about one thing: he was right to come to you. You've got a good head on your shoulders."

His father's praise filled Grayson's heart with a gush of warmth. "Good genes," he replied.

A couple who had finished dinner passed by the table. Grayson and Daryl acknowledged them with congenial smiles. The waiter followed right behind the couple, delivering sizzling plates of thick-cut steak.

"You know," Grayson said. "there's another aspect to this situation that upsets me."

"What's that?" Daryl asked, cutting into his beef and exposing a warm, deep-red center.

"This issue is pitting Wyoming against the US, but the fact is I'm an American, too. I love my country. I hate being forced to pick sides."

"Interesting," Daryl observed in between juicy bites of meat. "From the start, this issue's been framed as us versus them. Maybe that's the wrong approach."

"What do you mean?"

"I agree with you about our allegiance to the US. We should be searching for common ground, shared values."

"Fine by me, but tell them that."

Daryl fixed his eyes upon Grayson. "Instead of playing to win, maybe we should play to tie."

❧

Fury consumed Grayson, and he raged into his apartment. On the way home from dinner, a giant pothole had done a number on his 4Runner's front alignment. This incident by itself would ruin an otherwise good day. Combined with his dad's update and his ongoing depression, hopeless frustration had finally claimed its toll.

I've had it. My life in the last six months has been shit. Cicci's history, I have ongoing nightmares about Scottsbluff, and my home's being taken away. Enough is enough!

He stepped over to his desk and pulled up his government contact list on the computer. Grayson began to compose an email.

> *TO: Senator Barry Doolin*
>
> *FROM: Grayson Woodley*
>
> *SUBJECT: Wyoming*
>
> *You prick!*

Grayson considered the body of the message and rewrote it, using one simple word:

> *Why?*

He hit *Send*. A moment later, he considered his action. Grayson didn't regret it but realized it was a juvenile measure. He picked up a palm-size foam football and mindlessly spun it into the air. The *ting* sound of incoming email startled him.

> *TO: Grayson Woodley*
>
> *FROM: Senator Barry Doolin*
>
> *SUBJECT: Re: Wyoming*
>
> *I did your family a favor. The winters are much milder in Texas. :)*

That son of a bitch. He is behind this bogus pilot study. In an instant, Grayson understood his mission. *Yes, Dad, some causes are worth fighting for.*

Grayson remembered the governor's encouragement to break the rules. Up until this snotty communication from Doolin, he had blown off that suggestion as crazy talk. Now he bought into it wholeheartedly. *Time to get nasty. But how?*

Linsey was right about one thing. Washington, DC, officials required some sort of motivation to change their stance. They needed to be scared into action. What would scare them? Certainly not the threat of revealing uncomfortable personal secrets. Grayson had spent a year in Washington without hearing any scandalous rumors about Doolin or his close associates. Granted, the man was a slimeball, but that wasn't a crime. No, something else was necessary. What next?

A course of action perplexed Grayson for two sleepless nights. On Tuesday morning, he still had no definitive answer, but he'd seen a sign. Literally, he'd seen a sign.

❧

Rachel Smith opened the front door when Grayson rang the doorbell. Dressed in a bright-orange warm-up suit with black trim and wearing her blonde hair in a ponytail, Rachel smiled cheerfully with a mouthful of braces when she recognized the visitor.

"Hi, Grayson."

"Hello, Rachel. Are those new earrings? They look awesome." The fourteen-year-old's eyes brightened; her cheeks flushed. Having his own kid sister, Grayson knew how to nurture a fragile adolescent ego. "Are you going to or coming from practice?"

"Going. Our team drew the late shift at the gym this week."

"How'd it go on Saturday?"

"We took second. I played okay. The ankle's starting to feel better."

"Well, watch out world when you're back to full strength. I've seen your serve."

Another crimson wave spread on her face.

"Hey, ugly, come on in," Smitty said as he stepped next to Rachel. "Rachel, you need to be kind to dumb creatures. Don't leave them freezing outside."

"Oh, Dad," Rachel admonished him as she quickly separated from her father. Once across the living room, she turned and said, "Bye, Grayson."

"See ya."

"You want something to drink?" Smitty asked.

"Not right now." Grayson answered.

Smitty directed Grayson into the family room and offered him a choice of sitting spots—the exception being Smitty's personal recliner. Grayson sat at one end of an oversize sofa and began watching TV. A cable news channel was reporting the violation of Taiwanese airspace by two Chinese jet fighters. According to the commentator, the Chinese action was in retaliation to the proposed sale of advanced defense weaponry by the US to Taiwan. Smitty grabbed the remote and began channel surfing. He settled on a classic-movie station.

"George, remember, I'm going to book club after I drop Rachel at practice! She has a ride home with the Ortegas," said Mary, his wife.

"Yes, yes. We've been through this!" Smitty bellowed back. "Four times."

Mary poked her head in the doorway. "And there's lemon pie in the fridge—enough for two. Grayson, don't let him be a pig."

"Oh, you don't have to worry about that. If there's pie in the house, I'll get my share," he said, winking at Mary.

After Mary and Rachel left, Smitty turned to Grayson. "So, what's up?"

He relayed the news about the Woodley ranch being roped into the suspect pilot study. Smitty didn't react as surprised as Grayson had expected. "I figured some kind of shenanigans would start popping up in the rural world, given what's about to come down in the cities."

"What's going on?"

"Today, I learned the Feds plan to dismantle the state's institutional infrastructure. They plan to shut down virtually all of the state agencies."

"Who told you that?" Grayson asked, his eyes wide with concern.

"Smitty knows all," came the answer. He placed his index fingers on his temples.

"Seriously? How can they do that? The NRR will need some administrative oversight."

"They think they can run those operations at regional federal centers. They may need some of the state's office space, but not its people. A press release is coming out tomorrow. State employees are going to be out on their butts. Big job cuts. Cheyenne in particular will suffer."

"I never thought my state employment would be in jeopardy," Grayson complained. "Hell, I won't be allowed to ranch or work in the city. Guess I may have to go back to school."

"Not in Wyoming," Smitty said. "They're going to shut down UW and all the community colleges. They say with a much smaller population, higher education is an impractical expense. They'll still run some specific job-training programs, but the general-type education model is out the door. Oh, and all the sports will be gone, too. That's going to kill Rachel. She's been dreaming of playing for the Cowgirls since she was tiny."

Grayson stewed in contempt. For a short while, the room's only noise came from the black-and-white TV characters.

"That's my happy news," Smitty said. "What else have you got?"

"I've been racking my brain and confirmed what we already knew. If we try any conventional-type of resistance, we're screwed. Nothing gives us an upper hand."

"So, no progress," Smitty said with a bitter smirk. "Honestly, I don't think Linsey expects us to find a solution."

"But I did identify one potential advantage."

"What's that?"

"I've got nothing left to lose. They're taking away my home—and now my career, based on your news. A desperate man can be dangerous."

"Dangerous how?"

"I drove by a sign yesterday. It identified a potential savior."

"Trust in Jesus?" Smitty guessed.

"F.E. Warren."

Smitty pushed back with enough force to almost tip his recliner. "Are you serious?"

"Dead serious. We need something that will scare people, an attention-grabber. What they manage at Warren would definitely do the trick."

Smitty's furrowed brow indicated deep doubt. "Yeah, but how do you plan to gain access?"

"I have no idea," Grayson admitted. "Thought maybe you could help me out."

"No," Smitty said shaking his head. "Not a feasible plan, but I will give you a gold star for originality—and a referral to see a shrink."

"Hmm," Grayson said, disappointed but not defeated. "Is that drink offer still good?"

"Sure." Smitty stepped out of the room and returned with a couple of beers.

"I'm wondering," Grayson resumed, "do we actually need access?"

"If you want the goods, you do."

"I don't want to physically harm anyone. I just want to scare them. When I was little, there was never really a goblin hiding in my closet. I just thought there was. It was the thought that scared me."

Smitty stood and paced, putting his hands in his pockets. "Are you talking about a bluff?"

"Why not?"

"Well, you're gonna have to come up with one helluva story, and I suggest hiring P.T. Barnum to sell it." Smitty chewed on his thumb. "It's times like these when I think I should have taken up smoking."

"But you think it's doable?"

"I didn't say that, Grayson. What you're proposing would be extremely difficult."

"Difficult. Not impossible."

"So now you're the Godfather?"

"Speaking of movies, could you turn the sound down on the TV? That guy's screaming is driving me nuts."

Smitty grabbed the remote and silenced Marlon Brando ranting on a sidewalk while cupping his head with his hands. He sat back down, and the two men bounced ideas off each other for the next hour.

✑

The front door gently opened, and Rachel entered.

"Hey, babe," Smitty said. "How did practice go?"

"Fine," she said tersely, meaning it didn't go fine at all. She walked into the kitchen and reemerged with a sports drink and an orange. "I have a paper to finish." She walked upstairs, and a door closed.

"She's a great kid, Smitty," Grayson said.

"The best."

Grayson pushed himself up from the sofa and reached for his coat. "Tonight's been productive. It's a good start. I'll be able to take it from here."

"What's this 'I' stuff?" Smitty asked.

Grayson paused, his first arm in the coat sleeve. "No need to have more than one person hang his ass out to dry. My family's been directly threatened, so I'm committed."

"You think my family won't be affected? Didn't you just see my little girl walk through that door? She's the light of my life. She needs a daddy with a job and an opportunity to pursue her dreams."

"That won't happen if you're in prison. I've got no dependents. I'm expendable."

"Believe it or not, Grayson, you need me. This bluff thing may not work. If that's the case, we'll need a plan B."

"Which you miraculously have?"

"Maybe. I was just wondering, how big are you willing to go? Your F.E. Warren sign wasn't entirely off. You've identified the right resource; you just picked the wrong location."

Now Grayson was the one needing a cigarette. "Tell me where, and I'll go."

"You can't. You're too recognizable."

"But you can?"

"Uh-huh. It's time I got off my lazy duff and did something to save my home." Smitty stood and began clearing the coffee table. "Any other words of wisdom before you go?"

Grayson slid his other arm through the coat sleeve. "Yeah. My dad said because we're a bunch of cowboys and rednecks, Washington politicians will underestimate us. We should use that to our advantage."

CHAPTER 24

LENNY

GRAYSON WONDERED HOW long it had been since he'd last seen Lenny. Three years? It seemed strange to him how a person like Lenny winked in and out of his life. One moment they were practically joined at the hip, and then years rolled by without any contact.

Grayson shuffled through the set of nostalgic videos on his computer. Silently, he thanked his mom for harping on him to catalog all his life experiences as he was growing up. Those hours invested in organization enabled him to quickly find what he was seeking. He began watching a video of himself at the state science fair in eighth grade.

He was wearing the dressiest ensemble in his wardrobe: an olive argyle sweater and light-gray pants. The short-haired boy with dancing eyes laughed with a hint of nervousness. Grayson stood next to a table upon which an entry rested for the Wyoming Math and Science Fair. The project was titled "Fun with Probability," and it included an interactive computer application demonstrating probability's role in games such as poker, hearts, and backgammon.

At the opposite end of the table stood his towheaded friend dressed in a Day-Glow orange shirt and contrasting neon-green bow tie and suspenders. That outrageous getup puzzled those who knew Lenny Hibbs because it drew everyone's attention to him. On any other day, Lenny desperately tried to avoid attention. He suffered from an involuntary head twitch. His jaw uncontrollably jutted upward a few times each minute.

Lenny's condition necessitated twice weekly sessions with a special-needs counselor who quickly became Lenny's number one fan. The counselor showered Lenny with unconditional support and taught him techniques for coping with uncomfortable situations in a public setting.

Still, daily life with its social challenges wasn't easy for Lenny, but his counselor never wavered in her backing. Lenny was smart—off-the-charts smart. The counselor encouraged him to embrace his intelligence. She suggested he join the Math and Science Club and enter the contest. She called the club Nerdsville and told Lenny he was mayor. As such, he should dress with flair and boldly go forward. His eye-blinding ensemble was her idea.

Grayson was smart, too, though it was a different kind of smart. Basically, he was smart enough to choose Lenny as a partner. The boys worked together for weeks on their project. Lenny programmed the application while Grayson created data scenarios to test it. At the local competition, they won with ease. They qualified for the state contest in Gillette.

The state event consisted of two parts. In the morning, roving judges listened to informal presentations from the participants. Those judges scored all the projects, and the top five scores in each grade advanced to the finals. Lenny and Grayson made the cut.

For the finals, teams were required to make a formal oral presentation including a demonstration of key findings or features.

Prior to the afternoon session, the boys were captured on video in a discussion with their sponsor.

"Boys, congratulations on making the finals. How are you feeling?" the sponsor probed.

"Pretty good," Grayson answered.

"Lenny, you did a heck of a job with this morning's demonstration. Was it hard to do all that programming?"

Lenny answered, "Oh, not too hard. The hardest thing was learning about probability. That's a new type of math for me." The video captured Lenny's matter-of-fact confidence and his repetitious twitch. It also captured a set of onlookers standing behind him. They had initially been attracted by his outfit but now stared at his involuntary movement. On the video, Grayson could be seen observing the crowd's reaction.

The sponsor turned back to Grayson. "Are you ready for the oral presentation?"

"Um, yeah. I guess," he replied with an awkward hesitation.

"I'm doing the presentation," Lenny blurted out. The camera returned to his excited face.

"I thought we agreed that Grayson would make the presentation," the sponsor said in a calm voice.

"I'm doing the presentation," Lenny repeated.

"Yeah," Grayson muttered. "Lenny and I were talking last night, and he really wants to give it."

Looking at the camera, the sponsor ran a finger across his neck, and the video ended abruptly.

What followed was a heated exchange between the sponsor and the boys. Both the sponsor and Grayson had seen the uncomfortable reception Lenny was receiving from the crowd. They feared a similar occurrence with new judges could sink their chances of winning. Back home, people were used to Lenny's condition and accepted it. Unfortunately, acceptance takes a while, and these strangers were seeing Lenny for the first time. Even without Lenny's condition, Grayson was the better speaking choice for the afternoon session.

In the end, Grayson stuck by Lenny and his wishes. The sponsor was furious, but Grayson figured Lenny had masterminded the project; it was his call. Later that afternoon, Grayson left Gillette with a fifth-place ribbon and a devoted friend for life.

⁂

During their first year of college in Laramie, Grayson and Lenny shared extensive time together. Lenny had chosen computer science as a major and spent most of his waking hours at the computer lab. Grayson frequented the lab, too. He allocated some of his time to completing business programming assignments, but most of his hours there were devoted to playing a deluxe suite of computer games with Lenny. As semesters passed, Grayson's degree requirements sent him to other places on campus. Conversely, Lenny stopped going to class altogether. He became fascinated with the dark web and eventually dropped out of school. It was Lenny's acquired expertise in dark-web operations that Grayson now wanted to tap.

Reaching Lenny was going to take some effort. He had disappeared off the radar. Grayson possessed neither a current phone number nor email address for his friend—not that he would use either of those means to establish contact. Lenny's mom still lived in their Douglas home. He decided to contact her but needed to enlist the help of a sibling.

"Hey, Cin," Grayson said from his cell phone. "Is my favorite little sister playing hooky?"

"No, Grayson," Cindy answered. "School ended an hour ago. Geez."

"School's out at two thirty! Man, back in my day classes didn't finish until three forty-five. Of course, we were taking real classes."

"Oh, shut up! I *am* taking real classes. Why are you calling?"

"I wanted to hear your sweet voice—and ask a favor."

"Uh-huh, now the truth comes out. What is it?"

"I need you to get a message to a buddy of mine."

Cindy's voice rose an octave. "I may be able to do that, but it'll cost you."

Minutes later, the siblings struck a deal. For the mere sum of a new pair of trendy sneakers, Cindy would stop by the Hibbs residence and relay Grayson's desire to touch base with Lenny.

Several days passed with no response, and Grayson began to worry. Then one afternoon, a call from Cindy confirmed contact. According to her, she had been walking alone from school to catch up with some friends at Ollie's Creamery—home to the town's best ice cream—when a beat-up Jeep pulled alongside her. Cindy identified the driver as a bearded man wearing a camouflage baseball cap and aviator shades.

"Tell Grayson to meet at The Place of Worship next Tuesday morning," he said. Before she could answer, the Jeep lunged forward and turned right at the next street.

"Was it Lenny?" Grayson asked.

"No, I've never seen that guy before."

With his fishing rod in hand and a pack strapped across his shoulders, Grayson eased down the soft-earth embankment toward the water. As expected, he enjoyed the rippling stream to himself on this early-April morning. The temperature hung at a brisk twenty-two degrees, and an intermittent breeze chapped his face. He stayed near the water during his mile-long journey, sidestepping sporadic snow drifts and semi-frozen patches of mud. Of all the mountain streams flowing northeast out of the Laramie Mountains, this one rekindled his youth.

Grayson remembered his family's predawn departures from their house. Along with fishing gear, the Woodley boys would bring a tray of apple turnovers and two thermoses, one filled with steaming coffee and the other with hot chocolate, to kick-start the outing. Sometimes his dad let Zach and him bring a friend or two; Lenny was his frequent choice. When Lenny and Grayson turned twelve, Daryl permitted them to split off on their own.

One day when their angling luck was poor, Grayson spied a rock overhang roughly fifty yards up a steep hillside. After scrambling up the incline, Lenny and he were rewarded with the discovery of an eight-by-twelve-foot nook under the stone canopy. The site afforded a panoramic view of the stream and surrounding area. The location possessed a reverential type of mystique, and so they prayed for a change in their fishing fortunes. After waiting out a short rain squall in their protective fortress, they resumed fishing and landed five trout over the next twenty minutes. They attributed their excellent fortune to the newly discovered shrine and dubbed it, The Place of Worship. Thereafter, it became a reg-ular stop on any fishing excursion.

Grayson rounded the final bend and spotted his destination just as he had remembered it. Breathing deeply as he finished the climb, he stared into the natural sanctuary and was surprised to see Lenny dressed in an army-colored parka and black ski cap. He sat there in quiet seclusion on a sleeping bag and air mattress.

"Hey, man!" Grayson exclaimed, stepping into the protected area and patting his friend on the shoulder. "I didn't see any signs you were already here. No vehicle, no tracks. How'd you do that?"

"Practice," Lenny answered, followed by his signature head tic.

"When did you get here?"

"I came in during the night. Satellites can't see in the dark."

"Satellites?" Grayson whispered.

"And they can't see through rock. That's why I picked here. You've become famous."

Grayson expected some paranoid behavior, but this concern

about satellites suggested his friend had fallen farther down the rabbit hole.

"Anyone follow you on the road out here?" Lenny asked, staring at the horizon.

"No."

"Good. I didn't see any drones, either."

Drones? Jesus. Grayson noticed a pair of binoculars in Lenny's lap. "Why all the precautions?"

"You tell me. You sent Cindy to my mom's house instead of going there or calling her yourself. Given your new notoriety, I figured something was up. I'm guessing this meeting's more than just your desire to pay up on the six-pack you owe me."

"I owe you a six-pack? Since when?"

"That's the minimum it's going to cost you for whatever it is you want."

"I think my bill is going to be slightly larger than a six-pack," Grayson said. "I need your help in a big way, but it's risky."

"I'm guessing it has something to do with the Feds seizing control of our state. You want me to hack in and extract some dirt on certain congressmen?"

"Actually, that's not a horrible idea, but no. I have something else in mind."

Lenny's head ticked twice while he waited.

"I want to put a scare into the American people."

"What kind of scare?"

Grayson paused. "A nuclear scare."

Lenny sat back. "A nuclear scare. What does that mean?"

"It means we want them to think we will retaliate with some type of nuclear incident if they try to run us out of Wyoming."

"You have access to a nuclear weapon?"

"No, but they don't know that. What we do have is F.E. Warren Air Force Base in Cheyenne whose mission is to oversee hundreds of nuclear missiles. Accidents happen. Things get misplaced."

Lenny pushed to his feet and shoved Grayson into the uneven slab of rock wall. "The air force is not just some ragtag set of yahoos who misplace ICBMs! They're our country's best!"

Upon impact, a dull corner of protruding rock stabbed Grayson just below his shoulder blade. "Damn! Oh, damn! Ah, that hurts!"

Lenny stepped back while Grayson arched in pain. As he regained some semblance of composure, it dawned on him Lenny's dad had once served in the air force.

"Sorry," Lenny apologized.

"Your six-pack just went from hazy IPAs to Busch Light."

"An upgrade."

"You have to promise you're not going to drown me in the stream if I resume this discussion."

"Your idea is stupid. It's in no way possible."

Grayson extended his arm like a traffic cop. "Hear me out. I have no intention of actually heisting anything from the air force. I'm trying to fabricate a story—a rumor, if you will—that makes the public shit their pants."

"Grayson, you can't bluff the air force. They account for every screw. They employ all kinds of redundant fail-safe procedures. They have security out the wazoo."

"No! Lenny, you're not listening. I'm not trying to bluff the air force. I don't need to bluff the air force. I'm going after the general public. I need to scare Joe Average Guy enough to make him call his senator."

"Joe Average Guy relies on the military and our government to handle national security. If they tell Joe, it's safe, he believes them."

"Not necessarily. Nuclear accidents can happen. Remember Fukushima?

"Not the same," Lenny argued.

"I disagree. Joe has a connection to the internet, a lot of time on his hands, and a vivid imagination. Joe loves conspiracy theories, so let's give him one."

Lenny twitched twice.

"Think about it, Lenny," Grayson continued. "How long have UFO stories been bandied about? And look what happened during the pandemic. People scare themselves silly with rumors, and when people are scared, they demand action."

"Grayson, why not appeal to people's sympathetic side?"

"We tried. It failed. We're down to our last arrow. It's bent, but it's all we got. If this doesn't work, a lot of people are going to step in and fight. Some of them are going to die."

From the increase in Lenny's tics, Grayson knew his friend was agitated.

"Did I tell you? Dad's going to lose the ranch in less than six months."

Lenny's eyes widened in surprise. Grayson knew he thought the world of his dad.

"I hadn't heard that. I'm sorry."

Grayson nodded. "So, I was thinking maybe you could help me plant a rumor or two that work their way into social media. Done in a way that's impossible to trace."

His friend scanned the ridgeline on the other side of the stream. "Did you have something specific in mind?" Lenny seemed less combative.

"At first, I was thinking we suggest some type of leak has happened around a bomb silo. But now I don't think that's the way to go."

"Why not?"

"Because the damage would be confined to Wyoming. The nuclear part would concern people, but they wouldn't see it as directly affecting them. We want them to panic."

"I agree," Lenny said. "Not only that, a leak implies that it was an unplanned accident. We want to send a message saying we control the ability to create a crisis at a time and place of our choosing."

We. I like that. Lenny's on board. "Good point," Grayson said. "So now, the challenge becomes identifying some plausible scenario where we commandeer a weapon and either launch it from here or transport it and detonate it somewhere else."

Lenny frowned. "We're not going to pretend we can hijack a missile."

"I know. Believe me," Grayson replied while rubbing the bruised muscle in his back. "What if we somehow acquire nuclear fuel? What do they use in bombs?

"Plutonium, mostly. Uranium, maybe."

Grayson smiled in devious triumph. "Lots of uranium in Wyoming. Lots and lots."

"Yeah," Lenny argued. "In its natural state, but uranium has to be enriched to be used as fuel."

"Does it burn in its natural state?"

"I've never heard of a uranium fire. I don't think so, but I don't know for sure."

"Neither does Joe Average Guy. Roll with me here, amigo," Grayson said as his mind whirred. "What if a giant bonfire, or maybe a forest fire, was started, and a substantial quantity of uranium was added to the mix? The uranium burns, creating radioactive fallout in the smoke—smoke that rises high into the atmosphere and blows across the country like the California fires do. The eastern half of the country is exposed."

Lenny surrendered a meek smile. "You are batshit crazy. Do you know that?"

"Crazy enough to be believed?"

"Yeah, maybe."

"I think so, too." Grayson paused. "Give me a little time. Let me work out the details of our apocalyptic tale."

"You don't need to," Lenny answered. "Let them finish the story,"

"Huh?"

"We let them finish the story. I've done this before, and it works beautifully."

"D-d-done what?" Grayson stammered. "I'm not following."

"We let them infer. Our job is to plant some linked cryptic key words for them to discover. Maybe something like *Wyoming, uranium, retaliation*, and *radiation*. Then, we sit back and watch their imaginations run wild."

"Wow," Grayson muttered.

"They will take this story in directions we never expected. And the best part is, we'll get their full buy-in. You'll be amazed."

"So, my work is finished?"

"No," Lenny answered. "We're not scaring Joe just for the sake of jerking his chain. You have a different story to write. After we get his attention, you need to tell him exactly what we are asking for. We want a remedy to the current unacceptable situation, and you need to tell him exactly what that is."

Grayson protested, "Yeah, but if I do, won't that implicate me?"

Lenny interlaced his fingers and blew into his cupped hands. "Not if you're smart about it. I know you said you tried and failed to win the sympathetic battle, but I think you should try again. I'd get a PR campaign started pronto making the rest of the country aware of exactly what Wyoming wants. Then, after the public has scared itself with its own story, a majority of the country will remember our requests and think that's not such a bad idea."

"Okay. So how do we get this party started with the cryptic message?"

"That's my business." With a wry smile, Lenny added, "And you're right. It's going to cost a hell of lot more than a six-pack."

Initially, Grayson smiled, but that smile quickly gave way to worry. "Lenny, this is serious business. If we get caught, they'll put us away for a long time."

"I know. That's why we're meeting here. It's time for you to take off. I'll stick around until after dark."

CHAPTER 25

WHAT'S THE BUZZ?

ON THE DRIVE back to Cheyenne, Grayson replayed his rendezvous with Lenny. Prior to separating, he had informed his friend to wait for a go-ahead signal. In another part of the world, Smitty needed time to pursue plan B. Still, Grayson was anxious to see Lenny's upcoming magic show and wondered how long he would have to wait until his friend's handiwork appeared on the national stage.

As he watched Glendo Reservoir disappear in the rearview mirror, Grayson considered next steps. His skills as an influencer were about to be tested. He turned off the radio to concentrate.

His "Save Wyoming" plan would take place on two fronts. First, detailed protections for Wyoming citizens had to be established, articulated, and promoted. That effort ultimately fell in the governor's lap, but Grayson could help. Given that public relations were a key component of his job, he could openly engage with his boss to devise a plan.

The second step entailed a more delicate maneuver—one

excluding his direct involvement. After Lenny did his thing, Grayson needed Americans to connect the dots between the nuclear threat and Wyoming's unacceptable plight. He needed them to understand that by agreeing to his state's reasonable requests, the danger could be averted. The trick was in finding a neutral party to facilitate that understanding. He shuffled through a list of potential candidates and settled on one person.

❧

"Senator Mendenhall, Grayson Woodley here."

"Grayson! It's been a while," the South Dakota senator replied between bouts of coughing. "How are you doing?"

"Life's been a challenge, but I'm managing."

"I've thought about you and what you endured in Scottsbluff. I knew you were resilient and would push through it, but damn, you've had a tough go."

"One day at a time," Grayson said. "On a lighter note, I'm planning a drive across South Dakota and wondered if the Corn Palace is worth a stop."

Mendenhall laughed at his mention of the unconventional attraction just off Interstate 90. "Of course, it is. It's on the unofficial list of man-made wonders. At the very least, they serve icy-cold Coke, and you'll be thirsty after that long drive across the prairie."

"Yes, but is it part of your environmental tourism package?" Grayson teased. The senator raged into another coughing fit, and Grayson wondered if his friend might spit up a lung.

"Nothing more environmentally sound than recycled corn-cobs." Mendenhall steadied his breath and then asked, "Are you back in the environmental tourism business?"

"No. Actually, I'm working on the state's transition. A few simple changes to the Fed's NRR plan sure would make the effort easier. I'm working on a revised version palatable enough for our folks to accept. Unfortunately, our pleas seem to fall on deaf ears."

"Ah," Mendenhall observed. "That's a tough assignment. I'm afraid Doolin and company are adamant about achieving their vision for your state. Barring a lightning bolt from the heavens, I don't see them budging."

Grayson hesitated before casting aside a final doubt and making his pitch. "What if a lightning bolt were to strike? Wyoming would still need an outside interpreter to coax the masses toward the path of reason."

Now Mendenhall paused. "Have you been working on your weather forecasting?"

"No, just doing a lot of praying. Hail Mary in particular."

"Mmm, interesting," the senator mused. "No promises, but if some new writing on the wall appeared, I wouldn't be opposed to spreading the word."

"I appreciate that, Senator."

At the morning briefing in the Oval Office three weeks later, the President of the United States convened with his closest advisors.

"Let's discuss the elephant in the room," President Leonard Garcia began. "Every major news network is reporting some type of nuclear threat emanating from Wyoming."

"We're working on that, Mr. President," said Donna Fowler, his chief of staff. "So far, it looks like the network media picked up a story from a political blog. They're saying Wyoming is preparing for a terrorist-type strike in retaliation for the Twenty-eighth Amendment."

"That's quite an accusation," the president commented. "Any idea who's responsible for this message? Is this a formal threat? Is this a verified threat? Have we been in contact with Governor Linsey?"

Fowler answered, "We have not determined the source of the threat, but I did contact the governor just before this meeting, and he categorically denies any involvement."

Garcia raised his eyebrows. "Did he actually say, 'Categorically'? That's a word found in a prepared answer. Do you think he knows something?"

"His voice was odd," the chief of staff replied. "I sensed he had been expecting something to happen, but not this. He seemed genuinely distressed about a potential nuclear incident."

"Hmm," the president mused while he steepled his fingers. "Tell me the specifics of the threat."

Fowler shifted in her seat. "Mr. President, we have made this investigation a top priority, but we are still in the preliminary stages. So far, we've yet to identify any actual statement that expressly makes a threat. Instead, we've uncovered multiple interpretations of a chain of linked words coming from the dark web."

"A chain of linked words?"

"Yes, sir. Communication on the dark web is sometimes done in cryptic fashion. Many watchdog sites have programs searching the web for things like repetitive occurrences of seemingly random word strings. Usually, these discoveries are coincidental and harmless, but occasionally, they yield meaningful intelligence."

"You mentioned interpretations of this word chain. Who's doing the interpreting?"

"As I mentioned earlier, a popular political blogger posted last evening that plans for some sort of nuclear attack by Wyoming had been uncovered. Overnight, other media sources released similar stories."

"The newsclip I watched said some type of uranium-based contamination would take place," Garcia said. "They spoke of an airborne delivery. Are they talking about a missile?"

Fowler responded, "We don't think so. The word string suggests an environmental type of strike. Currently, we think the most likely method would be burning some type of agent that releases radioactive particles into the atmosphere. Prevailing winds would carry the particles eastward toward our primary population centers. Another possibility is the poisoning of reservoirs with the same type of contaminant."

"Word string! What exactly was in this word string?" the flustered commander in chief snapped.

Fowler looked down at her notes. "The common words identified were *vengeance, Wyoming, wind direction, uranium, reservoir,* and *chemical reaction.* They appeared multiple times but in varying order."

Sitting apart from the rest of the group, the assistant press secretary looked up from his phone and addressed the president. "Sir, a new story has just come across the wire. A radio station in Providence is speculating that the air force base in Cheyenne is a likely source for a weapons compromise."

President Garcia turned immediately to his national security advisor. "Is that possible?"

The stern lady with haunting gray eyes answered in an unwavering tone, "No. Intercontinental missiles are managed there under the most stringent security protocols. We've had no report of unusual activity. The story is preposterous."

Garcia nodded. "There was a time when the press actually fact-checked stories before releasing them. Now it's a race to see who can create the most sensational frenzy. Still, I want all weapon installations and inventories double-checked—make that triple-checked."

"Yes, sir."

"From what I've heard this morning, we may or may not be facing an actual threat; however, I am certain we have a rapidly escalating public-relations crisis on our hands. John Q. Public has embraced a fear-the-worst mentality, and we have to respond."

"May I suggest we immediately put out a statement saying we

are actively investigating all reports of a threat, but at this time, we haven't found any credible evidence that one exists?" Fowler asked.

The president rocked in contemplation. "Okay, today, let's keep the scare mongers at bay as best we can. But by this afternoon, I want a firm read on the threat—can it be carried out, and if so, by whom? Are we dealing with Wyoming leadership, or are we contending with a rogue group? I also want a detailed action plan to diffuse the mass hysteria. Does everyone understand?"

"Yes, sir," came a unison reply.

⁓

The buzz from gossip permeating the Wyoming State Capitol electrified the air. State employees scurried about the hallways with elevated anxiety. Silently, Grayson observed the shocked behavior of his colleagues. He had underestimated the effect his scheme would have on Wyoming residents. They were as surprised and frightened as anyone. On TV and computer screens scattered throughout the building, headline-worthy news stories such as Chinese warnings of retaliation in response to a Taiwan visit by US diplomats had been bumped into the background.

For the bulk of the morning, Grayson had remained at his desk and tried to manage the involuntary shaking of his hands. At one point, he looked up and saw the governor enter the room. His *genuinely deniable* boss offered him only a fleeting glance.

Grayson wondered how things were going for Smitty. His coconspirator had been away for several weeks without any communication. Prior to leaving, the pair had agreed Smitty was not to contact him directly but would somehow get word to his partner once his efforts had succeeded—or failed.

When Grayson thought of Lenny, he couldn't help but smile. *You hit the bull's-eye, my friend.* Americans across the nation were reacting just as Lenny had said they would. The media had predictably played their part and added oomph to the clandestine campaign. The assortment of concocted tales predicting immi-nent disaster amazed him. *So far, so good.* Now, he waited for Washington, DC, to respond and Mendenhall to come through.

❧

The next morning, Grayson read the headline and sat back in an unprecedented panic:

SOUTH DAKOTA SENATOR DIES FROM MASSIVE HEART ATTACK

❧

In Washington, DC, the president's team reconvened and awaited the commander in chief's arrival. In his double-breasted, charcoal suit and solid-red tie, the man at the nation's helm entered the room imparting a steady confidence—a trait voters valued and one they rewarded with high approval ratings. Unlike yesterday, when he had appeared to be thrown off-balance by the unex-pected rumors, Garcia had recaptured his mojo. The brisk pace of his entry conveyed a quiet resolve. "Good morning."

"Good morning, Mr. President."

"Donna, please give us a summary of what's been learned since yesterday."

"Yes, sir," Fowler began. "First, we are confident in saying no actual statement of a threat has been made. As we discussed yes-terday, the multiple instances of the cryptic word string are the source for all the speculation. That speculation has increased at least tenfold in volume and variety since yesterday's meeting."

"Have we identified who created the word string? Is it some-one affiliated with Wyoming? Could it be a foreign player—say one of Russia's disinformation ploys? Is it possible that all of these occurrences are random?"

"Definitely not random, sir. We've traced some links to two people." The chief of staff paused with a sheepish hint on her face.

"Who are they?" the president asked.

Fowler hesitated. "Congresswoman Blossom McKenzie and Great Outdoors America CEO Hector Devine."

"Two of the lead proponents for the Twenty-eighth Amendment," President Garcia said. "This was intentional. It's a sick joke. Someone is playing with us."

"It would seem so, Mr. President. Whoever it is, they're good at it."

"The jab at McKenzie and Devine is a clear connection to Wyoming, but it's too obvious," the vice president said. "Honestly, their folks aren't that sophisticated. I think we can rule out Wyoming as the source."

Fowler answered, "We can't be positive about that, sir. Vengeance is one of the key words. Still, no one affiliated with Wyoming has claimed responsibility, or knowledge, for that matter."

"What about Linsey?" the president asked. "His response to your call yesterday was weird."

"Complete denial," Fowler answered. "Same with all their other leaders. I checked in with a friend who works at the Capitol in Cheyenne, and she said everyone out there is stunned by the news."

Garcia tapped on his thigh. "Okay, so we can't verify a threat has been made nor do we have a definitive source making the threat. Let's discuss something we might have a handle on. Has there been any sort of weapons compromise at any of our military installations?"

"No, Mr. President," the national security advisor answered. "We have verified all weapons are accounted for, and security is firmly in place."

"That's good. Now, what about a uranium-based attack?"

"Our experts say it's highly unlikely," the national security advisor replied. "Uranium doesn't burn on its own. It would have to be mixed with oxygen. Also, the amount of uranium needed to cause an air-contamination issue is substantial and would be easily detected before it reached a dangerous level. Uranium is a heavy metal, and over a period of years it does contaminate water, but testing for that type of contamination is common practice. It's also radioactive and emits radon gas, but again, long periods of exposure are required before there are human health consequences."

The president winced as he massaged the bridge of his nose. "Yes, but rumors about these health hazards only take minutes to cause mayhem. The problem is panic sets in when people hear words like radon and radioactive. They respond emotionally. How do we counteract that?

The homeland security advisor, a lanky man with a bad comb-over and a white goatee answered, "Sir, may I suggest we calm the nation by assuming control of the assets causing the threat?"

"What exactly do you suggest?"

"First, we establish a military presence around all uranium mines and facilities. We justify the mission as an act of national security."

"And what else?"

"The next action is more aggressive, but I believe it's necessary to demonstrate we're in control and American citizens are safe. We occupy Cheyenne and establish martial law in the state."

Mouths dropped, and for a few moments, an eerie silence seized the room.

"Are you out of your mind?" the chief of staff finally asked.

"Not at all," the homeland security advisor countered. "At the very least, our nation is dealing with a vocally hostile contingent. Wyoming residents have threatened violence, and as in the case of Scottsbluff, we've seen that resistance spin out of control. Now the country is being menaced by some shadow enemy who hints at inflicting severe devastation."

"We haven't established where that shadow enemy comes from. It could be foreign, and it could simply be disruptive propaganda," Fowler argued.

The homeland security advisor snapped back, "We are trained and equipped to deal with foreign threats. A domestic insurrection is a new challenge and requires an unorthodox response."

The vice president chimed in. "Mr. President, if you enact martial law, this administration's actions will be lumped in with the Japanese internment camps of World War II and the nineteenth-century Native American abuses."

The homeland security advisor faced the president. "Sir, we are dealing with an imperfect set of information, so the question becomes, what type of mistake can we not afford to make? If we impose martial law and no actual threat materializes, the price is a reduction in freedom for a small minority for a short duration. But if we don't secure our vulnerable areas and, God forbid, an attack takes place, we will have a calamity on our hands."

"Sir," Fowler rebutted, "the cost of martial law will be far greater than a limited loss of freedoms. People in Wyoming will rise up in armed opposition. They will die in the tens or hundreds, perhaps even the thousands."

The president remained quiet for an uncomfortable length of time. "As I understand, the uranium mines are in desolate locations. Is that right?"

"Yes, sir," Fowler said.

The president nodded. "Secure the uranium facilities with military personnel, but let's throw out an olive branch. Donna, contact Governor Linsey. Inform him of our plan, and ask him to take the lead by deploying the Wyoming National Guard."

The homeland security advisor protested, "Sir, with all due respect, I think that's a dangerous move. We are opening ourselves up for sabotage."

Garcia accepted the challenge with self-assured calmness.

"Your objection is noted, but we can contribute advisory teams to the effort. We'll sprinkle in our people with theirs. I'm more interested in Governor Linsey's response to our request. It will give us a true read on where he stands."

"Yes, Mr. President."

"In the meantime, keep any occupation plans on the back burner. Let's pray calmer heads prevail."

When Governor Linsey received the president's request for assistance in securing uranium mines and facilities, he gladly obliged. It presented an opportunity for him to demonstrate that, at least officially, Wyoming was in no way part of the effort to intimidate the country.

He ordered the Wyoming National Guard into action. The governor then went on TV, radio, and social media imploring all Wyoming citizens to stay calm and exercise restraint. Linsey explained to his constituents that only uranium-related sites were being secured. Other property would be unaffected. He emphasized how the mysterious, dark-web threat affected Wyoming residents as much as other American citizens.

Overall, Wyoming citizens heeded his message; yet not everyone complied. After nearly two years of stress, a few disgruntled individuals had endured enough frustration. Two days after the governor's plea, a small contingent of self-appointed vigilantes ambushed a lone vehicle carrying three US Department of Energy civilians in the Powder River Basin. There were no survivors.

"Inexcusable!" Garcia raged upon hearing of the unwarranted attack. His face burned beet red with anger. White House advisors surrounded him in grave silence.

"How should we respond?" the vice president asked.

"I suggest a powerful retaliatory strike," the homeland security advisor said. "We need to nip these renegade actions in the bud. Anything less will simply encourage more violence."

The president silently counted to ten in an effort to regain his wits. "Do we know who the suspects are? I'm assuming there are multiple people involved."

"We have a pretty good idea about at least one," Fowler said. "Two guardsmen identified a vehicle leaving the scene. That vehicle is registered to a person who's been vocal about armed resistance."

"So, have the county sheriff arrest him," the vice president said. "This is a local jurisdictional matter."

"Is it?" the president asked. "Three federal representatives have just been murdered."

The vice president's posture grew rigid. "The Posse Comitatus Act restricts our use of federal military personnel in domestic matters."

"Exceptions are permissible if state authorities are unable to suppress the violence," the president said. "Eisenhower applied an exception during Arkansas' school-desegregation crisis. My understanding is numerous vigilante groups have organized in Wyoming. If so, it seems to me Governor Linsey and his law enforcement folks don't have a handle on the situation."

"Your analysis is correct, Mr. President," the homeland security advisor said. "Given the existing circumstances, military action is warranted."

"Prepare a forceful, targeted response," the president ordered.

The vice president stood in protest. "Sir, you are ordering the killing of American citizens!"

Garcia was blunt. "Someone threw this mass-destruction threat into our lap. We attempted to diffuse the situation peacefully, and now three civilians are dead. I am going to put a stop to this rebellion. If people die, that will be my burden to bear. In the end, I believe most Americans will understand."

News of the retaliatory drone strike sped through Wyoming. In response to the heinous attack on the Department of Energy employees, the US military destroyed a cluster of vehicles parked a mile off Highway 59. All the vehicles were destroyed, including the one identified by the national guardsman a day earlier.

In his office, Grayson accepted the revelation with sickening agony. He wanted to vomit. He had clearly overplayed his hand, and now armed conflict had begun. People were dying. He received more bad news while walking down the hall.

"Hey, Grayson, did you hear? Dusty's cousin is recruiting people for a border patrol. He got twenty-one volunteers in the first hour," a gangly man about Grayson's age said. "They plan on setting up a checkpoint at the state line."

This is really happening. God help us. Grayson realized hopes and prayers wouldn't be sufficient to quell the resistance of Wyoming's foolish brave. He needed to intervene. He rushed to his 4Runner and drove toward Colorado.

At the last exit before the border, Grayson spotted a large group of assorted vehicles parked along the overpass. He pulled off the highway and coasted along the exit ramp. People he didn't recognize peered at him with mixed emotions as he rolled past. Some looked skeptical. One guy gave him a thumbs-up. All were brandishing rifles. He parked at the end of the row and started his search for Dusty's cousin.

"Hey, I'm looking for Rowdy McCullough," Grayson said to the first man he met.

The man pointed down the road. "Big fella with red hair, long sideburns."

Three minutes later, Grayson found Rowdy. Against the background of darkening skies hinting at a spring thunderstorm, the big fella stood firm. He was younger than Grayson expected, maybe twenty-two, a purported age of invincibility.

Grayson extended his hand. "Hi, Rowdy. I'm Grayson Woodley. I work with Dusty at the Capitol."

While Rowdy shook his hand, a guy standing next to Rowdy was stuffing a wad of chew behind his lip. "I know you. You're the Scottsbluff fighter," he said.

Grayson cringed.

"Oh yeah," Rowdy said. "Did you come out to kick some more ass?"

"Actually, I was hoping to get you to call this off."

Rowdy stepped back and eyeballed Grayson.

"Rowdy, this is crazy. You can't take on the army. Look what they did up north."

"This is our home," Rowdy said. "We're tired of getting pushed around."

Grayson pleaded, "We all are, but a roadblock's not going to change that. It's just going to get somebody killed."

A crowd of Rowdy supporters gathered around the arguing pair. "Fuck you!" a voice in the group said. "We're holding our ground."

Rowdy nodded in agreement. "Mister, either grab a gun or get lost."

Grayson recognized the specter of irrational stubbornness and knew he'd lost his battle. He made the lonely walk to his 4Runner, drove across the overpass, and turned onto the highway ramp. He had just accelerated to cruising speed about a half mile from the overpass when he heard a whirring buzz. An eye-blinding explosion followed the noise. In his rearview mirror, the overpass had been reduced to ragged shambles.

✥

That night, President Garcia addressed the nation. He outlined the fateful events from the past few days and closed his speech with a warning to Wyoming citizens.

"Two missions have been conducted to thwart dangerous and illegal resistance by Wyoming residents. The first strike demonstrated superior US military capability. The second strike exhibited my resolve to use that capability as necessary."

In the Oval Office after the speech, Garcia ordered his staff, "Prepare to occupy Cheyenne."

CHAPTER 26

A WAKE-UP CALL

THE NEXT NIGHT, and sixteen hundred miles east of Cheyenne, a duty officer in the White House Situation Room picked up the first report of activity. Speculation had become reality. The officer was trained to react, and he did, but not before a few seconds of regret and angst flashed through his mind. *Could this have been prevented? What will be the outcome? How many people will die?*

Now, other personnel in the Situation Room were focused on the real-time incident. Chairs swiveled, keyboards were pounded, and a few bodies scurried into new places. The duty officer felt as if the room temperature had risen five degrees from intensity alone.

"Contact the national security advisor," the duty officer's superior commanded.

With a few finger movements on a secure line, the duty officer followed through with the order.

After nearly an hour of fitful stirring—an all-too-common, middle-of-the-night routine—President Garcia had finally dozed off when his telephone rang.

"Yes," he muttered.

The voice of the White House operator replied. "Sir, I have the national security advisor on the line."

The president sat up and turned on a table lamp. "Put her through."

A brief silence ensued. Then a female voice spoke. "I'm sorry to interrupt you at this hour of the night, Mr. President, but we have a situation."

"Go ahead."

"Five minutes ago, Chinese forces launched a massive assault against multiple defense sites in Taiwan."

CHAPTER 27

CARDS ON THE TABLE

IN THE SITUATION Room sometime after daybreak, President Garcia, in consultation with his staff, discussed possible responses to the Chinese aggression. During a pause, the homeland security advisor queried, "Sir, we are in position and awaiting your order to commence the occupation of Cheyenne. Shall I give the strike force the go-ahead?"

Red-eyed, yet keenly focused, the president waved him off. "Negative. Have the strike force stand down. Let's deal with one major crisis at a time."

⁓

Using a barrage of quick missile strikes, China destroyed much of Taiwan's counterattack capabilities. It also employed sophisticated spoofing and jamming techniques to temporarily disable the satellite-dependent navigational and weapon systems of the US Navy's fleet in the Philippine Sea. That critical downtime enabled China to encircle Taiwan with a naval blockade. In subsequent days, China made no effort to follow up its attack with a land invasion. Instead, it quarantined the island, initiating a dangerous game of military chicken. The next move belonged to America. An anxious world waited.

⁂

The president studied the latest intelligence regarding China's blockade of Taiwan. Once again, his Asian adversaries surprised him. Rather than choke the Taiwanese population into submission with physical hardship, China had actually permitted limited shipments of humanitarian-type goods to pass through their air and sea quarantine. It also allowed local government to function unimpeded by military action. On the flip side, China had stifled all passenger travel in or out of Taiwan. Nobody was permitted to leave the island. It also announced that any attempts to provide military aid would be denied with severe force.

These unusual tactics put the US in a quandary. The president faced a binary decision. He could go all in with a tactical nuclear strike, or he could pursue diplomatic channels, knowing the enemy held the stronger hand.

Having spent the past thirty-plus years preparing for reunification, the Chinese were willing to wait a little longer to achieve their goal. They painted the diplomatic option as the more palatable course. The world agreed.

Domestically, the president staggered from the backlash to his unprovoked attack outside of Cheyenne. In Denver, Salt Lake City, and Seattle, protestors took to the streets and voiced their opposition to the over-the-top use of force. Rather than uniting behind his national address and his resolve to quiet the Wyoming uprising, much of the country expressed sympathy for the beleaguered state.

Like millions of Americans, Grayson was glued to TV's nonstop coverage of the Taiwan crisis, now in its ninth day. For the time being, Wyoming and its dilemma had been relegated to the back burner. As he chopped vegetables for his dinner salad, his phone rang. Caller ID showed it was Mary Smith.

"Hey, Mary. How are you?"

"Well, considering everything going on in the world, not too bad," she answered. "How are you holding up? I've been worried about you."

"About the same. Have you heard from that ornery husband of yours?"

"Just briefly. He said the heat in Iraq is blistering, and the food's given him the runs."

Grayson laughed. *Typical Smitty.*

"He also said you had wanted to see one of Rachel's volleyball games. Her last two games of the season are this week, Tuesday and Thursday. I figured you could use an escape from reality, even if it's just a couple of hours."

"Yeah, that sounds great, actually. Thursday's good. At her school?"

"Yep. They start at four."

"See you there. Thanks."

"Bye, Grayson."

Rachel's team had just evened the match at one game apiece when Mary's cell phone rang. "Hey, there," she said. "You should be here. Your daughter's killing it." Mary nudged Grayson, who was sitting next to her. "It's Smitty," she whispered.

Grayson nodded and then scanned the half-full set of bleachers in the middle school gym. He tried not to listen in on the married couple's conversation, but he was anxious to know if Smitty had anything to say. A minute later, Mary passed him the phone.

"I need to visit the ladies' room before they start again," she said. "Smitty wants to say hi."

Grayson accepted the device from Mary and put it to his ear. "Hey, buddy! It's been a while. Where are you?"

"Back on friendly soil. I don't think I'll ever leave home again," Smitty said.

"Hard trip?"

"Yeah, did what we had to. Hey, is Mary or anyone else near you?"

"No," Grayson answered. "She went to the restroom."

"Good. Are you ready for my big news?"

"Sure."

"I got me a little girlfriend on this trip. Just dropped her off at her new place," Smitty revealed in an excited tone.

"Whoa!" Grayson answered.

"The thing is, she's a little kinky. I was telling her about you, and she wants to meet you. I'm guessing even you'll be able to score."

"Really? I could use some lovin'."

"Uh-huh. I'll send you a picture of her. You can show it to those blowhard friends of yours and do some bragging."

"Can't wait to see her," Grayson answered.

"Bye."

After returning home from Rachel's game, Grayson drew in a deep breath and dialed an all-too familiar number.

"Hello," the feminine voice on the other end said.

"Hello, Ms. Cicci."

A pause. "Hello, Grayson. How are you?"

"Surviving as best I can."

"Aren't we all. I've been thinking about you and this giant mess out your way."

"Sentimental thoughts, I hope."

"It's best not to ask," Cicci replied caustically.

"Right," Grayson said. "Hey, I hope my professional standing with you is solid enough to beg a favor."

"Depends. Let's hear it."

"I need to have a face-to-face with someone at an elevated status. I was hoping you could pass along that message in a very subtle way."

"How elevated?"

"High enough to have the president's ear," Grayson answered.

He heard a tongue click on the other end. "Here in DC?"

"No, Colorado. I'll give an exact location later."

"Uh-huh," Cicci muttered. "What's the topic?"

"Current events," Grayson replied.

"Current events as in mysterious nuclear threats?"

"It's best not to ask. Theresa, please keep this as quiet as possible. A lot's at stake, for everyone."

"I'll see what I can do."

◈

A pink, neon sign welcomed patrons to the Moose Breath Inn. A moose's head, including a handsome set of antlers, appeared next to a flashing series of parenthesis-shaped marks. The marks were arranged in a line and flashed on and off in a series to emulate the giant mammal's exhalation. The inn was one of five restaurants in the small town of Walden, Colorado.

At a booth inside, Grayson sipped his second cup of mid-morning coffee while waiting for his counterpart to arrive. Only one other customer was present, and he sat at the bar getting an early start on his daily quota of Coors. Though the calendar indicated the second half of spring, the temperature hung at forty degrees in this North Park town whose elevation exceeded eight thousand feet. The chill in the air warranted a fire in the inn's oversize hearth. Grayson indulged in both the fire's heat and its smell of burning pine.

This time of year in the Colorado high country was affectionately known as mud season, and it represented the low point for tourism. Grayson had chosen Walden for this reason. No one in the town knew him, and hopefully no one would be around to recognize his guest.

At 10 a.m., the front door opened, and two people entered. The first was a fit black woman, probably forty-something in age. She was dressed in a blue-and-white flannel shirt and a navy down vest. She wore her hair short, allowing her high cheek bones to stand out. Behind her came a pudgy, white gentleman of medium height wearing a tweed sports coat much too fancy for this region of Colorado. Grayson recognized the latter as Senator Barry Doolin but had no clue about the woman's identity.

Doolin spotted Grayson; the woman and he walked briskly to the booth and sat on the other side of the table. There were no handshakes, no pleasantries.

Doolin said, "I should have figured you would be in the middle of this mess. You were a troublemaker in Washington, the prime instigator in Scottsbluff, and now here you are, climbing out from under your rock again. We are going to lock you away for the rest of your life."

Grayson had prepared himself for this type of intimidation. After hanging up with Cicci, he realized he would likely be dealing with someone older whose political standing was far greater than his. The thought hollowed his stomach until he remembered his family, the ranch, and the sickening image of charred vehicles just a few days ago. *Feed off your anger, but manage it.*

He listened to Doolin's chastising remarks, then turned toward the lady. She was dissecting him with her disciplined eyes. They were eyes of experience and reason. Unlike Doolin's, he trusted those eyes. "I'm sorry. We haven't met. I'm Grayson Woodley. You can call me Grayson."

The lady matched him in tone. "Mr. Woodley, I'm Colonel Birdsong, commander of the 90th Missile Wing of the United States Air Force stationed at F.E. Warren. You may address me as Colonel."

Doolin sneered as Birdsong set the mood. "I thought you might like to meet the person in charge of the weapons you've allegedly heisted. I know she wanted to meet you."

The air force official's presence unnerved Grayson, yet he kept his cool. He had anticipated being accused of originating the nebulous nuclear warnings and had rehearsed a noncommittal response accordingly. Now, he ignored Doolin's baiting and put his preparation to work.

"Like most the folks in Wyoming, I understand why you clamped down on the uranium mines. Given the rumors, it was the prudent thing to do. What I don't understand, and frankly the reason I requested a meeting, is the excessive force being applied. Almost fifty people are dead."

Doolin snorted while wagging his finger. "No! No! Here's how this meeting's going to work. First, you are going to confess to initiating a threat against the United States of America. Then you are going to identify your coconspirators, including any Wyoming state officials. After that, you are going to confirm that this whole, dark-web campaign is nothing but a fabricated, bullshit story—or, if by some miniscule chance, you actually have something that can inflict damage, you are going to reveal what it is and where it can be found."

Grayson's heart pounded, but his voice remained steady. "Anything else? Fetch you a beer? Shine your shoes, maybe?"

"Look, smart-ass! You are in serious trouble! You are a traitor!"

Doolin shrieked as he rose off the bench. Furious heat radiated from both men's eyes.

Birdsong spoke. "Someone has behaved very recklessly, Mr. Woodley. Because you initiated this meeting, we suspect you have some part in it. The nation has been directly threatened and its citizens put through undue stress. Someone must be held accountable. Still, the fact you have come forward today will be looked upon favorably."

Once again, Grayson became transfixed by those ebony eyes. He regarded the colonel with mixed feelings. He despised her for sitting on Doolin's side of the table, yet he admired her as a military officer. Given the current Chinese crisis, he was grateful to know people like Birdsong were defending America.

Grayson looked around the inn. He noticed the two employees and the lone customer at the bar were giving his table their undivided attention. Nodding toward the onlookers, Grayson spoke softly to the colonel. "I could use some fresh air. Would you walk with me?"

She nodded back at him.

Grayson stood and pulled out his wallet. He left ten dollars for the coffee, waved at the waitress, and headed toward the door. The colonel walked close behind, and Doolin reluctantly followed.

Once outside, they turned onto a side street and walked away from the main road. After a block, they entered a small municipal park with some neglected playground equipment and scattered patches of grass. They were alone.

On this blue-sky day, Grayson drew in a deep breath and attempted a different approach. "Colonel Birdsong, as commander of the Mighty Ninety and a resident of Cheyenne, you know the Wyoming people. We're not traitors. We're decent Americans."

Doolin rushed forward and began to open his mouth, but the colonel halted his progress with a protruding arm. "Hold on, Senator. Please." Her judicious expression invited Grayson to continue.

"We accept the Twenty-eighth Amendment—at least, most of us do—and we're willing to be a team player. But what we won't accept is having our dignity and heritage stripped away from us. Not without a fight, anyway."

Birdsong answered, "I sympathize with the people of the state and their plight. It's a difficult deal, but I'm not the one who's making that call. Believe me when I say, there are many policies I disagree with, but I still choose to wear the uniform. Mr. Woodley, if you truly want to make a positive difference, convince your fellow citizens to accept their new status calmly. Urge these vigilante groups to disband."

Doolin could no longer stay quiet. "The president has quite clearly demonstrated the consequences of armed resistance."

Grayson regarded the colonel's words as sincere but bristled when Doolin spoke. "You have pushed us into a corner, and I'm sorry to say we are at a critical juncture. The way I see it, we can come up with a plan that's acceptable to both sides, or we can jointly suffer the consequences of a terrible loss."

"What are you talking about?" Doolin bellowed. "Is this another threat? You don't have squat. I'm so fed up with your bluffs."

"It will be devasting for the entire nation. For the world, even."

"Stop it!"

"And it can be avoided if you would just sit down with the governor and hash out a simple deal."

"You go to hell, Grayson!"

"Unfortunately, hell is where we'll all be."

Doolin kicked the dirt beneath him. Then his signature smirk reappeared. "Okay, wise guy, I'll play your little game.

Tell me where this catastrophe happens, and I'll consider talking to Linsey."

Grayson reached into his shirt pocket. He pulled out a pen and a recently received photo. He scribbled something on the back of the photo and passed it to Doolin. The New York senator read the word and quickly flipped over the photo. He viewed it, and the color immediately drained from his face.

CHAPTER 28
THE WOMEN WE KNEW

(Many Years from Now)

CICCI SCOWLED IN aggravation as she reentered the bar. She paced back to the table where Mr. Tang and Grayson sat.

"Trouble in paradise?" Grayson asked.

"You would think a highly educated person could follow a simple set of directions, but apparently, it's necessary to write out the words verbatim," she stormed.

"Doolin couldn't order his own Happy Meal?"

Grayson's remark drew a half smile from Cicci. "No, a junior-level genius gave a logging outfit in Oregon permission to cut before receiving a written copy of the judge's approval. That approval contained some added conditions before logging could start, but Junior only listened to half the conversation when he spoke to the judge's office. Now we have a lot of upset people." She clasped Grayson on the shoulder. "I'm sorry, but I have to clean up this mess."

He frowned. "I'm sorry, too. We didn't get a chance to catch up."

"What's your DazzleDollar account?" Cicci asked as she pulled her phone out of her jacket. "I'll send you money for my drinks."

"Don't worry about it."

"Seriously, Cowboy. I don't want you tapping into your retirement fund."

"But I enjoy making you feel guilty. It's one of my few remaining pleasures."

Cicci grimaced and then addressed the third person at the table. "Goodbye, Mr. Tang."

Mr. Tang stood. "Goodbye, Ms. Cicci. It was a pleasure getting to know you."

Grayson also stood. "I'll walk you out."

He followed Cicci around some high-top tables and out the front door of Gerry Manders. Daylight had softened in intensity, but the temperature remained warm. He placed a tender hand on her shoulder when she stopped under the awning. His sometimes friend and former lover turned and extended a melancholy smile. He reciprocated.

"When are you headed back?" she asked.

"Tomorrow morning," Grayson answered as he surveyed the exterior of the building. "This place hasn't changed much."

"No, it hasn't, but the people in it have gotten much younger."

"That's true wherever I go."

The corners of her mouth drew downward.

"Did you ever make it to the Tetons?" Grayson asked.

"I never did."

"The invitation's still open."

Cicci gazed off into space. "I still think of that day in Scottsbluff. Not often, but sometimes. You know, it's funny, but instead of the Tetons, I've thought about going to Fort Laramie to see the grave of Claude's little boy. Isn't that strange?"

"Not at all," he said. "Did you know Claude is buried there as well?"

"I didn't."

Cicci's cell phone interrupted the conversation. Her forehead wrinkled as she identified the caller. "These guys aren't going to leave me alone. Sorry, Cowboy, I've got to run."

The pair indulged in one last sentimental moment. So much still to be said, yet nothing was. Cicci stepped forward and kissed her cowboy. What couldn't be transmitted in words was communicated by touch. The length of her embrace expressed, "I've missed you." Her abrupt separation said, "Go home."

Grayson watched as she turned onto the sidewalk and walked up the street. He smiled as he considered their reversed roles in this scene. He was the classic Westerner, but Cicci was the one headed into the sunset.

Once she was out of sight, he ambled back into the semi-dark establishment. As he approached the table, he observed Mr. Tang checking his phone, still nursing a half-full mug of Yuengling. Grayson quietly took his seat.

Mr. Tang finished and placed his phone back into the inside pocket of his suit jacket. Then he simply looked at his beer and remained silent as if in deference to Grayson's current reflective state. When their glances finally met, Mr. Tang smiled and said, "The female persuasion. So powerful."

"She's a good woman,"

The pensive silence resumed.

Finally, Grayson said, "So, what about you, LeRoy? I imagine with your stature and worldliness, you've enjoyed the company of many ladies."

Mr. Tang blushed in awkward embarrassment. "Oh no, Grayson. My work has always been my mistress."

"Oh, come on!" Grayson egged him on. "I've told you plenty

of stories in the last three hours. Throw me a bone. Tantalize me with something scandalous."

Mr. Tang responded to his phrasing with an uncharacteristically high-pitched giggle. "You are so funny, my friend. I haven't laughed this hard in a long time."

Grayson folded his arms. "Well?"

After Mr. Tang's laughter played out, he drew in a breath and gathered himself. Then, Grayson detected the most subtle change in his demeanor. It was as if a deep-seeded memory had struck a nerve. The diplomat's physical reaction passed in a flash, but it had happened. He was sure of it.

"There was one acquaintance," Mr. Tang began.

"Yesss," Grayson encouraged as he leaned in with his elbows on the table.

"She stood apart from the rest," Mr. Tang continued. "Yet from the very beginning, it was a one-sided admiration, something I'd previously experienced many times. Even so, I was captivated."

Grayson appreciated the emotions of hopeless devotion.

"I was working in the Middle East when we met. Our introduction was brief but oh so memorable. When I think about it, I actually only saw her a few times after that. It's strange how imagination inflates one's memory."

"Was she native to the region?"

Mr. Tang paused in reflection. "I believe she was of a mixed background, but she yearned to travel. More than anything, she longed to see America."

"And she couldn't have accompanied you on your journeys?"

Mr. Tang smiled at Grayson's question. "No. For numerous reasons, it would have been inappropriate for us to be seen together during international travel."

Grayson recognized the delicacy of affairs regarding one's family or profession—or country.

Mr. Tang continued. "She was also limited by her own

country's travel restrictions. There was a great deal of distress because she had connections in the United States yet was prohibited from going."

"What happened?"

"What happened?" Mr. Tang echoed. "I understood our relationship was limited, so I decided the best I could do was help her fulfill her destiny. I was fortunate at the time to be in a small position of influence, and I arranged for her to leave the country."

"Wow!" Grayson cried. "Unrequited love."

Mr. Tang looked blankly into space.

"Did she make it to the United States?"

"She did. From time to time, I received news about her. She settled in the mountains." Mr. Tang smiled wistfully. "Like so many immigrants eager to assimilate in their new surroundings, she changed her name to an American one. I understand she now goes by Stella."

CHAPTER 29

SMITTY KNOWS A GUY

(Seventeen Years Earlier)

TAIWAN WASN'T THE only flashpoint in world events. When Iran announced it had achieved offensive nuclear capability, other Islamic nations in the Middle East embarked on a mad dash to attain similar power. Intellectual know-how and equipment passed freely along both formal-diplomatic and black-market channels. Unlike the United States, where hazardous material was carefully accounted for and secured, things fell through the cracks half way round the world. Dangerous things.

While Grayson had been establishing contact with Lenny to hatch the dark-web scheme several weeks back, Smitty had set out in another direction. If Grayson's bluff failed, Wyoming's future would depend on a more radical solution.

Smitty understood the two key components required for

his task. He needed to secure funding, and he needed to enlist a person who knew how to get things done. The first step entailed meeting a handful of Wyoming's most successful businesspeople without drawing undue attention. The majority of contacts who had reaped financial riches during the state's minerals heyday were eager to step up with monetary support. The effort's second component was now sitting next to him in the business class section on a flight to Baghdad.

Remi Bartholomew, popularly known as Remi B, carried legendary status in the oil patches on three continents. The burly man laughed from the depths of his soul. His tone rang infectious and inspired a zest for living in those around him.

"That little stunt cost me ten days in the Uintah County jail," Remi B chuckled. "Even so, we still met our deadline and struck oil at sixteen thousand feet."

Smitty sat mesmerized by the man's countless tales of adventure. "Looking back, did you really have to tattoo *SCUMBAG* on the guy's butt?"

Remi B frowned. "Did that guy really have to bring my mother into our conversation? I should have stamped it on his forehead."

"Nowadays, it wouldn't be ten days; more like ten years," Smitty said. "And you'd certainly be fired."

Remi B was a man out of place, a throwback to days gone by. There wasn't a hair-coloring product on the market capable of disguising the wear and tear of sixty-eight grueling years. The former three-sport high school standout from the Oklahoma panhandle sipped on his Sprite. Raised by a Baptist mother, he abstained from drugs and alcohol. Remi B believed his professional success was due in large part to the avoidance of those temptations. This practice certainly enhanced his stature within the Middle East's Muslim community.

Smitty imbibed the airline-size mini bottle of distilled spirits and considered all the stories he'd heard about Remi B. "So what was your most outrageous venture: stealing an entire oil rig or sleeping with the CEO's wife?"

Remi B responded with a sideways glance. "Mr. Smith, I believe you are baiting me."

"Just some idle chatter I heard around the water cooler."

"Hmm," Remi B retorted. "The two examples are not comparable. First, I did not steal that rig. Its arrival at my well site the day I needed it was pure coincidence. I can't be held responsible for someone else's shoddy paperwork."

"And the fact the rig was transported by your flatbeds?"

"You can't just leave a bunch of steel lying about in the desert. That's a desecration of nature." Remi B paused. "Despite my good citizenship, I do recall the regional administrator making it clear I would not be invited back for any further mineral exploration. That's contrary to the other aforementioned affair. There, I definitely remember parting on the friendliest of terms," the oil field pro said with a wink.

Smitty compared his mundane existence with the fantastic tales from this modern-day swashbuckler, part in admiration and part in envy. His own life achievements of rolling a 603 series in bowling and legging out a double in the regional softball semifinal paled by comparison.

"So, we'll stay in Baghdad tonight?" Smitty asked.

"Yeah, it's better that we wait until daylight to drive to Basra. Less suspicious."

"And you're comfortable with the shipping arrangements?"

"As comfortable as I can be. The front end through the Persian Gulf is solid. Vancouver could be a bit of a trick because I'm less familiar with it, but my boys will come through. Once we're on land, we're golden."

"How long is the ocean voyage?" Despite his age, Smitty was new to this game.

"Normally, an oil tanker takes about seven weeks to sail from the Persian Gulf to North America. Given that we have a smaller vessel dedicated to our need, I think we can make it in five weeks, maybe a few days less." As an afterthought, Remi B added, "Don't worry about transportation logistics. Our primary challenge is acquisition."

That reminder threw Smitty for a loop. He flagged the flight attendant and ordered another Dewar's. Nervously, he rubbed his mouth with his hands. "What are our chances for success?"

Remi B considered the question. "I'll have a better feel when we're on the ground. I need to see what's changed since the latest dustup." He lifted the window shade and peeked out at the darkened world from thirty-eight thousand feet. "If I had to put a number on it, I'd say our chances are one in five."

A gloomy mood seized Smitty. "That's not very hopeful."

Remi B turned back to him. "Smitty, you worry too much. Hell, I've operated under a lot worse conditions. I remember coming through a situation when my odds were barely one in ten."

"Yeah?" Smitty replied. "What situation was that?"

"The one with the CEO's wife."

The two men shared an unapologetic grin.

"It all comes so easy for you," Smitty observed. "How do you do it?"

"I learned critical life skills early on," Remi B answered. "Stroking egos, greasing palms, and busting balls when necessary."

✦

Smitty watched as Kamal operated simultaneously in three environments. Remi B's contact in Basra sat with the American pair at the small, unadorned table while his thumbs nimbly worked the keypad on his phone. In addition, the slight man in a white dress shirt and dark slacks answered Remi B's questions while tracking the comings and goings of customers in the traditional restaurant located in the Al Ashar Bazaar, one of the city's busiest trading places.

"It is very dangerous, what you are asking," Kamal said. "I'm sure you already know that, but I must impress upon you the gravity of the matter."

"But it's possible," Remi B answered. Smitty wasn't sure if Remi B was asking a question or iterating a belief.

Kamal's eyes darted toward the entrance as two new men arrived for an afternoon meal. He set his phone down and began biting a thumbnail. "Maybe. Possible."

"Please get in touch with Majid Rahim, and let him know we would like to discuss the matter with him," Remi B requested.

Kamal's face darkened. "No. Majid Rahim cannot help you. He was arrested by the authorities last month."

The older man's jaw tightened. "Who's his successor?"

"No successor," Kamal answered. "His family and close associates were also taken down." He glanced about the room. "Haidar Abdul-Jouda is your best bet."

Remi B's eyes widened. "After the oil rig redirection, I haven't been on the greatest of terms with the sheikh."

A half smile formed on Kamal's face. "I remember. Still, Sheikh Abdul-Jouda is a businessman. If the transaction is attractive, he won't let personal biases get in the way."

The phone on the table vibrated. Kamal frowned as he read his latest message. "Forgive me. I must attend to another matter." He gazed earnestly into the brown eyes of Remi B. "I worry for you, my friend. Is this adventure really necessary? Is it so important to risk the well-being of you and Mr. Smith?"

"It is."

Kamal carefully folded his napkin and placed it on the table. "God be with you." He stood and quickly left the café.

After Kamal disappeared, Smitty finally spoke. "I have difficulty understanding these people."

"What? The way they interweave religion and business?" Remi B queried.

"No, not that," Smitty said. "I can't understand how they drink hot tea when it's 105 degrees outside."

Remi B laughed. "The same way you down them chili peppers at home."

Smitty grunted. "So what is Kamal's status? Is he any sort of royalty, or is he a government official?"

"He's neither. He's a gatekeeper. He knows the system, and he keeps his ear to the ground. He specializes in information."

"Kind of like you."

"Kind of, only he's not as handsome." Remi B interlocked his fingers behind his head and yawned deeply.

"I'm still not real clear on the roles over here. Who runs the show? Is it the government or the tribes?" Smitty asked.

"Good question. It depends. Control varies by resource and by region, and it can change over time. Power is a murky thing. Given what we're trying to do, murky is our friend."

⌁

The receiving room in Sheikh Haidar Abdul-Jouda's home dazzled the visitors' eyes. A sectional sofa in hues of orange, red, and brown rested atop a tile floor arranged in geometric patterns. Above, gold drapes swooned inward from all sides and were clasped together in the center with an alabaster chandelier. Candles burning fragrances of white musk and saffron offered guests a soothing welcome. Smitty sat in dumbfounded awe while Remi B leaned forward, ready to engage with their host.

With his hands steepled against his lips, the sheikh considered the purpose of the Americans' visit. Wearing his keffiyeh, the traditional checkered headdress, and a simple white gown, he probed his audience for answers.

"An ambitious pursuit, even by your standards, Remi B," Abdul-Jouda began. "I thought the heist of an oil rig was your pinnacle feat, but once again, you have surprised me."

Remi B politely smiled. "We live in an extraordinary time. Duty carries us in unexpected directions."

"Duty? Indeed," the sheikh remarked. "Tell me, what kind of duty demands the quest for a dirty bomb?"

With an erect posture, Remi B answered his host, "In the western part of the United States, an internal conflict is underway. People in a state called Wyoming will soon be forced to unfairly relinquish their land. Perhaps you have heard of this incident?"

"I am vaguely aware," Abdul-Jouda admitted. "But it seems unusual for a man of your—how should I phrase it—free-spirited nature to take such an extreme interest in political events. Are you really willing to risk your life to acquire this device?"

"The device is an equalizer for a cause I believe in."

The sheikh's semi-smile held a hint of admiration. "Interesting. The oil field legend has a heart after all."

"I'd appreciate it if you kept that between us," Remi B answered as he tried to keep the discussion evenly matched.

"Mmm, I'm curious. My understanding is you are seeking a bomb that is modest in yield."

"Yes."

"Why? Given the risks you are taking, I would think you would want a weapon that could deliver extensive damage."

Remi B understood his logic. "We're not concerned with the total amount of potential damage. Our aim is to jeopardize a delicate place."

Abdul-Jouda's eyes enlarged. "And that would be?"

Remi B wiggled his finger between Smitty and himself. "Our little secret."

The sheikh stood and assessed his guests. He folded his hands and walked to the window. After a few moments of gazing outward, he turned and addressed the big man. "I am sorry, Remi B, but I cannot help you in your effort. Go well."

Shit!

*

Back at their hotel lobby, Smitty moped in dismay. "No success and no liquor to ease the disappointment. I hate this place."

Remi B sipped his tea with a steady hand. "We knew the odds were long," he said.

Smitty considered his partner's calm behavior and grew irritated. "You surprised me. I expected you to fight harder for a deal. You never pushed the sheikh on his stance."

The oil field wizard's graying eyebrows rose slightly. "There was no point. Abdul-Jouda had made his decision prior to our meeting."

"Then why did we even bother?"

"I didn't know until we were together in the room."

"Why won't he deal with us?"

"I'm not sure he has access to what we want. The government may have a better grip on the situation than I anticipated."

Smitty folded his arms, sticky with sweat like the rest of his body, and wished he was back home in Cheyenne. "Well, we blew our cover and revealed our intentions. That sucks."

Remi B shook his head. "We didn't tell the sheikh anything he didn't already know—or will soon learn."

An adolescent boy weaved through the hotel lobby, stopping briefly at each table. When he reached Remi B and Smitty, he laid down a business card and boasted with a large smile, "Zahir's Bakery. Best baklava in the city." He glanced deliberately at Remi B and then moved on to the next table.

"So, what's next?" Smitty asked.

Remi B examined the card the boy had left. In addition to the bakery's name and location, a handful of pastries were listed. He noticed the *k* in *baklava* had been circled in pencil. He showed Smitty the card and answered, "Dessert."

Remi B accepted the small paper sack containing the pastries from the man behind the bakery counter, presumably Zahir. The baker took Remi B's money and placed it in an antiquated cash till.

"It is important that you taste the baklava at its most fresh," the baker declared. "Is your residence far?"

"Maybe fifteen minutes away," Remi B answered.

"That is no good!" the baker shouted. "You must try it here. I have a room in back with a table. Please be my guest."

Smitty scowled at the bizarre request, but Remi B obliged without objection. They followed the baker through a small door into a dimly lit room. Along two sides, built-in shelves with assorted baking utensils and bowls stood. Large containers of flour, sugar, dried fruit, and other ingredients were stacked near the door they had entered. A wooden table with four chairs sat toward the back.

"Please." The baker beckoned them to sit. "I need to attend to the counter, but I will return to hear of your satisfaction with my beautiful baklava."

Remi B smiled courteously while Smitty remained baffled. "Is this a local custom, or is that guy off his rocker?" Smitty asked.

His partner shrugged and bit into the gooey combination of honey, nuts, and phyllo dough. Before he could take his second bite, another person entered the room.

"Kamal!" Smitty blurted out.

"Hello, my friends," the newcomer said. "Obviously, you received my message."

Remi B nodded while Smitty indicated the opposite with a shaking head. When Smitty observed Remi B, he stopped. "W-w-what the h-h-hell?" he stammered in his partner's direction. "You knew he was coming?"

"Relax, Smitty."

Relaxing was the furthest thing from Smitty's mind. "You led us down a dead end," he said while staring at Kamal.

"I am sorry," Kamal apologized. "But it is no longer of any matter."

"Why's that?" Remi B asked, leaning forward in his chair.

Kamal walked to the table and sat. His eyes narrowed as he addressed the Americans. "If you are willing to pay the same sum you were prepared to pay Sheikh Abdul-Jouda, I have your solution."

"Who? How?" Remi B quizzed him.

"I'm not at liberty to say," Kamal answered. "But the weapon fits into your specified parameters."

"You're being straight with us?" Remi B asked. He concentrated on his counterpart's mannerisms, scanning for signs of deception.

"No," Smitty insisted. "Not unless you give us more detail. I'm not spending the rest of my life in a foreign prison."

Kamal snapped back in agitation, "What I offer is genuine."

Smitty resisted. "Not enough information."

"God is great! He provides! Do you want the item or not?"

Remi B summoned all his instincts regarding human behavior as he contemplated the most dangerous decision of his life. Those instincts suggested Kamal's offer was the real deal.

"How exactly would this work?" Remi B asked.

"I will be your sole point of contact. I will have the item delivered to a place of your choosing where you can inspect it. When satisfied, you will provide payment as I specify, and the item will be yours to take."

"I don't like it," Smitty declared. "Too many unanswered questions."

"Smitty, we both knew there were no guarantees when we signed up for this assignment. I'm out of options. We either take our chances here or go home empty." The veteran dealmaker gestured to his partner with an open palm. "It's your call."

Smitty threw his head back in exasperation while an agitated leg rapidly bounced up and down. "You'd do it?"

"Yes, I would."

❧

Kamal was true to his word, and after careful inspection, the American weapon seekers accepted the package. Now in possession of the equalizer, Remi B orchestrated his logistical magic. The container was transferred from land to ship at the deep-water port of Umm Qasr without incident.

During the ocean journey, Smitty monitored Grayson's progress on the home front. Though details were sketchy, the bluff had clearly failed. Instead, the situation had escalated into violent confrontations.

As Grayson and he had agreed upon prior to his departure, the failure of Grayson's efforts meant Smitty would position the dirty bomb and prime it for activation. He longed to speak with Grayson but remained faithful to the plan. He would only make contact once the bomb was in place.

After twenty-nine days at sea—better time than had been anticipated—the transport ship entered the Port of Vancouver. From Vancouver, the cargo was hauled eastward by truck. The smugglers entered the United States at the Porthill-Rykerts Border Crossing just north of Bonners Ferry, Idaho, and then proceeded southeast until they reached their destination.

Even with assistance from Remi B's men, the final leg of the journey was brutal. They had to negotiate sections of choppy, off-road paths with steep inclines and downed timber. Finally, weeks after leaving Cheyenne, Smitty's quest had been realized. As a light rain drizzle tapered in the dense set of pines, the career civil servant pulled an antiquated Polaroid camera from his pack and photographed the bomb—a photograph that couldn't be tracked with GPS. Once he was back at the motel and miles away from the current location, he would take an image of the Polaroid with his phone camera and send it to Grayson.

"Hey, Smitty, move your ass. I'm tired and hungry!" Remi B bellowed.

Smitty acknowledged the request with a nod of the head. He turned back and gave the bomb one final look. "Welcome to your new home, Stella."

CHAPTER 30

STELLA

"YOU CAN'T BE serious!" Doolin cried.

He passed Grayson's photo to Colonel Birdsong. She turned the picture over, read the one-word caption, and froze.

"Yellowstone," she whispered.

Grayson watched two entirely different reactions unfold. A downshifting semi on the main road growled and diluted the sound of Doolin's obscenity-laden rant as he gyrated like a satellite spinning out of orbit while the colonel assumed a battle-stations stance. She flipped the piece of paper back to the photograph side and examined it. Looking up at Grayson, she asked, "Exactly what type of device is this?"

Grayson shivered, his body succumbing to the pressures of this telltale moment. "It's a dirty bomb. One with enough potential to contaminate that entire ecosystem for decades." He focused on the colonel. She was clearly processing, oscillating between shock and contemplation.

"How do we know this isn't an idle threat?" Birdsong asked.

"It's easy enough to mock up a bomb look-alike with some wires and hardware."

"Exactly!" Doolin spewed. "This is just another scare tactic."

"Your experts will be able to confirm its authenticity," Grayson answered. "But I think in your heart, you already know it's legit."

Those amazing dark-brown eyes transmitted her belief in his story. "Why? Why destroy a place beloved by all?"

His father's words—*Maybe we should play to tie*—raced through Grayson's memory. "Precisely because it is beloved by all. If Yellowstone is contaminated, everyone suffers. We all would share a horrible misery. That's why we all should do everything possible to not let this happen."

"You're insane, Woodley!" Doolin bawled. "Where's the bomb?"

Grayson bristled in defiance. "Somewhere in the Absaroka Range," he snarled. "Or is it in the Gallatin Mountains? Maybe somewhere on the Two Ocean Plateau? Gee, Senator, I don't remember. It's a pretty big park."

"Listen, smart-ass. We'll retrace every moment of your pitiful life for the past six months to learn what we want. You're not that bright, kid."

Grayson laughed with pure belligerence. "You think this is a one-man show? We have eyes watching Stella, and if you get close to her, she'll blow."

"Stella?" Birdsong asked.

"Stella," he confirmed.

She waved Grayson off. "I don't even want to know."

As if God was indicating halftime, a substantial gust of wind swirled through the park and distracted the combatants. Birdsong used the break to reset the conversation. "So, Mr. Woodley, what exactly are you asking of us?"

"First, the president needs to call off the military attacks, and he needs to assure us there'll be no attempts at an occupation."

"The military attacks were a response to the killing of

innocent civilians," the colonel replied. "We will never relinquish the right to defend our people. However, if you can demonstrate control over your vigilantes, we may be able to accommodate your requests."

"We have a functional state judicial system. I can't promise to control the actions of every Wyoming resident, but if someone breaks the law, we have the resources to arrest, prosecute, and punish any offender. If we need assistance from the federal government, we'll ask for it." What Grayson didn't mention was the impact the two military strikes had had on the psyche of Wyoming's population. Given President Garcia's willingness to retaliate, would-be rebels were now far more reluctant to commit violence.

"That still doesn't address the genesis of this situation," Doolin said, his voice resuming the more even tone of a statesman. "The initial veiled nuclear threat remains unsolved. Given that you're knee-deep in the dirty-bomb business, I'm betting you could fill in all the blanks."

Careful not to incriminate himself, Grayson chose his words carefully. "Uranium facilities have been secured. Have there been more threats? Was there ever actually a threat in the first place?"

"You know damn well there was."

"I know what the media reported," Grayson said with his best poker face. "I don't know what to tell you. Maybe this ordeal was a figment of some blogger's paranoia. Maybe it goes away as quickly as it came."

Birdsong interjected. "This argument is moot. Given what you've just handed us, Mr. Woodley, we have a new priority in threats. By your own admission, you are threatening the United States with a dirty bomb. You, Mr. Woodley. You are directly responsible."

"Yes." Grayson tried to swallow the enormous lump forming in his throat.

"Besides assurances Wyoming will not be occupied, what else are you asking?"

"Like I said earlier, those of us living in Wyoming who want to stay should be allowed to do so with the same quality of life we currently enjoy. I can't tell you the specifics—that's for the senator and the other head honchos in Washington to work out with Governor Linsey.

"Linsey!" Doolin said. "I knew he was in on this."

"Actually, no," Grayson corrected him. "He's only recently been informed about Stella. Frankly, he's as shell-shocked as you are, but he understands an opportunity has been created to sit down and talk. He's anxious for the two sides to work together and find a happy medium. Surely a compromise can be reached."

Doolin rejected the proposal with folded arms. "When the world learns about a radioactive bomb ticking somewhere in Yellowstone Park, they'll go berserk. And your name will live in infamy for putting it there."

Grayson fired back, "And your name will be right there with mine for allowing it to happen. The difference between us is I'm trying to preserve a way of life. You're looking to score political points. We'll see who's judged more harshly."

"Gentlemen! Stop!" Birdsong intervened. "This isn't helping."

Grayson felt the heat pouring off his face, but the colonel's interruption gave him a chance to regroup. "The public doesn't have to know. As of this moment, only the two of you, the governor, and our little group of Team Stella are aware of her existence. Our side will keep our mouths shut. If you can do the same, we'll be fine."

"And what do we tell the press? That we received a message from the heavens and now intend to change policy one hundred eighty degrees?" Doolin asked.

Grayson had been considering this hurdle for weeks. "Publicly, tell them the cryptic nuclear scare prompted the president to have quiet conversations with Governor Linsey about a peaceful solution. Tell them the horrific violence we've witnessed in Wyoming makes that quest more urgent. Tell them the Taiwan incident made him realize a unified America is more important than ever. Privately, suggest to them that polling showed most of the nation was in favor of cutting Wyoming a break or two in the transition, and you're worried about the upcoming election."

For the first time, Doolin smiled, albeit weakly. "Have you ever considered running for office?"

Grayson remained serious. "We're all in the same predicament here. Whether we sink or swim is up to you."

Doolin's face sobered. "Well, obviously, I can't make this decision on my own. How should I get back to you?"

"You need to negotiate with the governor. I'm just observing the action from the sidelines."

"Any solution will require you to turn over the bomb," Colonel Birdsong said.

"When we have a signed agreement," Grayson replied. "Oh, and immunity from prosecution for me and the rest of Wyoming's citizens is another stipulation."

"Mmm," Doolin grunted. "Anything else?"

"I think that's enough for today." Grayson said.

"Colonel, I'll meet you back at the car. I need to make a stop at the restaurant." Doolin turned and began walking back to the main road and the Moose Breath Inn.

When he was out of the park, Birdsong addressed Grayson. "You are walking a tightrope."

"Tell me something I don't know." He paused. "Hey, I'm glad you were here this morning. Help Doolin convince the president. Please don't let them force my hand."

"Mr. Woodley, I'm not sure how you'd respond if you're forced into a corner, and that's what I'm going to tell them. That type of doubt can be great motivation to reconcile differences. I'll do what I can."

"I appreciate it."

Colonel Birdsong started back toward the main road. She stopped and turned to Grayson. "You left one party out when you listed all those who know about Stella: your supplier. Would you care to share?"

"No," Grayson said. He couldn't tell her because he didn't know. He wondered if he ever would.

CHAPTER 31

FRIEND OR FOE?

(Many Years from Now)

A FEW SECONDS passed before Grayson grasped the meaning of Mr. Tang's last word, "Stella." Like water plunging over a series of waterfalls, the significance of the Chinese diplomat's love story cascaded down the steps of his mind—first recognition, next surprise, then understanding and, ultimately, anger. Wyoming had been played.

Grayson's face flushed as he stared at the man across the table. "You! It was you. You supplied Stella."

Mr. Tang didn't smile. He didn't gloat. He pushed the rim of his glasses higher on his nose, absorbed Grayson's scrutiny, and responded in kind.

Grayson slammed his fist on the table with a bang loud enough to capture everyone's attention in the room, including Billy, the waiter, who walked to the booth. "Everything cool here?" he asked.

Grayson didn't answer nor did he look at Billy, so Mr. Tang replied. "My friend just received a surprising bit of news, but he'll be okay. He needs a moment, Billy. Thank you for your concern."

Billy evaluated Grayson, looked at Mr. Tang, and then gave Grayson another once-over. "Okay, okay," he said. "Let me know if you need anything."

Mr. Tang nodded gratefully, and Billy walked back to the bar.

Grayson folded his arms and stared vacantly at his currently empty gin glass while playing out past events in his mind. Of course, it all made sense now. Mr. Tang had been dropping hints the entire evening. When it came to high-stakes diplomatic missions, he was China's Johnny-on-the-spot—India, Djibouti, and Iraq. The Alabama-trained engineer understood the big picture and how all the pieces fit.

Finally, Grayson said, "You used us against our own country."

Mr. Tang interlocked his hands in his lap. "Sometimes, there is opportunity in partnering with the adversary of your adversary. Back then, the US government was our common opponent. It worked out well for both causes. You acquired your sought-after equalizer, and we added a major distraction to pull attention away from Taiwan."

Grayson wallowed in the embarrassment of being so badly duped. China, and Mr. Tang in particular, had understood the entire chessboard and had executed moves to perfection. For all these years, Grayson had blindly believed his team had pulled off the coup of the century, when in fact they were no more than a pawn in a much bigger world game. He strained to put any positive spin on the ordeal.

"You don't know that my ultimatum was the reason the US backed off Taiwan."

"True," Mr. Tang said. "Nor do we know that it wasn't. It was one of many pressures applied to dissuade the US from retaliating against us. Together, those pressures had a cumulative effect. Exactly which one represented the final stroke is hard to say."

Grayson unfolded his arms and circled the rim of his gin glass with a finger.

Mr. Tang continued. "What we know with certainty is that our cooperation led to favorable terms for Wyonation's creation."

Grayson bristled. "We never would have cut the deal had we known China was behind it. We're not traitors to our own country."

"That's why Kamal was forbidden from revealing the source to your friends," Mr. Tang agreed, nodding his head.

The man from Wyoming lightly tapped his teeth as he continued processing the information. "You know, Mr. Tang, there's a big difference between us. Your side uses people in whatever way necessary to achieve its goals. We are more principled."

Mr. Tang's response was terse. "You are only kidding yourself, Grayson. We are very much the same. You have no love for the Arab people. Your oilfield colleague, what was his name?"

"Remi B."

"Yes, Remi B. He made a career out of using people, Arabs and others, to acquire what he wanted, and I think it is fair to say you used him in your pursuits."

Grayson reeled as his moral veneer was stripped away by the foreign diplomat.

"I'm not criticizing," Mr. Tang added. "We do what we must to advance our cause."

"Why are you here?" Grayson asked bluntly. "This appearance of yours is no accident."

The question softened Mr. Tang's expression. "I wanted to get acquainted with you," he said simply. "This afternoon's session was a serendipitous occurrence. Fate granted me the opportunity to meet an old partner face-to-face for the first time, a partner I've long admired."

Grayson could only summon a puzzled expression.

"In my years of experience, I've only known a handful of people like you. People who act courageously for a cause in the face of great odds. Though sometimes naive, you always behaved honorably in the fight for your region."

The praise stunned Grayson.

"Your efforts likely saved thousands of lives, and yet you took no credit for the achievement. You are a hero, Grayson, a hero that no one knows. You are not even an asterisk in the history books."

CHAPTER 32

THE BIRTH OF WYONATION

(Sixteen Years Earlier)

THE BALL POPPED into Grayson's mitt and stung the palm of his hand. He burst out of his catcher's crouch while wildly waving the softball glove. "Damn, Rachel! That hurt."

The blonde-haired teenager's grin revealed pure delight. "You said, 'Fastball.'"

"Yeah, but I wasn't expecting lightspeed. Where did you learn to pitch like that?"

"I've been practicing," Rachel admitted as she blew an expansive bubble with her gum.

The front porch door swung open, and Smitty, adorned in a full-length, white cook's apron, poked his head out. "Get in here. The press conference is about to begin."

From opposite ends of the yard, Grayson and Rachel met at the sidewalk leading to the house. They high-fived, Grayson being careful to avoid using the hand that stung. Both climbed the three steps onto the porch.

"Rachel, you look amazing without braces. Not that you weren't amazing before, but your smile's so pretty."

Smitty's daughter gobbled up the compliment while letting her shoulders bounce. "And I getta chew gum, I getta chew gum."

"Hey, Rachel!" her mom yelled from the kitchen. "Get in here and help me out."

Grayson waved bye to his softball buddy as he entered the Smiths' home. He sniffed the smoky aroma of barbeque ribs permeating the screen windows from the backyard. "Man, that meat smells incredible. I am hunnn-gry."

"Dinner after the show," Smitty replied. "Head on into the den. Want a beer?"

"Sure," Grayson agreed before plopping down on one end of the large, comfy sofa. Smitty soon appeared with a couple of beers in hand and occupied the other end.

Grayson fixed his gaze upon the Smiths' oversize TV screen and observed a female reporter smartly clad in a pearl-white, linen suit standing at the edge of the White House Rose Garden. The camera then panned to a speaking podium with rows of chairs facing it. Saturday afternoon was an unusual time to conduct a high-profile signing ceremony, but President Garcia was committed to attending an economic summit in Geneva, Switzerland, on Monday. He wanted to arrive there on the wings of a reunified and invigorated nation back home.

Grayson recognized several faces in the background who were assembled for the ceremony. US Senator Emma Shelton, Wyoming Senate President Carl Biddle, and Wyoming Speaker of the House Winnie Lopez milled around Governor Linsey. For Shelton, this event was her final act in Washington, DC. The natural range region to be known as Wyonation would have no representation in Congress. On the other side, Senator Barry

Doolin and Congresswoman Blossom McKenzie were among the many in attendance. Dressed in beaded and feathered Lakota regalia, Hiram Dancing Grouse conversed with Hector Devine. Soon the audience of VIPs seated themselves, and the president was introduced.

In his confident and congenial style, President Garcia addressed the crowd in attendance and the nation at large.

"My fellow Americans, today, we celebrate a new chapter in our country's illustrious history. Beginning in 1776, we have been a collection of individual states bonded together by a common desire for freedom. That journey began with thirteen colonies lying along the Atlantic Ocean. Over the next two centuries, our country expanded westward, culminating in a union consisting of fifty states, fifty white stars on our American flag. During that time, we have thrived as a republic, maintaining a careful balance between state and national governance.

"But what exactly is a state? Historically, it has simply been a collection of citizens living in a bounded geographical region with a desire to join existing Americans in the pursuit of life, liberty, and happiness, and a willingness to abide by the laws of our land. However, in recent years, many have argued the characteristics of a state should meet certain objective standards. In particular, to enjoy privileges afforded all states, the population of any given state should be large enough to represent a materially significant proportion of the nation's total population.

"To meet the ever-changing needs and values of our people, our forefathers in their wisdom, bestowed upon us a constitution and set of legal procedures to create or modify laws and regulations. In the past year, those tools were employed to pass and ratify the Twenty-eighth Amendment, an amendment requiring states to maintain a minimum population relative to the population of the United States.

"The enactment of that amendment produced

immediate consequences. Because it failed to meet the Twenty-eighth Amendment's population minimum, Wyoming was no longer eligible for statehood, and for the first time, we were confronted with the task of converting a state into something new.

"Change can be a scary time, especially for those most affected—in this case, the people of Wyoming. However, change also represents an opportunity for betterment. In dealing with Wyoming's transition to something new, our challenge was to balance the interests of both sides. We worked to right past wrongs and create a sustainable land going forward while simultaneously recognizing the rights of Wyoming's citizenry.

"That goal was difficult. It required all sides to negotiate with an open mind and a level head. It demanded statesmen from both sides to step forward with leadership, and it begged all Americans to remember we are a nation based on compromise."

"But mostly, it needed the ticking voice of Stella to scare the hell out of 'em," Smitty whispered to Grayson.

The president continued. "I'm delighted to say that after many grueling months, we have succeeded in our quest. Today, we witness the creation of America's first natural range region, Wyonation."

The seated audience rose to their feet with nearly a minute's worth of enthusiastic applause. Feigning humility, Garcia accepted the praise before resuming.

"This effort has come to fruition due to the tireless work of thousands of dedicated individuals. However, two gentlemen stand out in this pursuit and deserve special recognition. Senator Barry Doolin and Governor Hogan Linsey, would you please stand?"

As the two men stood, Smitty mimicked gagging.

"Ladies and gentlemen, when the threat of an armed confrontation seemed imminent, these patriots, two of America's finest, cast aside their differences and hammered out the blueprint for

Wyonation's existence within the realm of the United States. Please show them your gratitude."

Again, the crowd responded with a standing ovation.

"The guiding principles for Wyonation forged from the efforts of so many have been well publicized. I won't specifically address them now, but they are available on the Wyonation website for anyone wanting to learn more. At this time, I would like to execute the formal change of status. Governor Linsey, would you please join me at the podium."

Linsey made his way next to the president, who greeted him by placing his hand on Linsey's shoulder before resuming his spot in front of the microphone.

"Governor Linsey, please raise your right hand. As the representative for the State of Wyoming, do you recognize the validity of the Twenty-eighth Amendment of the US Constitution and willingly relinquish your claim as a state in the United States of America?"

"Yes."

"And do you as representative for Wyonation, a proposed natural range region, agree to abide by the principles and laws set forth in the Wyonation Constitution?"

"I do."

"I hereby nullify Wyoming's status as a state and now welcome Wyonation as a designated natural range region. To the citizens of Wyonation, I say join us in peace, in freedom, and in friendship."

Grayson glanced over at Smitty. "Well, buddy, I guess that's a wrap."

Smitty sulked. "Doesn't it piss you off those guys are getting lavished with all the praise?"

Grayson agreed. He remembered those who hadn't completed the journey: Claude Mullin, Swede Mendenhall, Rowdy McCullough and his bunch. Yet like most days, he chose to make the best of the situation. "Well, maybe they're getting the praise, but they don't get to taste those fine ribs I'm smelling."

❧

Later that evening, Grayson returned to his apartment and started sorting through a mail pile. As he began tossing junk items into his recycling bin, he spotted a different stack: a collection of working papers on his desk. Like a moth to candlelight, he was drawn in its direction. He sat in his wheeled office chair and reread the culmination of a two-year struggle.

WYONATION NOTES

Physical Description: Wyonation will consist of the entire geographic area formerly known as Wyoming and the portion of South Dakota between latitudes 43.0° and 45.0° north and longitudes 103.6° to 104° west. This area includes the towns of Belle Fourche, Spearfish, Deadwood, and Lead.

Prime Directive: While adhering to the guiding principles, Wyonation, a federally recognized natural range region, will exist as a distinct and autonomous political entity within the United States. It will regulate and oversee its own domestic affairs. It may conduct business and other affairs with the United States Government or individual states. However, it will have no representation in the federal government, nor will it maintain any relationship with foreign nations.

Guiding Principles

1. *Return Wyonation to its natural state through the reduction/cessation of industrial and agricultural activities deemed harmful to the environment.*

2. *Limit human population in Wyonation to a size (ideally fewer than five hundred thousand) that can be supported by the environment without undue stress. Reduce the non-Native American population through attrition.*

3. *Establish a Wyonation constitution and create governing bodies at both the regional and local levels to oversee and administer domestic affairs. At least fifty percent of these bodies must be federally recognized Native Americans.*

4. *Enact policies to expand Native American ownership and management of land and businesses. In particular, establish policies whereby Native Americans play a majority role in the administration and ownership of new renewable energy ventures.*

Concessions to Wyoming Citizens

1. *Citizens who currently own or rent homes will be permitted to stay in Wyonation at will.*

2. *Citizens who currently own land or private businesses will be allowed to retain them. Corporate land and business owners will be given a two-year window to sell the property/entity to Wyonation's governing body, who in turn will redistribute to the Native American population.*

3. *Children who are Wyonation citizens will be allowed to inherit homes, land, or businesses. Should no qualifying children exist, land will be offered to Wyonation's governing body for purchase and redistribution to the Native American population or returned to its natural state.*

Grayson's cell phone rang, interrupting his concentration. "Hey, Dad."

"Hello, Grayson. I wanted to check in and see how your life in the new country's going. The cattle look the same here."

Grayson laughed. "Did you watch the ceremony this afternoon?"

"Nope," Daryl answered. "I still gotta work. Damn thunderstorm came in last night and blew down that old cottonwood at the bend in the creek. I had to clean up that mess. Just got back to the house a few minutes ago."

"Long day."

"Long day." There was a pause, and when the voice on the other end resumed, it choked up. "Listen, son. I want you to know how proud of you Mom and I are. I don't know exactly what your involvement was in this whole compromise business, but I am sure we'd be in a lot worse shape without you."

Grayson's heart soared. His dad's words outweighed two hundred standing ovations.

"Things will definitely be different going forward, but I think we're gonna be okay," Daryl said.

"I do, too. Get some sleep. Say hi to Mom and Cindy."

Grayson set his phone on the table and noticed an undisturbed letter from his mail pile. Recognizing the Washington, DC, return address, he ripped open the envelope and extracted a simple card with a black-and-white rendering of the Capitol on one side. He flipped the card and read a handwritten inscription:

Cowboy,

Best of luck in Wyonation. I hope you enjoy the life you fought so hard to attain. Should you choose to do something brilliant like declaring gin as the official drink of the land, let me know. I'll join you in celebrating.

Cicci

CHAPTER 33

IDENTITIES

(Many Years from Now)

"YOU PRESENT THE situation like I was jilted by my country—both of them," Grayson said. "I don't see it that way at all."

Mr. Tang smiled in deference.

"It's true only a few people knew of my involvement, but that was out of necessity. Stella's existence had to remain a secret, but to say I wasn't rewarded is wrong. I benefit every day when I wake up to a mountain view in my home and live the life I've chosen. I'm also grateful when I make the occasional trip here to DC and walk along the National Mall. I'm proud to say I'm still part of the greatest country on earth."

"Such an optimist. Another one of your admirable traits," Mr. Tang praised him.

Grayson accepted the compliment silently. He looked around the bar and observed what once was a bustling crowd had dwindled into a handful of patrons.

"Stella lived a short but impactful life," Mr. Tang remarked.

"Those of us who knew her, sing her praises often."

"There are rumors Stella had children."

Always probing. Grayson couldn't decide if he admired or was annoyed by the diplomat's perseverance. "She was of child-bearing age," he offered.

Mr. Tang's pressed lips acknowledged the creative counter to his inquiry. "Stella," he mused. "I've often wondered why that name was chosen."

"Oh, that," Grayson answered. He hadn't given the naming any thought for years. "The night Smitty, my colleague, and I were brainstorming ideas to fend off the takeover, the TV was playing in the background. This guy kept screaming, 'Stella! Stella!' It was driving me nuts. The movie, *A Streetcar Named Desire,* was from way before my time, but that scene is very famous. Marlon Brando was the actor. When the idea for a bomb came up, Smitty said we should call it Stella. The name stuck."

Across the table, Mr. Tang exhaled, "Oh, my friend!" What began as a sheepish grin ballooned into a boisterous chortle. "Grayson, you have no idea the resources expended to decode your naming convention. Now to find out it was random…" The diplomat's genuine surprise combined with an evening's consumption of Yuengling threw Mr. Tang back into his high-pitched fit of laughter and again drew the waiter's attention.

When Billy reached their table, he clasped his hands and displayed a charismatic smile. "How are we doing?" he asked.

Pondering his empty mug, Mr. Tang replied, "Billy, you are just in time. We need a refill."

"Why don't I arrange some transportation home for you gentlemen?" Billy suggested.

"No, Billy," Mr. Tang protested. "Let us enjoy another drink so I can toast my friend."

"I think you've had enough for tonight. Believe me, you'll thank me in the morning."

"Billyyyy," Mr. Tang whined.

Grayson evaluated the interaction between the waiter and his drinking companion. At last, he said, "Billy, one small beer, and split it into two glasses. Then close us out."

After a brief pause, Billy agreed. "Yuengling?"

"You had to ask?" Grayson joked.

He watched Billy snicker as he swept the empty glasses from the table and walked away. Then he winked at Mr. Tang and said, "We'll pretend we're in Tuscaloosa, LeRoy."

Mr. Tang enthusiastically flashed his crooked-tooth smile.

"You know, the offer I made to Doolin—to live together or suffer together—wasn't exactly an original thought. I got the idea from a scene in another Clint Eastwood movie, *The Outlaw Josey Wales*."

Now, Mr. Tang laughed uncontrollably. "Ah, your affection for cinema is truly remarkable."

When Billy returned with two small beers, Mr. Tang clutched the nearest glass and raised it in the air. "I would like to make a toast: to Americans and their movies."

Grayson failed to raise his glass. Instead, he stared back stoically.

"Is something wrong, Grayson?" Mr. Tang asked in dismay.

Grayson let the silence linger a bit longer before speaking. Finally, he said, "Wyonational. I'm a Wyonational."

Slowly, Mr. Tang's frown transformed into an apologetic smile. "Ah, yes, yes. Of course, you are right. Let me rephrase: to Wyonationals and their movies."

The two glasses clinked, and the men downed half their ale. With his glass lifted, Grayson spoke. "My turn." One last time, he studied the mysterious man with whom he'd shared the evening. "To the Chinese and their beer."

Now it was Mr. Tang's face that remained blank, but only for a moment. As the edges of his mouth curled upward, he crowed, "You mean Alabamans!"

ACKNOWLEDGEMENTS

I would like to recognize all of the people who helped me along this writing journey. Thanks to my family: Doug, Sandy, Gene, Christy, and Craig for providing constant encouragement during each chapter's rough creation. Many thanks go to the dozens of my fellow writers in the Rocky Mountain Fiction Writers' critique groups for offering their weekly insight and expertise to my submissions. I am grateful to my beta readers: Dan, Jason, John, Mark, Mary, and Nancy for your thoughtful and candid feedback. I would like to recognize the folks at Damonza for their fine book cover and formatting services and say thanks to Kirkus Editorial Services and Readers' Favorite for their editing and proofreading contributions.

Last but not least, I want to acknowledge my three special girls. To Karen, my wife and life partner, thanks for letting me follow the road less traveled. To Natalie and Shannon, thanks for bringing a smile to my face each and every day. Love you all.

ABOUT THE AUTHOR

Dallas Jones was born and raised in Casper, Wyoming. He is a graduate of the University of Wyoming and the Georgia Institute of Technology. Dallas developed technical-writing skills as a business systems analyst and consultant, but he didn't catch the creative-writing bug until age forty.

In 2017, he released his first novel, *MEET THE BOYS OF CASPER*, a nostalgic remembrance of growing up in the 1970's. The novel was awarded a CIPA EVVY Book Award for historical fiction by the Colorado Independent Publishers Association. In *WYONATION*, Dallas switches to a forward-looking focus with his near-future, what-if speculation.

Currently, Dallas lives in Colorado where he enjoys outdoor activities, traveling, and spending time with his family. You can reach him at *authordallasjones@gmail.com*

WELCOME TO OSPREY

Charles Howard

Hat Maker Press

WELCOME TO OSPREY